D1210417

A Heart in Sun and Shadow

Annie Bellet

Terri—
Thank you!
♡
Annie Bellet

Copyright 2011, Annie Bellet
All rights reserved. Published by Doomed Muse Press.

This novel is a work of fiction. All characters, places, and incidents described in this publication are used fictitiously, or are entirely fictional.

No part of this publication may be reproduced or transmitted, in any form or by any means, except by an authorized retailer, or with written permission of the publisher. Inquiries may be addressed via email to doomedmuse.press@gmail.com.

Cover designed by Ravven.
Formatting by Polgarus Studio.

Print Edition #2, 2014
ISBN-13: 978-1461059158
ISBN-10: 1461059151

Part One

Prologue

"Something isn't right," the young slave said. She looked up from rubbing ointment onto the swollen belly of her mistress who squatted beside the huge wooden bed, her body shuddering with each contraction, each heaving moan echoing through the stone building. The dim interior of the hall was choked with the metallic taste of blood and the hot stench of sweat.

"Och, child, I know. The baby's coming backwards," the midwife said, shushing the girl. There was little she could do at this point but hope the baby inside still lived. The feet had come down into the canal. It would endanger both child and mother to push the babe back in and turn it. The amount of blood worried the experienced midwife; however, she knew all birthings were hard.

"Garb, I feel another," the gasping mother said. Her cheeks sucked in as the pain of the contraction hit her and she gripped the shoulder of her servant with bloodless fingers. The contraction brought more blood spilling down her legs to seep into the once clean rushes on the rough-hewn floorboards.

"Good, Cellach, good. Breathe child." Garb smiled with a confidence she didn't feel. A breach birth on the first babe was not a good omen. She whispered an old prayer to Corchen, the serpent goddess of birth and making, as she took shallow breaths.

3

The men milled about outside, each trying not to glance at the heavy tapestry curtain covering the wide entrance to the hall. The day had dawned bright and clear, a rare thing this early in spring. *A good omen*, thought Fingan, nervous still about his beautiful young wife and their first child. They'd opened all the chests, shot a green arrow into the air, and untied the sacred knots, tossing the special red rope into a fire. The womb would open, the baby would come.

A horrible cry sounded from behind the bright curtain. The men turned toward the door, waiting. Then the scream of a very cold and angry baby greeted them. Fingan unclenched his fists and yelled with triumph. His first child was born alive.

Inside the far end of the hall, in a sleeping area partitioned by finely carved wooden screens, the midwife caught up the child and neatly tied a red cord around the umbilical cord, cutting both with a sharp knife. She bathed the child in an earthen basin filled with warm water. A girl, with a strong set of lungs at that. Garb smiled.

"Had a hard birth, didn't you child? You'll be strong for it." The baby stopped screaming at the sound of her voice and opened her large eyes for the first time. The midwife sucked in a shocked breath and looked the baby over more closely. Her eyes were not newborn blue like most, but instead a bright green, the color of new leaves. The child was pale once the blood was washed away, save for a bright and thick thatch of hair. The midwife had thought the color of the hair was marred by blood, but no matter how much warm water she rinsed the crown with, the hair stayed that deep dark red.

"My baby, is my baby all right?" Cellach had moved to the bed with the help of her slave. She looked as an injured animal might look, distended and bloody, sprawled on the rich greens and warm yellows of the woolen bed coverings. With a sickened, terrified expression, the slave girl tugged a blanket over Cellach.

"She's beautiful," the midwife lied, hiding the child behind her body as she swathed her tightly in the linen strips laid by for the purpose. She couldn't lie and say the baby was dead; the whole world must have heard its lusty cries, but neither could she bring herself to tell the young woman the truth. It was too much to tell her that her first child was a changeling.

"Garb," the slave said with the same urgency as before.

With the child safely swaddled and no longer crying, the midwife turned toward the bed. Blood soaked through the woolen coverlet over the mother's legs. Garb looked down to the birthing rushes and saw that the afterbirth was already delivered. That was too much blood.

Fingan fretted when no one came out to get him. He brushed off the congratulatory arms of his men and stood near the doorway. His child was alive. Why hadn't the midwife announced it? Minutes passed as he dug a small divot in the packed turf outside the threshold with one boot.

After what seemed far too long, there was another scream. This time it was one of anguish and grief. Moving too quickly for any of his men to stop him, Fingan burst into the birth chamber. He stopped cold at the sight of all the blood and the miasma of cold sweat and death that hovered as an almost tangible cloud around his marriage bed. His eyes rose from the soaked rushes and stained boards to the bed where his lovely wife lay still in the way that only dead things can be still. His own wordless cry joined the slave girl's.

The midwife considered slipping out with the child, but the man turned hollow eyes to her before she'd managed and asked, "My child? I heard the cry. I want to see my child."

"It's a girl," the midwife said and wished she could spare him this second pain. Knowing she could hide it no longer, she held the swaddled changeling up.

"Kill it." Fingan stared at the unnatural babe in the midwife's hands. "It killed my wife. It deserves death."

"That would be unwise, Ríbenn," the midwife said. She knew the shock of grief clouded his judgment. "This child belongs to the fey folk; they won't take kindly if we slay her."

"Take it away then, do what you think best. I don't want to see it. I'll tell them the baby died with her mother." He turned away, anger and pain marking every tense line in his face, in his body.

The midwife tucked the child into her cloak and slipped out. People looked at her with questioning eyes as she passed, but she paid them no mind. The path to the sea lay beyond the village, down a rocky bluff. She ignored the beach where someone might bear witness and instead chose a small stand of windbent trees near the shore. She laid the infant, still swaddled, at the base of one.

"There, child. Your people will come for you. Sleep now." With a final prayer, the midwife left.

The sunlit day passed and the child stared up into the branches, watching the shifting patterns of light. She slept now and again, lulled by the rhythmic waves striking the rocks nearby.

Night fell and with it came a storm. The tide rose, bringing angry waves with the power of the wind behind them. The sea touched the grove, a wave lifting the child away from her resting place and pulling her back into the cold and raging water. The shock scared the baby and she screamed in fear and discomfort. She sank below a wave, green eyes wide.

A warm dark body lifted her to the surface again. Then a second body joined the first, keeping the child aloft and out of the waves. Heat radiated through her from the soft skin of the seals. Huge dark eyes and curious whiskers poked above the waves as they carried their burden further out to sea.

The storm died, as quickly as one wave follows the next. The sea turned to dark glass beneath the sudden stars. The seals swiftly bore the child across the smooth surface, swimming through the night.

The dawn found them near a beachhead. The seals let the tide and waves carry them into the shore. As soon as the water got to standing height, one seal disappeared beneath the surface and a woman, pale of skin and dark of hair and eye, emerged to take the child from the back of her kin. The selkie tucked the baby into the loose sealskin slung over her arm and walked from the water to the sunlit beach to sit on the rocks. The child was hungry, its mouth working in futile hope against the damp air.

The selkie woman lifted the babe to her breast and let her suck. Thick milk poured into the babe's mouth and she drank deep. After a time, as the sun rose further, the seals watching in the shallows barked a warning. The selkie woman looked up from the beautiful child and saw a figure making its way down the beach. She slipped the baby from her skin and laid her gently on a stone near the water's edge before returning to the sea.

Tesn waved to the woman down the beach, but as she drew near where she thought she'd seen her, there were only rock and waves. No, that wasn't right; there was something on one of the stones. The wisewoman picked her way carefully to the wide, flat rock. A baby lay there, large eyes green as new leaves, with a thick shock of hair as red as fresh blood.

"Well, you're a baby of the fey, and no mistake." Tesn smiled down at the child. "Child of the Isle by those eyes, though you bear the red and white of our own fair folk." She shook her head over the mystery, which only deepened as she noticed the seals milling about just offshore. The child's mouth and chin were wet with milk.

"And fed by a selkie." She'd looked after children before in her profession as wisewoman. Fair folk or not, this was a baby, and it needed someone to care for it. She gently removed some of the salt-stiff swaddling. Her, she'd need someone to care for her. Tesn pulled her cloak from her pack and wrapped the child in the clean cloth.

"I'll see this child is raised with love, as befits a gift of the fair ones," she said aloud, both to the selkies and to any other Unseen that might be lurking near. "Now girl, let's go find you some milk, hmm?" The baby gurgled and fell immediately to sleep in the old woman's strong arms.

One

"This hoof is near the size of my hand." Idrys laid the hand in question alongside the depression in the rocky soil.

Emyr pushed his crouching brother playfully. "Come on, slow one, our prize went up that hill."

Idrys flashed a wide smile at his twin. The boys were in good spirits. It was high summer, the sun shining hot in the lazy afternoon but with a cooling breeze coming down from the rocky hills. Standing, which put him exactly of a height with his brother, Idrys ruffled Emyr's unbraided black curls and took off up the slope. They'd been chasing the same large buck since the early dawn hours, their quarry always ahead, just out of sight.

They were nearly two days travel from home, nearing the boundary of the Cantref of Llynwg. If the stag crossed into Arfon, they'd have to turn back. The twins knew they'd gone further than they should have, but the large hart beckoned. The forests of Llynwg opened up here, turning to scragling brush amid tall grass and stones. The trail led them to a steeper hillside covered in loose soil and larger stones.

The stag stood at the base of the hill, his proud head raised in alarm. Nostrils tasted the air as the twins laid down their short spears and carefully knocked arrows to their light bows. Moving as silently as possible they crept to where the tall summer hay turned slowly to shorter growth.

Idrys looked at his brother. No words were necessary. Emyr nodded and moved to the left. The stag waited, still as an etching against the backdrop of boulder and sky. His rack boasted six points, a little velvet still clinging in ragged strips, and his fur a rich caramel. He was in his prime and a true prize.

In perfect unison, the twins broke their cover. They stood up smoothly and each let fly an arrow. The stag twisted away in a desperate leap, foiling both shots from a killing wound. Emyr's arrow struck the shoulder instead of the neck. Idrys's arrow fared no better, striking the flank. The injured deer leapt to the nearest boulder, springing up the hill and away from his assailants.

Emyr turned back toward where they'd left the spears with a shake of his head. Idrys, however, ignored the spears and started climbing up the steep slope after the hart. The stag had left a trail of bright blood that would be simple to follow.

"Idrys!" Emyr called, realizing his brother was moving swiftly away. The stag had almost reached the crown of the hill.

"He's hurt, he's slow. Come on brother." Idrys paused atop a boulder and waved to his twin.

"We'll find some other way up. That hill looks unstable." Emyr slung his bow over his shoulder and walked with both spears to stand at the edge of the rocky slope.

"Coward," Idrys said, laughing, "You'd leave our prize for the wolves for fear of a few rocks?"

Emyr's dark brow knit in anger and he opened his mouth to make a rude reply. His eyes shifted past Idrys as a low rumble caught his attention. The stag had loosened stones with its mad rush up the hillside and now a large boulder was free and gathering momentum. The whole hill began to tremble.

"Idrys!" he cried in warning. His twin felt the tremors of the slide and looked behind.

"Emyr, run," Idrys yelled as he leapt down from his boulder and skidded over the rocks down the hillside. He lost his balance as the soft soil beneath him gave way and tumbled down at the head of a wave of grit and stone. Idrys kept rolling, hearing his bow snap beneath him with a wince. Strong hands caught him and pulled him to his feet. There was no time for thanks. The twins ran across the scrub meadow and did not pause until they'd crested another hill.

Turning to look behind, Idrys whistled softly. He grabbed his brother's arm and pulled him to a stop. The meadow below them was nearly gone, covered now in a blanket of dust and stones. Somewhere beneath the haze and rock was their deer. Idrys sighed.

"Gwydyon's balls, Idrys," Emyr said, leaning over to catch his breath in the dusty air. "You can't seriously be sad over the loss of the stag. You nearly died."

Idrys, also still breathing hard, grinned at his brother. "But it was a magnificent beast, eh? We almost had him." He sighed again, more for dramatic effect than real sorrow.

"Sorry father, I didn't mean to get my brother killed. But what do you know? We were after such a *magnificent* beast!" Emyr straightened. He wondered if he looked near as terrible as his twin.

Idrys's tunic was torn on the right shoulder revealing his tanned skin beneath. His trousers had fared a bit better, though only a strip of leather remained hanging forlornly off his belt where once his quiver had been. His bow hung from his shoulder, its limbs snapped just above the riser. Idrys had a small cut on his chin just below his generous and grinning mouth. A deep purple bruise was forming above his right eye along the ridge of his brow.

"Admiring how I'm still prettier than you, brother?" Idrys's clear brown eyes flashed with amusement as Emyr shrugged.

"You're explaining the loss of the spears and all when we get home." Emyr made a face at his brother. Idrys shrugged and started moving toward the dark line of the forest.

The twins hadn't brought much with them since it had been a spur-of-the-moment decision to go out hunting the morning before. When it looked as though they might have a race over open ground for the stag, they'd tied their light packs up in a spreading oak at the forest's edge.

Emyr, being the less bruised of the two, nimbly climbed up into the branches and cut free their gear. He climbed down and sat with his brother at the base of the tree.

Idrys grabbed the water skin and drank deep before passing it to his brother. He then began to gingerly prod his bruises and take stock.

Emyr leaned against the tree and said nothing as he watched his brother. The adrenaline had worn off and he was hungry and tired. Idrys cheered him, however, by making exaggerated faces of pain and consternation over his condition.

"Well," Idrys said after a few minutes of prodding, "nothing's broken save my bow." He pulled off his boots and dumped a fair amount of gravel from them with a sigh.

"You're bloody lucky." Emyr shook his head and winced as a small cloud of dust and a few tiny stones came free from his hair. *I must be a sight as well, though without the bruises. He's going to complain the whole way home and then play up that cut on his chin as him heroically saving me by the end, I imagine.* Emyr grinned despite himself.

"I recall a stream not far. Let's go wash up and maybe get a fire going. There's daylight enough to fish since, thankfully, you didn't manage to lose our hooks in that tumble." Emyr rose and shouldered his pack.

They found the stream and walked along it until they came to a little heugh. The stream pooled in the overhung glen and the wide roots of the trees would make a good camping place. With the unspoken communication of long habit, Idrys dropped his pack and began to gather deadwood from the forest floor around them as Emyr dug into the loam near a stump for worms.

Night fell and the stars emerged to wink between the branches. The boys had a little fire going and the picked-clean bones of their dinner were neatly piled on a flat stone near the blaze. The boys curled into their cloaks back to back with heads resting on their leather packs.

"Em," Idrys said softly.

"Eh?" Emyr answered him sleepily.

"Thank you. For pulling me up and all."

It was as close to an apology as Idrys would come. In the dark Emyr smiled.

Two

Idrys woke as the sun pierced the canopy. He felt every bruise and scrape from the day before. With a groan he stood carefully and prodded the fire with a booted foot. It had died in the night. Cold breakfast it would be. Emyr woke when his brother moved and sat up.

"How're the mighty hunter's wounds this morning?" He smiled as he opened his pack and pulled out the leather-wrapped bundle of dried venison. Taking a long hard strip, he sawed off one end with his small knife and popped the meat into his mouth to soften.

"Give over, Em." Idrys sat back down on his cloak beside his brother. "I feel like Govannon tried to reforge me overnight." He took the strip of meat out of Emyr's lap and cut himself a piece.

"Or perhaps like someone rolled you down a mountain?" Emyr was smug and not the least bit sore.

"I said leave off. Or I'll give you a split chin to match mine."

"I'd never wish to be so pretty as you," Emyr said around his mouthful of meat, unperturbed.

"Is it really that bad?" Idrys tried to keep the vain whine from his voice without much success. Both twins were acclaimed for their height, their dark curling hair, and their strong and handsome faces. They'd just reached the age where the opinions of woman had begun to matter and they enjoyed the blushing attention.

Emyr glanced at his brother. It was really that bad.

The cut on his chin had scabbed in the night and now marred the clean line of his jaw. The purple bruise over his right eye had expanded its territory as well, reaching down to his cheek and up into his hairline.

Idrys had rinsed in the stream the night before, so at least his hair was clean in its braids. Pulled back from his face, however, his hair did nothing to hide the swelling of his forehead or the dark bruising. Another scrape that Emyr hadn't noticed the night before graced his twin's neck below the ear in long oozing weal to the shoulder.

Likely from his bow, Emyr thought. They hadn't brought a change of clothing, meaning only to be gone a night at most and Idrys still wore his dusty tunic, the soft, deep brown weave streaked with dust. The threads were beginning to unravel around the torn shoulder.

"You should mend that. I think I've a needle," Emyr said, trying to cover how long he'd been silent.

Idrys sighed as Emyr dug through his pack for the little stitching kit. He hated sewing, though he'd learned at his mother's knee just like his brother. He knew better than to complain of "women's work" around his fierce and stubborn mother. *She's going to laugh when she sees my stitching and probably not let me be until I admit she was right to make us learn.*

It was high afternoon again when Idrys spotted the snow-white buck. This deer was smaller by at least half than their prize of the night before with only two points on his antlers.

Idrys motioned silently to his brother and crouched at the edge of the clearing. The buck was pulling the fresh growth from the low brush here and apparently oblivious to the presence of the twins.

"Oh no," Emyr whispered. "We've got only one bow between us, Idrys. We're going home."

"Look at his coloring. He's small, but with a coat like that! We'll be better received if we bring such a gem." Idrys's eyes filled with stubborn fire as he glanced at his brother.

"I can't believe I'm even listening to you." Emyr carefully strung his bow even as he shook his head.

"You won't regret it," Idrys promised.

"If we had a deer for every time I've heard that, we could feed the entire cantref," Emyr muttered. His reluctance faded as the joy of the hunt took over. He crept closer and took aim.

Something warned the deer. It raised its delicate head and bounded away into the trees. Drawing his knife, Idrys gave chase.

Cursing, Emyr followed after his twin. They dashed through the woods after the white shadow of the hart. Idrys curved off to the right, aiming to cut the deer off from that side. Emyr took the left, running headlong through the trees. They leapt a small rushing brook and dashed between the leaning boles of the mighty oak and slender popular and ash.

The deer stopped abruptly and stood quietly shaking in a clearing near a second, wider brook. The boys slowed and circled the edge, Emyr taking aim. Just when he would have loosed the arrow, the buck sprang away again, disappearing into the underbrush near the stream.

The boys dashed after it again. They broke through the underbrush and saw no sign of their quarry. Idrys checked along the banks for hoofprints or a sign the buck had crossed. There was nothing.

"Deer don't just vanish," he muttered after some minutes of frustrated searching.

"That one did. Did you see his hocks? Red as blood they were." Emyr shivered despite the warm summer light.

"Fairy stories again? I've never seen one of the fair folk, have you?" Idrys said and made a face.

"Stories eh? Then where did your deer go?" Emyr's mouth set in its own stubborn line, his expression mirroring his brother's.

Idrys balled up his left fist and advanced toward his brother in mocking threat. He paused suddenly and looked around. Emyr was about to ask what it was when he too heard the sound.

Singing. It was a woman's voice, lovely and pure. They couldn't quite catch the words but the tune was both merry and haunting as it rang through the wood. The notes came from upstream and Idrys moved toward them.

For once Emyr didn't argue with him and followed his brother wordlessly. They moved quietly through the forest along the stream until they came to where it pooled in a deep stone basin. A rushing waterfall spilled over the stones into the lovely glade, its bubbling joy a sweet counterpoint to the haunting beauty of the song. The boys crouched low in the brush, frozen by what they saw.

A woman bathed in the water, naked to her waist. Her hair was red as fresh blood and her skin even in sunlight glowed as pale as white stone. Her face had high cheekbones and full red lips. Her eyes were silvered, the pupils dark pools within swirling depths. Her breasts were full with high pale nipples peeking out between the long silken strands of red hair.

Transfixed, the twins stared their full. Here was one of the fair folk, they were sure. She could not be anything but Other. Their mother was widely considered a fine beauty, but next to this woman, Hafwyn's tanned skin and dark features would be as impressive as a candle lit in daylight.

The Lady ceased her singing and the clouds cleared from the mind of the two boys. Emyr tugged his brother's sleeve and motioned with his head that they should leave. Idrys shook his own head and refused to look away from the lovely creature.

"You don't have to hide, children. Come, speak with me a while." The Lady's voice rang out in a welcoming caress.

Idrys stood immediately, giving Emyr no choice but to follow suit.

"We greet you, Lady, though we did not mean to disturb you," Emyr said formally, bowing.

Idrys bowed alongside his brother, grateful that at least one of them was capable of polite speech in this moment.

"I am not disturbed, as yet, young prince." She walked from the pool toward them.

"We are no princes, Lady," Emyr responded, flushing as the water grew shallow and her body was revealed. Every inch was as pale as the rest, save a nest of dark red curls between her slender thighs.

"Are you not the sons of Brychan, Chief of Llynwg? Perhaps I was mistaken and rude boys have instead come upon me?" Her words held a bite though her smile did not as she tilted her head to one side.

"We are, I mean, there is no mistake. I am Idrys, my brother is Emyr, Lady." Idrys found his tongue.

"Come then, sit with me a while and comb my hair." She turned and walked along to the bank to where a pale blue coat and matching shift lay warming across the rocks. She dressed, wringing the water from the ends of her waist-length locks. Then she picked up a carved bone comb and held it out to the boys.

"As it please you Lady, we meant no harm. We were hunting deer and came upon you by accident," Emyr said as they both walked to her.

The Fair Folk could be dangerous. Tales ran of them abducting youths to attend them for centuries in their halls or of the Folk playing cruel tricks on foolish mortals. There were tales also, however, of fairy maids who would take a mortal lover for a time. Emyr nervously remembered the former tales; Idrys excitedly recalled the latter.

"My name is Seren, princes. Attend me and we shall speak of how you may repay your rudeness. I believe it was only an accident, do not fear." Her smile was open and so bright it hurt to think of anything else.

The twins dropped their packs and came to sit beside her where she indicated. Idrys sat up behind Seren, perching on a stone where he could pull the carved comb through her hair. She smelled of honey and tilled earth fresh after a rain.

She asked them questions then, about their family and their lives, listening to their stuttering replies with a tinge of amusement. Emyr did most of the talking, Idrys fascinated by the softness and beauty of the Fairy's hair as it poured over his hands like blood stroke after stroke.

The shadows deepened and grew long. Emyr raised his head and looked about them.

"I beg your leave, Seren," he said, for she'd insisted they call her by name. "But we're going to be sorely missed if we don't start home. We've already been gone a day too many."

"Nonsense, my princes, it is near dark. You cannot travel in these woods by night; it would be most dangerous. Stay with me and we shall speak of this come sunrise." She motioned and a small hut appeared on the other side of the pool where they were certain none had been before.

Rising, she walked around the water to the door. Idrys looked at his brother and shrugged. Neither wanted to anger the Fairy, so they followed.

The inside of the hut was far larger than its exterior suggested. Woolen tapestries in bright colors hung on the walls. They told the tale of a hunt, with a large red and white boar the centerpiece of each panel as it ran before a flood of hounds. The hunters depicted were all of the Folk, tall and graceful even in stitching.

A wide platform covered in the fur of many creatures was arranged against the back wall while a lush spill of sewn pillows and sheepskins surrounded a bronze firepit in the middle. Over the pit hung a large pot from which delicious smells emanated. The princes, having not eaten since their meager breakfast, salivated at the sight of the bubbling stew.

Seren laughed. "Sit, my guests, and make yourselves comfortable." She picked up two copper bowls from a smooth wooden shelf near the door and dished up the soup.

The twins hesitated for a moment, the stories once again clouding their minds. Was it safe to eat the food the Fairy offered? Both decided with a shared look that angering Seren by refusing her hospitality would be far more dangerous and gave in to their empty bellies' demands.

It was venison stew, full of fresh summer roots and herbs as well as tender savory meat. The twins ate their fill, marveling how the pot never seemed to empty despite the second and then third helpings. Seren reclined on the pillows, watching.

"I fear we've been rude, Seren," Emyr said when he finally noticed she touched nothing of the meal herself.

"I do not gain my strength from mortal fodder," Seren answered his unspoken question. "You are my guests. It is proper you should not hunger."

"Thank you," Idrys said, nudging his brother.

Emyr's face remained clouded with thought, however. *Not from food, but from what? Where are we really? Oh, Idrys, what have we stumbled into now?* Emyr shivered again, though he tried to hide his fear and returned to eating. Seren missed the tremor and the dark look.

Idrys did not and watched his brother out of the corner of his eye, suddenly worried himself. Emyr always thought things through and he listened better than Idrys had ever been able to as well. Emyr noticed things and his instincts were usually good, though often Idrys paid them no heed in favor of action.

Seren rose and picked up a small bone jar from her shelf. She knelt then beside Idrys and opened the lid. The jar held an unguent of some sort, its pungent herbal smell not unpleasant, though strong.

"You two would be as alike as raindrops if not for this bruising," she murmured. Idrys held still as she gently rubbed some of the ointment into his bruises and wounds. He braced himself for pain, pain that never manifested.

Her touch was warm and gentle, the pungent ointment seemed to coat his aches and they began to fade immediately. He heard Emyr gasp as Seren rose and stepped away.

"Still pretty?" Idrys said, trying to make a joke to wipe the astonishment off his brother's face.

"Feel your face, Idrys," Emyr said softly.

Idrys raised a hand to his face, touching his chin. Where there had been dark scabbing there was nothing now but slightly slippery unblemished skin. He felt above his eye then and his neck. The bruise was gone, as far as he could tell, and the oozing weal as well.

"Thank you, Lady," he said in wonder to Seren. He too felt a chill now, for the Folk were not generally known to give a gift without a leash attached. He looked back to his brother and saw that same fear in his dark eyes.

Seren walked to the bed and sat gracefully at its edge. She beckoned to the young men. "Come, princes, let me show you how I am nourished. Let me sate your curiosity while you may perhaps sate me." Her voice purred, the tones of her earlier song reflected in the inflection of her words. Her silver eyes smiled at them, heavy lids and long lashes lowering seductively.

The twins glanced at each other once more and silent thoughts flew between them in that gaze. Apprehensive, but also excited, they rose together, each feeling flushed and confused at the tumult of emotions. Then Seren's slender arms opened to welcome them to her bed, and there was no more thinking.

Three

The sun was already sailing high over the branches by the time the twins woke. They found themselves alone in the Fairy's bed. Idrys rolled over and propped himself up on one arm to look at his brother. Emyr's eyes opened and a small smile played across his generous mouth. The smile faded, however, as he recalled all of why they were there and not just the mysterious and beautiful events of the night before.

"It's too bad they won't ever believe this story," Idrys said with a wistful sigh. "How many can claim that one of the Fair Folk made them men, eh?"

Emyr gave his brother a light push. "I don't feel any more a man today than I did yesterday. Besides, father will be sick with worry."

He rose from the bed, suddenly uncomfortable with his nakedness around his brother in a way that he'd never been before. He ruefully thought of his words a moment ago. *No, not like a man, but still, she's changed us somehow.*

"True." Idrys yawned and stretched. "But ah, I think it worth it."

Emyr threw him another amused look and found his tunic. Pulling it on he went to the door and reached to pull it open. The door didn't budge. He put his full weight against it until he finally fell back into the sheepskins, his arms burning.

"Quit playing, brother." Idrys rose and walked to the door. He set his weight against it and got the same result as his brother. They shared a look and then both tried, gripping the smooth wooden handle hand over hand.

The door stuck.

Both men sat down then, the sense of dread from the evening before returning full force. They were stuck in a fey home, trapped by a lady of the Folk. Emyr and Idrys looked at each other with apprehensive eyes.

"I think I like stories better when they stay stories," Idrys said.

"No argument here. I tried to tell you we should leave that white buck well enough alone, didn't I? But no, you just had to go running after every bleeding whim of yours, as usual." Emyr's words held more bite than he intended, fear turning what was meant as a gentle rebuke to something crueler.

To his surprise Idrys dropped his gaze and curled up with his arms around his knees, mouth pressed into an unhappy line.

Unaccustomed to this lack of fight from his twin, Emyr sat for a few minutes in silence, thinking. He took stock of the small cabin. There was a covered pail, much like the indoor privy buckets he was used to at home. At least their captor had provided for that need, though it cut off an excuse to leave the house.

He looked finally to the small window. The windows at home were usually shuttered or covered in leather scraped thin enough for light to come through. This one looked too smooth and clear for leather.

Rising, Emyr went to investigate it. The pane felt like stone under his fingers, warmed from the sun and very hard. He rapped on it with his knuckles just in case. The stone reverberated a little but otherwise didn't budge. He dug with his nails around the edges, seeing if there was a way to dig free the pane. Emyr thought they might be able to squeeze out of the opening if he could remove the barrier.

"Emyr." Idrys's voice held a warning and none too soon.

Emyr stepped free of the wall near the window and turned to his brother just in time as the door swung open and Seren entered carrying a basket under one arm. She closed the door behind her and smiled at the twins.

"You're awake, lovely. I've brought a present for my loves." Her smile was brilliant and for a moment chased away the shadows of fear in their minds.

Idrys, still naked, and Emyr, in his dark brown tunic, both moved to take the basket from her. It was a beautiful basket, woven of dyed rushes in twisting knot-work patterns that evoked images of long-legged birds.

Having reached her first, Idrys removed the covering of fine linen and found to his delight the basket was laden with fresh berries and ripe pears. Forgetting his earlier melancholy, he turned to his brother and they sat down with the gift to break their fast.

"Thank you," Emyr said and Idrys echoed him with a mouth stuffed with berries, the red and purple juice running down his chin.

Seren smiled benevolently down at them and then moved to sit on the skins beside them. Her fine-boned hands gently played with Idrys's dark curls. She'd unbraided his hair the night before, remarking on how perfectly similar the twins were in visage.

They were so different in personality, however, she mused. Emyr had loved her with determined concentration, touching her as though she were fragile. His passion had come as reverence more than sexual desire.

Idrys was different. Once over his initial shyness, he'd explored her like a man hunting a rare creature. His touch was full of raw desire and an almost selfish need. He'd taken as much as he'd given, his long-lashed eyes wide with the wonderment of the act.

When the final moment of consummation had come, Emyr's eyes had been closed.

Seren had taken mortal lovers before, but never twins of such exquisite youth and strength. She had little doubt she'd tire of them soon enough, though perhaps not soon as these humans measured time. For the moment, however, she intended to keep her new pets and teach them well how to please her.

The twins ate their fill and then looked at their captor.

"We need to go home, Seren. May we leave?" Emyr spoke, asking the question that hovered on the mind of both, hoping the answer would dissipate the fears that loomed once again.

She laughed, the sound like the burbling of the waterfall outside her house. "You'll go home, of course! But it is nearly night now, too late to make a start of it this eve. Stay another night with me." Her silver eyes grew hard and her gaze sharpened. "Unless, perhaps, you grow weary of my company so readily?"

"It is not that, Lady," Idrys spoke up. "It is only we've been gone so long, we don't wish to kill our father with worry."

"Such lovely and dutiful sons he has." Though she smiled so beautifully it made their hearts and loins ache, they were not oblivious to the mocking sting of her words.

She rose then with a gesture that forestalled any further queries and closed Emyr's mouth before he could say aught. She removed her gown, letting it slide seductively down her hips as she undid the clasps and lacing. Her skin, luminescent and pale as moonlight, rekindled the twin's desires.

At Clun Cadair, they'd both begun to play the adolescent games of discovery and courtship. The speculative whispers in their shared bed at night and the stolen and deliciously furtive kisses of Caron and Efa, the two girls closest to their age at home, were only explorations of a desire they hadn't yet entirely manifested. Until Seren. She'd imparted a knowledge and a need that, once roused, was a fire nothing might quench.

Idrys rose first, naked and hungry for her flesh. He was accustomed to shrugging off doubts and consequences and used his experience to banish the nagging voice in his mind. One more night, what could that harm? His father's fretting would be a tiny price to pay for such mysteries as the Lady might show them in the softly lit interior of her magic home.

Emyr watched his brother rise without hesitation and envy stole over him. Idrys was always so sure of himself, so able to act without the weight of doubt. *Or*, he thought bitterly, *without consideration.*

He watched his brother's tanned body entwine with the tall pale beauty of their host. The sight of them kissing in focused hunger shoved away the doubts in Emyr's mind. *He's right, maybe. Enjoying himself like this. We can't change the situation immediately anyway. Perhaps she'll let us free on the morrow.* He stood and pulled his tunic back off as desire burned away his fears.

Still, there in the back of his mind, hovering like an insect he couldn't quite catch, lurked the tiny voice whispering that she'd never let them go.

Four

Idrys woke first, lethargy and deep exhaustion pervading his limbs. He could scarce keep his eyes open long enough to register that the little cabin was sunlit. He felt his brother breathing next to him on the wide bed. Furs, damp with sweat from sleeping, matted against his skin, itching slightly.

The bed was soft and warm beneath him, his head pillowed on more furs, his brother's soft dark hair brushing along his cheek with every breath. It was warm and comfortable and he could not resist the pull of sleep as it reclaimed him, though the nagging sense of apprehension followed him into his dreams.

Idrys dreamed of fire and the smell of burning leather and fur. Then smoke, thick enough to burn his eyes and sting his lungs. An owl, silent and pale, landed on the shifting stones beneath his bare feet. It turned its head halfway around and spoke to him in a chorus of voices.

Run.

Idrys awoke again, this time with adrenaline coursing through his blood. He sat straight up, the lethargy and comfort of earlier purged and only urgent fear remaining. Emyr was awake beside him, also sitting up and breathing hard. They looked each at the other.

"A dream," Idrys whispered.

"I dreamt, too," Emyr said. "I saw fire and much smoke."

"And an owl." Idrys nodded. They'd shared dreams before, though none quite so clear as this.

"She's not like to let us go anytime soon, is she?" Emyr shuddered.

"Not likely. Though really, is it so bad? We're living a dream of many young men, eh? All the food and, well, and other things that anyone could want. No chores, no one making us learn sums or sit through boring hearings on the grievances of this sheep farmer or that one." Idrys gave his brother a weak smile.

"Perhaps, Idrys." Emyr sat then for some minutes in silence, pulling the furs further up over himself although the little room was warm enough with the clear sunlight pouring in the window and the little smokeless coals glowing in the brazier.

After a time he turned his head to his brother and rested his cheek on his drawn-up knees. "But how much time passes out there? I remember in the stories the places under the domain of the Fair Folk mark the passage of time differently from our own. What if we stay here only a few weeks before she bores of us or consents to release us and time has passed so quickly in the world that it is more like years? I remember tales where the youth lived with his lover and when he emerged from their realm, centuries had passed and all he knew before was gone."

Idrys turned to sit facing his brother with legs crossed. He thought a moment on what his brother said. If it were true, then he might never see his mother again or his father. He thought on his mother's dark eyes and the soft swish of her skirts as she walked. She never raised her voice to her sons or to anyone else for that matter, always gentle though often stubborn, a green stalk that will bend but never break.

He thought too of his father, Brychan, a chief in more than just name. His father often raised his voice, quick to passionate anger, but also quick to kindness and understanding after, his moods flashes of flame in the dark, there and gone again. He might never see gentle Efa or sweet and sarcastic Caron, never win his bet that he could outrace Llew to the weeping tree and back.

Even as he recalled each face languor slipped back over him. Warmth, sudden and unnatural pervaded his body and seeped into his thoughts. Desire rose unbidden, clouding the memories, pulling away the faces he conjured in his mind.

"Idrys!" Emyr knelt over him, shaking him roughly by the shoulders.

Idrys shook his head to clear the cobwebs of need and want from his mind. He took a few deep breaths.

"We need to escape," he said, shoving away the strange sadness that gripped him. He was unused to such gripping, deep emotions, being much like his father. Feelings came quickly as whims struck him and rarely stayed long.

"Where did you go just now? I swear I spoke your name three times before you heard me," Emyr said, releasing his shoulders.

"I don't know. I feel very strange, Em. I think that's why we have to go."

Idrys rose, climbing over his brother. He walked to the door and found it locked as tightly as before. This did not surprise him and sighing he moved to relieve himself and find his clothing.

"How? She'll not let us out." Emyr found his own tunic folded neatly on a shelf near the door.

"Mayhap if we lull her into thinking we no longer wish to leave she'll let us bathe outside. I could use a bath, as could you." Idrys gave an exaggerated sniff.

"It's worth a try, eh?" Emyr grinned, feeling better now that they had a plan. "I wish I knew what she'd done with our knives and my bow." He looked around, but no weapons presented themselves. "We might be able to cut that window pane, whatever it is, if we had something heavy or sharp."

"We could try to smash it with the kettle, but she's likely to be back soon if yesterday is any indication. I don't think she likes to leave us alone for long. And if that's some sort of stone, it will make a fearsome racket even if it cracks." Idrys shrugged, feeling adverse to action for once, yet unsure of what it might mean exactly.

"It's too hard to think when she's around." Emyr shifted uncomfortably as thinking about Seren brought on a wave of mingled desire and confusion.

Idrys moved to his brother and wrapped his arms around Emyr's slim form. "Indeed. But think what a tale this will be once we're home."

"If any believe us."

"I'll make them believe. Besides, mother always knows when we lie. She'll at least believe and if she believes, father will cleave to her. He always does."

Emyr chuckled at this truth spoken and the twins laid a head each on the shoulder of the other as they waited for the Fairy to return.

"Of course you may bathe." Seren smiled so warm and so sweet, her teeth flashing like white stones in the dimming interior of the little house. She motioned to the door. "Idrys, why don't you stay and help me prepare our meal while your brother washes? Then he can come and tell me more stories of your exciting hunts while you take a turn?"

The twins exchanged a look. They'd expected she might not let them go together but disappointment still wormed its way into their young hearts at hearing their expectations fulfilled.

Emyr went to bathe. He emerged from the hut and saw the same burbling waterfall, the same pond. The trees looked much unchanged as well. The sun had dipped quite low, though the air remained warm enough.

He gratefully stripped off his tunic again, having not bothered to pull on boots or trousers, and plunged into the cold water. He used sand from the bottom to scrub himself clean and then finally rested on the same wide, flat rock Seren had laid her own clothing upon the fateful day they'd met.

There was birdsong as the winged creatures settled for the evening. A light breeze ruffled the leaves, twisting them from green to silver and back again in the fading light. The hut perched next to the pond, looking for all the world like any normal cabin save for its lack of a chimney.

It never even occurred to him to run. Even if he'd had boots and supplies, Emyr could never leave his twin. He glanced to the sky again, watching the sun sink lower. Was its angle different? How much time was passing? Was the air cooler than it should be at high summer?

He sighed and pulled on his tunic. Idrys still needed to bathe and it would be selfish to take all the daylight moments for himself. With a deep breath, Emyr walked back to the cabin, pushed open the door, and stepped across the threshold.

They gave themselves wholly over to Seren that night, all doubts pushed aside as the twins did their best to make their host believe their whole hearts lay with her and only her. Neither asked when or if they might go home but instead told boisterous stories, well embellished, of their various hunting and fishing conquests as well as tales of the pranks that, while mostly Idrys's conception, they'd both pulled around the llys.

When Seren finally let them sleep, they fell into exhausted and satiated slumber. If they dreamed, neither could recall in the morning.

Idrys awoke first again. He forced himself to wake fully this time, slapping at his arms and finally biting his lip so hard it bled. The stinging pain pushed away the final clinging vestiges of sleepy comfort.

Emyr beside him slept on through it all. Idrys shoved at his brother to no effect. He finally pulled Emyr off the bed and left his twin lying there, tanned and muscled limbs in disarray, as Idrys grabbed the pitcher of fresh water that was set out for them. With a smile and a prayer, he dumped the contents over his brother's head.

It worked. Sputtering, Emyr awoke. He sat up naked on the floor and stared about himself with a confused look that slowly cleared.

"Was that necessary?" he asked, annoyed.

"Probably. You weren't waking. Be glad I didn't bite you." Idrys pulled down his lower lip to reveal the red, swelling sore.

"Indeed. I should be glad my twin is so determinedly strange." Emyr offered a small smile as he used a skin from the bed to dry his face and chest.

"We're still stuck in here, though I think we've more time 'til she realizes we're awake if that languor was any indication," Idrys said and his own smile faded. He collected their clothing and the twins dressed, donning their boots as well.

"Let's break the window. It's worth a try, mayhap." Emyr nodded toward the cooking kettle.

Idrys gripped the kettle and heard the sudden rush of wings in his mind. He ignored the strange touch and swung the kettle at the pane as hard as he could.

The window rang with a strong clear tone and the kettle split cleanly in half.

The boys stood, ears aching from the reverberating sound. It faded and they stayed still as rabbits spotting the shadow of a hawk, waiting for their captor to storm through the door. Moments passed and she did not appear.

Slowly they both exhaled and stared at the kettle, half of which Idrys still gripped mutely in one hand. He released it.

"What now?" Idrys said softly. At Emyr's shrug and lost look, Idrys' strength crumbled and he sat heavily onto the skins before the brazier. "Come on, Em, you always have some brilliant plan or another."

"Usually because you've gotten us into some bind or another," Emyr said bitterly. "Oh look, back here again are we?"

Idrys's eyes flashed with anger and he half rose before falling back with a shake. "Fair enough, but fighting gains us nothing. What would father do?"

"Throttle her, probably." Emyr sighed and sank down across from his twin. "Better to ask what mother would advise. She's far more practical."

"She'd outwit the Lady. Or turn things about so that Seren might think letting us go was her very own clever plan." Idrys shrugged.

Idrys stilled suddenly and then jumped up. "That's it! Emyr, we know what to do."

"What are you talking about? If you're about to suggest we kill the Lady, I think you know how badly that would go. I'm not even sure how to kill a Fair One, not to mention I'm not sure I could face her with malice in my heart." Emyr folded his arms across his chest and raised his brows.

"No, no, of course not. I'm not bloodthirsty, you loon. But we dreamed it, don't you see?" Idrys motioned at the brazier excitedly.

"Set the hut on fire?" Emyr rose as well so that he could stand eye level with his raving twin. "What will that do other than kill us? The walls look to be stone and earth; they'll hardly burn."

"The door is wood, those shelves are wood. We can pile them against the door and set the whole thing alight. Once the wood weakens, we can break through." Idrys turned and started to empty the shelf of its earthen cookware and various little shells, bone carvings, and other pretty sundries.

"What about the smoke? There's no chimney, stupid. What about us? We're going to what, just leap through fire? You dumped the water on me, remember?" Emyr didn't move.

"We'll wet the skins from the bed with our piss and use them to damp the fire so we can get out. Once the door burns through, we can use the brazier itself to bash a good opening. It's large and heavy enough I think." Idrys had that specific determined look on his face that only came with the more daring or harebrained of his plans, the ones he wouldn't be rationally talked away from no matter the arguments against.

"Urine and fire? Gethin said that sex made men mad, though I'd thought he meant it less literally." Emyr shook his head again and closed his eyes.

He could see the flames from his dream and feel the choking smoke in his lungs. Wings beat in his mind, soft and nearly silent but for the telling rush of wind. Idrys might be right, but from a practical perspective, setting the only door in a small space on fire seemed too risky.

"Think, Emyr. How long will we stay here? Already I struggle to hold familiar faces in my mind. How long 'til I forget? What if we forget each other?" Idrys stopped moving items and held his hands out in supplication.

Emyr sighed, his resistance crumbling under the weight of that plea. He too, during the telling of tales the evening before, had found the familiar stories and comforting faces of home slipping like fish from the grasp of his memories.

"If you get us killed when we could have settled for a century of having our every desire filled, I'll never forgive you," he said even as he moved to help.

Idrys laughed, relief flooding through him. "I'll never forgive myself either, never fear."

Their minds set, the youths worked swiftly. Soon they had the shelf pried apart and the planks set against the door. They used sheep's wool scraped from the skins as tinder. Emyr used a broken pottery shard to gouge the door, roughing the thick wood that the fire might take purchase more quickly.

Wrapping their faces with strips of cloth torn from the pillows and their hands with leather ripped from the bedding, they lifted the brazier and dumped the coals onto their makeshift pyre. It took both to lift the heavy bronze and tip it. Emyr grunted and nearly dropped it as his leather hand coverings slipped. He fixed in his mind their goal and hung on despite his awkward grip.

They'd both emptied their bladders into the chamber pot and then used the contents, smelly though they were, to wet down a couple skins. The skin that had been underneath Emyr when Idrys dumped the water pitcher on him was still quite wet and they took it also.

Hunkering down on the bed, wet skins ready, they waited as the flames leapt and ate at the shelving and finally the base of the door. The splinters they'd managed to raise in the wood of the door caught flame and curled in the heat. Smoke, thick and acidic from the wool and wood, spread out over the roof of the hut, finding no outlet. Soon they were coughing behind their crude masks.

Emyr pulled Idrys off the bed and they lay on the floor, struggling to breathe.

It was too hard to see, though the fire looked to be burning fiercely enough despite the dwindling air supply. The boys closed their eyes. Breathing was getting harder and harder. Idrys gripped his brother's arm tightly with one hand, the other resting on the wet, stinking skins.

There was a rush of flame suddenly and the smoke abated. The sound was much like the sound of the owl's wings and it roused the twins from their dazed and labored state.

Idrys raised his head and forced his stinging eyes open. The fire burned brighter than before, the flames eating hungrily at the door. And beyond it was daylight. The fire had eaten through the thick old oak.

Unable to form words from his dry throat, Idrys tugged at his brother's hand and pulled on the leather. Emyr squeezed back and leaned over to grab a wet hide.

They struggled to their knees, crawling toward the oppressive heat, each holding a damp skin out like a shield. The power of the fire's blaze was such that they had to avert their faces. They tossed the thick, soaked leather onto the flames, which damped the fire's fervor but did not quite quench it.

It was enough.

They'd left the brazier near the door. Ignoring the heat, they lifted the shining bronze and heaved it into the leather, flame, and charred wood.

It crashed through, leaving an opening in its wake large enough for a man to dive through.

"Go, you first," Idrys said.

"You, what if she returns? You run faster." Emyr shook his head. His voice sounded graveled and strained despite the sudden gasp of fresh air to breathe.

"I'll not leave you, nor you I, so what does it matter?" Idrys glared, his throat raw and painful as well.

Emyr, scared and full of adrenaline, shook off the desire to argue further and rose. He dove through the opening head first, coming to his feet in a neat roll on the grass outside. He turned and moved to the side as his brother quickly followed him.

Their tunics were smoke-stained and their hair around their faces singed. Above the strips of colored cloth, now blackened with soot and smoke, their eyes were red-rimmed but clear and bright with hope.

"Run," Idrys said, taking his brother's hand as he tore away the strips of cloth from his face.

They ran. It was mid morning judging by the sunlight that filtered down through the forest. They set their path to the south and west, toward home and all things known and normal. Fleeing the Lady and their own confused desires, they plunged through the wood in a strange parody of the mad hunt that had brought them to her doorway.

Fatigue, hot and persistent in their muscles, forced them to slow eventually. The sun had risen past the midpoint and begun its long descent toward the night.

The twins slowed to a fast walk, picking a more careful path through the wood. About them they began to notice changes they'd been oblivious to before in that first mad rush of freedom.

The leaves had started to change. The green of high summer was fading and the wood was now tinged with gold and brown. Not fully, for it was not yet fall, but still, the beginnings of the shift in seasons was evident around them.

"It's been three days. But how long out here?" Emyr lifted a golden leaf, fresh fallen, from the ground as they walked.

"I'd say late summer, perhaps," Idrys said.

"Good we left when we did, then."

"Aye. Though the time passing will lend truth to our story."

"They probably think us dead." Emyr shivered.

"Don't think it, brother. They'll still be hoping, searching. Our parents won't give up easily without answers." Idrys clapped Emyr on the shoulder and then took up his brother's hand again. Their fingers entwined, each clinging to that familiar comfort.

It was late afternoon before they heard the pursuit. The forest grew mysteriously quiet around them. Then, just as they noticed this unnatural stillness, the far-off cry of hounds sounded through the wood.

Emyr looked at his brother. "Father's hounds?" he said hopefully, though they were at least a day's hard travel from home.

"I think not," Idrys said, pausing to listen.

"I think we'd better run again," Emyr said with a shudder.

The twins kept their grip on each other's hands and ran at a more sustainable though no less urgent pace. The woods here were open under the thick, old canopy, with only small patches of fern and hazel blocking their path.

The sun was dropping and gloom rising when the hounds got close enough to sight. The chilling baying struck renewed energy into the exhausted twins and they pushed their already burning legs to further speed.

Idrys wasn't sure he could have outpaced his brother at this point even if he was considered the quicker of the two. His lungs labored and his throat was choked with thick phlegm. His lip throbbed where he'd bitten it, though now it seemed such a small ache compared to the rest. He glanced behind and wished he hadn't.

A score of hounds flowed perhaps fifty meters behind the twins like a wave breaking over the landscape. Their bodies were tall and lean in the way of hunting hounds, but their fur was bright and shining with the white of the moon and the red of fresh-spilt blood.

"Find a tree," Idrys cried. "We've got only moments."

"Gwydyon's balls." Emyr looked behind as well and pressed his speed further.

Ahead of them a spreading oak loomed out of the descending darkness. Its branches started just above their heads and reached out to create a clearing of sorts. The brothers veered and made it to the tree with the hounds so close they could hear the dogs breathing as they ran.

Idrys jumped, catching the lowest branch with sore hands. He hauled himself up and swung a leg over. Emyr jumped as well, his hands catching the limb. Idrys wrapped a leg tightly around the branch and grabbed his brother's tunic with both hands and hauled him up.

A hound, the first to reach them, leapt as Emyr heaved upward. The jaws of the creature caught his trouser leg, ripping free as its teeth found no purchase on the thick spun cloth.

The twins climbed to a deep crook in the tree where they were well above the snapping jaws and frustrated cries of the fairy hounds. They rested there, breathing hard as they clung to each other.

"You think she'll come and call them off?" Emyr gasped finally as the painful ache in his chest eased a little with each breath.

Idrys thought of Seren's face when they coupled the eve before. She'd had a look of detachment, yes, but also one of desire, the kind of possessive passion he usually acquainted with owning a particularly fine horse or a rare gem.

"She'll come," he said.

"Promise me, whatever she says, whatever she does, you'll stay with me. Don't let me go, Idrys." Emyr shook, his voice trembling.

Idrys wrapped his arms tighter around his brother's shoulders. He felt as scared as Emyr sounded but steeled himself against his own tremors.

"I so swear, Emyr," he whispered into his brother's dark hair, breathing in the familiar scent of his twin beneath the lingering smell of smoke.

"I so swear, Idrys," Emyr echoed, feeling at once both too old and too young.

The twins sat in the tree, each with their head on the other's shoulder, waiting as the red-and-white sea of crimson-eyed hounds circled and sang beneath them.

Five

The last shaded rays of sunlight lingered on as the twins clung to their perch in the spreading oak. One moment the air was filled with the baying of the excited hounds, the next all was still as though the entire world had taken a deep deep breath and now held it.

Out of this immense calm, Seren appeared. Her hounds sat still as stone carvings, lazily arrayed at the base of the tree. The Fair One walked out of the growing gloom wearing a simple white dress with a small wreath of blue summer flowers circling her loose, rippling scarlet locks.

"Come down from there," she commanded. Her voice was clear and cold as a winter night, her face impassive giving no hint as to her mood or will.

The twins shook their heads, each keeping a tight grip on the shoulder of the other.

Emyr spoke, "Lady, we greet you. We have enjoyed your hospitality, but we must return home."

"Decided that, then, have you?" She laughed and there was a cruel, mocking note in the clear tone that they'd never marked before.

"Aye," Idrys and Emyr answered as one.

"Since you are so set on this, I'll make you a bargain." She smiled, the mocking expression fading in the light of her iridescent beauty. "One of you may go; the other will stay with me and be my love."

Her words sounded at once warm and reasonable. A bargain indeed. Emyr and Idrys looked at each other and their promise in the frantic moments before her arrival echoed in the eyes of each.

"And if we refuse this bargain?" Idrys asked. He'd grown wary in a way he'd never have been only days before.

Seren shrugged. "Mayhap I'll see if my hounds care for further sport then. You gave them a merry chase, and I doubt you'll make a home of that lovely tree."

She tried to look disinterested. These young mortals clearly did not know that in truth once they'd refused her she'd lost her power over them. She chose to let them think she could take them against their will, so long as she didn't have to voice the lie. Centuries of practice let her comfortably couch all statements in the realm of the possible instead of the actual, allowing her to avoid having to tell the truth entire.

The Fair Folk could not lie, but they'd talk circles to avoid the truth.

"No matter what," Emyr whispered to his brother and Idrys nodded.

"I quite like this tree. Such lovely leaves this time of year," Idrys called down to the waiting Lady.

"Idrys," Seren guessed, for she could not tell the one from the other, filthy as each was with soot and ash. "I will make you a prince in truth, my love. I can teach you things no mortal has ever known."

She walked to the base of the tree and leaned a slender hand upon the bark. Her inner light grew then until it spilled cool and clinging over the lowest branches of the oak.

Desire, hot and unbidden, rose in Idrys. His blood sang with remembered passion, her words arousing sensations along his skin as he lost himself in the memory of the most tender caress he'd ever known.

Emyr's arms closed more tightly around his brother as he saw the anger fade to rapture in the gleam of the Lady's power. The air around him was too heavy to breathe and he struggled to draw it into his lungs. *Idrys. You promised. Don't leave me brother. Not like this.*

Idrys started to pull away.

Emyr managed a strangled cry and, clinging to his brother, threw them both from the tree.

They hit the ground hard, Idrys slightly under his twin. It worked. The look faded from Idrys's eyes and he groaned and blinked as though waking from a deep sleep.

"No," he croaked, eyes on his brother who still held his shoulders.

At the word there was a sound like a harp string snapping, a clear and broken note. The light winked out leaving only Seren standing there in her cold beauty. The hounds were gone, slipping back somewhere into the oncoming night.

"Very well," she said. All kindness was gone from her features. "So loyal, each to the other. Much like a dog. In fact, I think you shall live as dogs, since you have broken my hospitality like wild curs."

Idrys and Emyr, their hands still clasped, fingers intertwined, rose slowly to their knees before her. The power of speech had fled them both in the face of cold terror and their iron resolve.

Seren smiled and the twins shivered. "Yes, quite fitting." She looked to the sky. "By night, you Emyr, shall serve your brother, his faithful mutt. And you, Idrys, I think by day it shall be your fate. As you've shared your lives, so shall you split the burden of your fate." Again the mocking laugh, quick and soft in the gloom.

Emyr doubled over, pain stretching along all his limbs. Horrible screams burst from his lips as his body twisted. Idrys held on, finding his own voice as he screamed as well in horror, screaming for her to stop, to take him, to leave his brother alone.

It was over in the space of a breath, between one scream and another.

There, standing in a puddle of tunic and trouser, Emyr was no longer a man. Instead he bore the form of a tall hunting hound, his coat sleek and black. But his eyes, staring in shock up at his twin, they were Emyr's eyes still, clear and brown as polished wood in firelight.

Emyr the hound threw back his head and howled. Idrys leapt to his feet and sprang at the Lady with an unintelligible curse. The hound followed on his heels, teeth bared. Rational thought fled in the face of terrified anger.

Seren disappeared. It looked as though she only took one backward step but somehow the oncoming night swallowed her whole, leaving only whispering leaves and an empty wood behind.

Idrys stumbled about, thrashing through the woods, yelling for her to come back and undo her curse. He collapsed, exhausted, his throat closing off with choking anguish.

Emyr crept up along side his brother and licked his face, laying a large paw on his brother's thigh. Idrys grabbed onto his twin, pulling the hound half into his lap as he let himself sob into the warm, silky fur.

"I'm sorry, Em. Gods I'm sorry. I'll make it right. This is all my fault. Emyr. All my fault." They lay curled together on the forest floor until the pervading fatigue of grief claimed them both.

A strange tingling woke them both. False dawn lent the surrounding trees a grey corona against the pale sky above. Emyr lifted his narrow head and tasted the damp air with fresh senses. He'd hardly noticed the night before the panoply of scents and sensory input that assailed his new form.

He shook himself and wagged his tail at his brother as Idrys sat up. They were both stiff from sleeping on the ground and cold from the dew that now clung to their bodies and dampened their hair.

The tingling grew as Idrys scrubbed at his eyes with dirty hands. The fear and anguish of the day before combined with the intense physical exhaustion and left him empty. He shoved down the irrational and entirely childish hope that somehow this was all still a strange dream and that his true waking would come.

"Emyr. What do we do? Go back? Find her hut? Maybe she'll change her mind." Idrys looked at his brother but found no human expression to read on the narrow face that returned his gaze. Emyr yipped and turned his head to the east.

The first rays of sunlight slipped into the sky and with it came a strange pain riding the wave of tingling sensation in the limbs of each twin.

The change that hit them felt less violent than it had looked the night before, and far quicker.

Emyr knelt on the ground, human and naked in the morning light. Idrys stood entangled in his own pool of clothing, looking around with a very human, surprised expression on his narrow hound's face. It almost made Emyr laugh. Almost.

"Idrys, it's all right. Give it a moment. Your senses will be overwhelming for a moment if you're feeling like I did."

Emyr took a deep breath and tried to offer what comfort he could to his brother. Ever practical, and rather chilled, he gently pushed his brother out of the way and began to pull on his twin's discarded clothing.

He stood and took in the forest. They were a long day's travel from home, if his bearings were correct. Knowing by his own experience that his brother would retain his human mind while confined to the hound form, Emyr turned and spoke.

"We can't go back to her. The gods only knows what else she might think to do. We have to go home. They'll be worried sick. Mother must know, at the least. She's clever, she'll think of somewhat." Emyr tugged on his boots, pulling the soft leather over his sore heels.

Idrys tucked his tail into his body without thinking and whined high in his throat. He walked forward and licked his brother's outstretched hand. He knew Emyr was likely right, and the folly of not listening to Emyr lay fresh and painful in Idrys's mind.

The brothers walked side by side toward the moors and the sea as the forest woke up around them and the sun rose to cast green and gold shadows among the turning leaves.

They reached the edge of the wood as the sun sank low. The weather held despite heavy clouds that blew in from the sea toward the distant taller hills of Eifon that rose like shadows against the mercurial sky to the north and east.

Emyr got their bearings again as the wood faded into the low heath and brushy grass of the moors that spilled from the tall old forests down to the rocky shore of the western sea. Near the edge of the forest stood a tall standing stone, called a carreg, bone white with its northern face thick with moss. It was a well-known landmark to the twins; the shepherds called it the talking stone, though the tales about how it came to be varied with the telling.

"There, Idrys." Emyr pointed to the white carreg. "Though I think we should wait here for a while yet."

The tingling had started again in his body strongly enough that he was able to differentiate it from the burning of his muscles. Night was coming and with it he'd change. They were only perhaps an hour out from Clun Cadair, but it was too close to dark to be sure they'd make it before the curse took its terrible effect once more.

Idrys stood alert next to his brother. His black form came to Emyr's waist and a light wind lifted the dark fur from his long back. Swallows dipped and circled in the meadow ahead as the sun dropped down over their home.

He too felt the singing in his blood and tensing of his muscles as the light faded. He raised his eyes to his brother and nodded his narrow head in a very human gesture, trying to signal he understood. It was too frustrating, this inability to communicate. He was accustomed to the easy if sometimes argumentative banter that Emyr and he had always shared. Its loss stabbed keenly as despair threatened to fill the hollow of his heart.

The twins retreated into the trees and Emyr stripped off his clothing. He folded each piece carefully and laid them on his boots. Shivering despite the lingering warmth of the day, he sank down beside his brother and slipped an arm over the hound's shoulders. Idrys licked his cheek, his tail thumping the packed earth.

"Tell them both, Idrys. Mother and father. We owe them the truth," Emyr said as the sun dropped out of sight.

Again the strange shifting feeling, a pain that was both inside and out at once. The terrible stretching and the sudden sense of *otherness* as the change completed itself with the final dying of the day.

Idrys dressed quickly and walked back out to the edge of the wood.

"Tis only fair, I suppose, that you'd leave me the task of telling them," he muttered. "This whole mess is my fault, after all."

Emyr butted his sharp head into Idrys's hipbone hard enough to stagger his twin.

"Ow. Leave off, you." The gesture jolted Idrys out of his deepening self-loathing. A tiny smile shifted across his lips only to fade into a grim and determined line.

Together they set out for the holding, hugging the line of the trees as they made for Clun Cadair and a very strange homecoming.

Six

The shout went up through the holding as the slender form of a son long lost appeared like an apparition at the opening of the low palisade that defined the border of the llys.

"Be you spirits, come to torment us?" asked Gethin, the aging head of Chief Brychan's flocks. He eyed the tall black hound and the filthy, gaunt youth he barely recognized as one of the twins who'd so merrily set out hunting nearly two months before.

"I'm not a spirit, Gethin. A spirit wouldn't be half so dirty or tired, I'd hope." Idrys halted at the sight of the men gathering with spears.

It might have been funny if he weren't so weary. Here they'd wished for nothing but home these many days and now home was proving hard to enter. Truthfully, he'd given precious little thought to what his reception might be, instead focusing on how he'd explain his terrible folly to what he imagined would be angry, worried parents.

"Emyr?" Gethin motioned the two young men behind him back toward the cluster of dwellings. "Gods boy! What's happened to you? Where's your brother? What's with that great black beast?" He stepped forward, peering into the youth's face in the light of the standing torches that marked the entry to the holding.

Idrys didn't bother to correct his mistake and instead answered, "I'll tell my tale to mother and father first, if that's all right. It's long, I'm afraid."

Tears threatened to spill as a lump rose from his heart to his throat. Gethin clapped the boy on the shoulder and escorted him to the main hall without further questions.

Emyr pressed close to his brother's side. The myriad of human and animal smells and sounds overwhelmed him again. Sheep, horse, fresh-cut rushes, cooking meat, and wood smoke, the smells of home. The llys would be near empty this time of year for the summer grazing of the flocks and the tending of the harvest fields and fishing in the seasonal villages near the sea.

The outer cluster of wood and stone houses were mostly boarded up. They both were grateful for this small mercy. It meant less people to stare and shrink away as they passed.

A slim figure broke away from the light doorway of the great hall. Her skirts flying around her, Hafwyn ran to her children and threw her arms around Idrys. He clung to her tightly, the tears that had been gathering for the last few hours welling over with a strangled cry. She smelled of lanolin, wood smoke, and fresh pears. She smelled like his mother, tall and strong, solid and real.

Emyr pressed his narrow head into her skirts as he too drowned in her familiar scent and warmth. Their mother pulled back suddenly and stared down at the large black hound. He looked up at her with desperate eyes, willing her to know him, somehow, through special motherly magic or intuition.

Hafwyn tentatively reached out her hand and stroked the silken head of the hound. She looked then at her son and saw the same sad desperation mirrored in the brown eyes of both boy and dog. She knew then, though her practical mind forced away the thoughts of the impossible.

"My son has returned," she said, her voice loud and clear though full of un-invoked emotion. She put her arm around her son's slim shoulders and led him inside. Brychan stood, a rough, hirsute hulk of a man, in the doorway to the hall but moved aside as his wife and child entered with the unnaturally sized black hound. His blue eyes searched Idrys's own dark ones for a long moment.

Once inside the light of the long and thankfully empty room, he reached for his son. Idrys went to him and fell into his thick arms with another grieving cry. He tucked his head against the bristling beard. His father was stiff, caught between relief and anger and wondering, but he embraced his son for a moment before pushing back the red-eyed lad.

"Where is your brother, Emyr?" Brychan asked, making the same mistake the others had.

Idrys realized his hair lay unbound against his shoulders. He'd always worn his own hair braided, a habit ingrained to help everyone tell him apart from his brother. He shook his head slowly.

"It's not a tale I can tell here." He glanced behind to where the courtyard outside was slowly filling with the permanent folk of the holding.

"Food, and a bath. Then we'll hear the story," Hafwyn said firmly, putting a hand on her husband's arm.

She ordered Melita, her maid and companion, to help her fill the copper tub before the hearth in the twins' old room. Brychan, after a look from his beautiful wife, fetched a bowl of thick stew from the hearth and sat quietly with his son as the boy ate.

Idrys looked down at Emyr, who waited patiently beside him at the headmost table. When he'd half-finished his food, Idrys took the bowl and set it onto the bench beside him for his twin. Neither had eaten in at least two days, though it felt far longer. The warm stew soured in his stomach as he faced his father.

Brychan had more grey in his hair than Idrys remembered. "I'm sorry father," he began.

Whatever Brychan might have said in reply was forestalled by Hafwyn's return. She beckoned him away from the table toward the private rooms built into the back of the hall.

It was strange to return to his room. A fire burned in the hearth and the large copper tub steamed on the stone floor in front of it. The bed was made, a state it rarely found itself in when the twins had slept here. Idrys shivered. *Two months gone, it feels like yesterday and like years all at once.*

Melita and Hafwyn both left the youth and the hound alone to bathe. A small pot of soap lay next to a soft cloth and a change of clothing on the hearth. Idrys stripped with a sigh and sank down into the bath. He had to tuck his knees up to his chin to fit, but it was heavenly just to relax into the hot water.

He took up the pot and scraped up a bit of the soft, crumbling soap. It smelled of roses, his mother's favorite scent. Idrys scrubbed himself, finally dunking his hair into the now tepid and filthy water. Reluctantly he stood and dried himself with the soft cloth.

"I guess I'd better explain it to them, because things will be strange when you request a bath tomorrow morning after sunrise." He grinned down at Emyr who had flopped onto the bed as soon as they were alone. His mirth lasted only a moment as there came a soft knock on the door.

"One moment," he called. He wrung the excess water from his curling hair and pulled on the clean tunic and trousers.

Going to the door, he opened it. Hafwyn stood with bowls of the thick stew in each hand, Brychan looming behind her. Both parents carried a mixed expression of worry and curiosity, though the chief's was tinged with anger as well.

The twins sat on the bed, Emyr sitting up so he could eat from the bowl that Idrys tucked between his long forelegs. Idrys also ate, thinking that if he were chewing, he'd have excuse not to speak. The stew didn't last. Exhaustion pulled at his limbs and he sighed. It was best to get it over with.

"I don't know where to begin," he said, hating the way his voice broke and wavered. He was so tired and this tale was too great a burden to bear alone.

Emyr leaned against Idrys's side and tucked his narrow head under his brother's arm. The soft heat of the hound lent Idrys strength. *I'm not alone. I have to speak for us both now. Well, at least 'til morning.*

"Start at the beginning," Hafwyn said and her gentle tone combined with the understanding and sympathetic gaze of his twin broke the dam of words inside.

The story poured from him then, though he fumbled with some of the parts in Seren's house. He could see from the slight flush in his mother's cheeks and the knowing cast of his father's look that their imaginations filled in the more seductive details that he left unspoken. Neither of his parents spoke nor broke the spell his tale wove in the little room. He related the details of their daring and doomed escape and the mad flight through the wood for home. Finally, Idrys reached the end, speaking of the horrible curse and subsequent transformation.

So loyal, each to the other. As you've shared your lives, so shall you split the burden of your fate.

He stopped then, Emyr beside him sitting up on his haunches now, head raised as each watched their parents.

Hafwyn nodded. She'd half-suspected something of the sort the moment the tall black hound at stared up at her with her son's own eyes. She opened her mouth to speak words of comfort to her children but her husband went rigid beside her and cut off what she might have said.

"Idrys." His face had turned red as he absorbed the tale. "This is your fault, boy." He rose to his feet with an angry gesture, thick hands balled into fists. "If you hadn't led your brother on that mad chase, none of this would have befallen you. Why don't you ever listen? Look what you've done to your brother!" His voice boomed in the tiny space, his blue eyes bright and hard as stones.

"I know, father," Idrys said softly before his mother could chide her husband. He bowed his dark head and gripped a handful of Emyr's silky coat. "I'm so sorry. I don't know how to make it right."

He looked up then, toward his mother. Emyr had promised that telling the truth would help. Hafwyn was clever, she always thought of something.

Hafwyn recognized the look of a child expecting his strong parents to fix the world and sorrow welled from deep within that they would learn the truth in such a terrible fashion. She spread her hands, finding her body too heavy with emotion to stand. Helpless, she shook her head, hating to see his gaze fall as tears replaced the faint glow of hope in his red-rimmed eyes.

"You are dead to me, Idrys," Brychan said as he too sat back down on the narrow bench beside his wife.

"Brychan! You cannot say such, even in anger." Hafwyn grabbed her husband's arm.

"I can." He looked at her with grief-hollowed eyes.

He'd thought both sons dead these last two months. Oh, he'd held hope dear but with each searching party that came back without trace or news; his hope had faded further into despair. He felt every ache in his bones.

"I can," he repeated, "I will. We can't tell others this story; it'll bring suspicion on my sons, on my heirs. What man wants to be ruled by one who is cursed?"

Hafwyn sighed. She could see the practical merit in his words even if she did not agree with the anger that drove the hurt deeper into Idrys's heart.

"All right." She smiled at Idrys and Emyr, her gaze moving between the two. "Here's what we'll do. We'll tell part of the truth." She took a deep breath.

"Idrys, you were killed in a rock slide while hunting. Emyr was knocked to the ground and taken in by a kindly hermit. There are rumored to be such wise men of the wood about, after all. He gifted you the hound and helped you remember who you were. That's where you've been these months." Her agile mind formed the story even as her heart sank at the thought of spending the rest of her days pretending her son was dead and gone. *'Tis better than having him actually dead and gone, you twit*, she told herself.

Idrys struggled to grasp the plan in his despair. He was dead, then. He laughed mirthless and sudden.

"Well, Emyr, I guess I'll have to learn to run slower, eh?" He tried to smile at his brother as he refused to meet his parents' gaze.

Emyr yipped and butted his head into his twin's side. He did not care for the plan and his father's anger had torn a larger wound in his already aching heart. Perhaps Idrys had been reckless, but wasn't he, Emyr, as much to blame? After all, he'd followed his brother willingly enough. But what was there for it? He looked to his mother and nodded his narrow head in exaggerated fashion to make sure she understood.

The twins collapsed into exhausted slumber on their bed as the fire died in the hearth. The tale was slowly told in the hall to the curious folk by Hafwyn. Her husband had stormed to their bedroom and slammed the oaken door behind him without facing the people.

In the morning, Brychan, Chief of the Cantref of Llynwg emerged early. His hair had turned overnight to pure white.

Seven

Áine skipped down the rocky shore with her basket clutched tightly in one small hand. It was a blustery autumn day and the sky couldn't make up its mind about whether to cloud over and rain. Clouds moved slowly overhead, reflected in the choppy waves. It was low tide and kelp decorated the shore in long brown ribbons.

Áine slowed as her first burst of energy faded and she began to look for the slick green seaweed that was her mission for the afternoon. The child, though only eleven, took her duties as the wisewoman Tesn's helper very seriously.

A piteous cry sounding over the rhythmic lull of the waves caught her attention. Áine raised her head and searched the shore with her large green eyes. There, down the beach near a cluster of boulders, she thought she saw movement.

She glanced behind at the small fishing village where Tesn and she were staying until one of the village wives had given birth. The little sod huts tucked into the scrub high above the tide line were too far away for her to yell and the men were long gone from the shore with their round boats. She shrugged slender shoulders and walked fearlessly toward the strange sound.

It was a grey seal. It lay on the rocks and barked in warning at her as she approached. She stayed very still and observed the situation from a safe distance. Tesn always told her to collect what you know before you act. She took a deep breath and heard the pitiful cry again. It was not coming from the seal but from something nearby.

"I greet you, seal," the red-headed child said solemnly.

She circled the creature who watched her quietly with large liquid eyes. She finally spied the cries origin. A seal pup, no more than a few days old, was caught between two large stones. Áine decided he must have slid down between them when his mother left him to hunt.

Áine set down her basket on a rock and moved slowly toward the seal and her pup. She kept her eyes averted and her body facing slightly sideways.

"Sah, sah, mother seal," she said softly over and over. The mother backed away, offering no further aggression to the strangely fearless and unthreatening child.

Áine knelt in the silty muck beside the stones without a thought for her rough-spun dress. Pushing up a sleeve already now too short with her last spurt of growth, she reached between the stones to try to grasp the pup. He squealed as her hand came near, but though she pushed her arm in to the shoulder, she could not quite reach deep enough to get a grip on the slippery seal. Her fingertips brushed his thick fur but could go no further.

"Silly pup." She shook her head at him in a crude imitation of Tesn's gently chiding manner. "Found yourself a perfect little cave, haven't you?"

She pulled at the stone nearest herself, since it was flatter and thinner than the boulder behind it that it rested upon. It barely shifted.

Áine rolled back her other sleeve and dug into the rocky muck around the seal pup's trap. It seemed for every stone she removed to a pile beside her, she found two more. Her hole began to fill with water.

She rose and glanced at the sea behind her, feeling guilty that she'd broken Tesn's rule about never turning her back to the waves.

The tide was coming in. It had crept up the shore while she dug and was nearly to the waiting seal mother. Áine considered running for help, but if the tide reached the seal before she could, she wasn't certain he'd be able to swim out the narrow opening before he drowned.

She stood and gripped the stone with both hands. Setting her weight against it, Áine pulled and pulled until her fingers were numb and scraped from the rough, cold stone. It was no use. She could not shift the rock, for much of it was buried far below the surface of the beach.

Áine did not like to give up easily. She continued to strain and pull. Her tears bleared her vision as the tide rose to lick her bare heels. A few dripped from her chin and bounced from the stone to sink into the water, turning to perfect shining pearls as they touched the rock. Áine was too focused on the seal and her effort to notice, much less heed Tesn's warning about not letting her remarkable tears hit the earth.

Strong, pale hands reached over her and gripped the rock. Áine jerked her head up in surprise. Bending over her stood a woman with dark brown hair and smiling liquid brown eyes. Her skin was as white as Áine's own and she was fully naked.

She spoke to the child in a language Áine'd never heard, the syllables sibilant and lilting. Her meaning seemed clear enough, however.

Together the woman and child pulled on the stone. The woman's arms rippled with muscle beneath a sleek layer of fat and grudgingly the stone moved away from its resting place under the assault of their strong persistence. The opening grew and though the water flowed now around the rescuers' ankles, soon enough the seal pup was free.

He swam in the shallow water to his mother. Reunited, the pair rode the waves out to deeper water and disappeared.

Áine stepped from the circle of the woman's arms and walked up the beach to get out of the water. She retrieved her basket and turned back to the woman.

"I greet you," she said politely, remembering her manners belatedly in the excitement. "I thank you for your help."

The dark haired woman laughed then, at least, Áine thought it was a laugh, for she threw back her head and barked not unlike a seal, though singularly human mirth threaded through the sound and her face as well. She walked out of the water toward the girl.

Áine held still; she did not think the woman meant her harm for all she acted strangely. Áine wondered how she could be out on the shore in the wind without a stitch of clothing on her body. She didn't even have cold bumps on her skin. Áine was shivering and had cold bumps all along her legs from her soaked and muddy skirt. She pulled down her sleeves and wiped her skinned and dirty hands self-consciously on her dress.

The woman touched Áine's blood-red hair, coming loose now from its braids, with one long-fingered and big-boned hand. She smiled and Áine noticed with a start that the woman had small sharp teeth behind her bloodless lips. The child reached up with a curious hand and touched the woman's face. Her skin was warm and very soft. Her eyes were round, large and dark with strange pupils. *Like a seal,* Áine thought, dropping her hand.

The woman spoke again in her strange but beautiful tongue. Áine shook her head looking up at her in confusion. Then the mysterious woman bent as she tipped Áine's chin up. She kissed the child full on the lips, her mouth cool. The woman stood back up and turned away.

Áine licked her lower lip, tasting where the stranger had kissed her. She tasted of salt, as though she'd licked a stone that had soaked in the sea or perhaps swallowed a tear.

She watched silently as the woman turned and walked back into the sea. Her dark head disappeared beneath the waves with barely a ripple. Áine, her seaweed-collecting mission long forgotten, took off down the beach toward the village to tell Tesn what she'd just witnessed.

She glanced back at the ocean before she turned up the path to the huts. Out in the white and green waves, swimming through a rare shaft of sunlight, watched a seal with its dark head round and glistening above the water. Áine waved and then ran up the path.

"Tesn!" She stopped as she crossed the threshold of the low main lodge and blinked as her eyes adjusted to the dim interior.

Tesn sat by the hearth where her old bones could stay warm away from the autumn damp and chill. She smiled as she took in the muddy and frantic appearance of her adopted daughter.

"I'm here, Áine."

Áine nodded politely to the three women who sat in a semicircle just inside the open door, using the light of the afternoon to mend nets by. She walked past them and sat on the rushes at Tesn's feet, folding her cold feet underneath herself. She glanced at the circle of women and leaned in to whisper to her mother. She told her in hushed tones of her encounter on the beach.

"Was she a selkie, Tesn?" Áine said the word with reverence.

She knew the story of how she'd come to the wisewoman. Tesn had told her as soon as Áine was old enough to form sentences of how a selkie had carried Áine across the sea and given her as a special gift to the healing woman to raise as a daughter and apprentice. Áine had many years ago ceased to tell the tale to anyone else, for the children made fun of her and the adults regarded her with either condescending indulgence or keen suspicion.

"She likely was, my dearest heart." Tesn smiled at the girl, her dark eyes kind in her wrinkled face. "We'll talk about it more tonight. You should go and change your dress. If you ask sweetly, I think Dydgi means to do wash this afternoon and she might help you."

Áine nodded and stood. She went to the low cot she shared with Tesn and pulled her leather pack out from under the bed. Her second dress was better mended than the one she wore, though no less plain.

She went outside and walked the short distance to the freshwater stream. She hissed at the cold water but dutifully scrubbed her feet. She pulled off her soiled dress and rinsed the mud from her legs and arms as well. For good measure she splashed her face, recalling the touch of the selkie. She wondered if it were the same one who had carried her across the sea and nursed her on the shore.

Shivering, Áine pulled on her second dress as she fought to recall any of the selkie's words. Perhaps Tesn would know the language if Áine could remember something about how it had sounded.

The girl tucked her dirty dress under her arm and tugged free the leather ties on her braids. She ran her fingers through her long red hair and pulled it back into a single braid as she walked.

Áine returned to the lodge and found the women circled around the very pregnant Wladus who lay on a makeshift padding of deerskin before the warmth of the hearth.

"Her water's broken," Tesn told Áine as the girl walked to her side. "What should be done now?"

Áine knit her brows as she concentrated. "If her contractions are weak, we should make a tea of raspberry leaf. For pain we can give a tea of chamomile and water elder. Liniment of lavender and chamomile should be rubbed on the belly and lower back to help ease tension and make pushing easier." She looked up at Tesn and relaxed a little as the old woman smiled.

"Very good, love. Fetch my things. We've a while yet 'til the babe starts to come, but we should be ready."

The men returned and the rain followed on their heels falling in large cold sheets that swept across the sea and up the beach toward the mainland. They repaired to a hut to wait out the birth, leaving the lodge to the women who held quiet vigil within.

Áine nodded off, curled on the cot before the fire. She woke to Tesn's gentle touch.

"It's time." Tesn turned back to the women.

Wladus crouched now over the clean rushes. Blood dripped from between her legs. Áine knew this was normal enough, for it was not the first birth she'd assisted. She hovered near Tesn as the wisewoman intoned gentle prayers and rubbed sweet-smelling oil into the stretched skin of the pregnant woman's belly.

The night deepened and still the baby did not come. The woman's pains intensified until she could hold herself up no longer and lay back instead with a pad of soft leather clenched between her teeth. Tesn felt her belly and then eased her fingers into the birth passage to feel for the baby. She could just touch the crown of its head. The child was the right way round yet still not passing as it should have. She sat back on her heels to think.

Áine knelt beside her mentor, recognizing that look of deep concentration. Something was definitely wrong.

Wladus looked up at them both between painful contractions, her dark eyes full of worry and pain. Áine reached out and touched her knee, smiling in reassurance as she'd seen Tesn do many times.

A strange jolt went up her arm, almost like a muscle cramping. Suddenly it was difficult to breathe as her belly filled with pain and the blood rushed in her ears. She grabbed at her neck with both hands and tried to free herself from the phantom strangling cord she felt there.

The pain faded immediately and she could breathe again. Everyone, including the exhausted mother, stared at her.

"The baby," Áine said with strange certainty, "the birthing cord is twisted around his neck. I felt it."

One of the women backed away from the group, her fingers crossing in front of her heart to ward off evils. The other two looked at Áine with a mix of fear and awe on their faces.

"Could the child be right?" Dydgi asked as she looked to Tesn.

"Aye, more than right I think. The babe is crowning but going no further. It would make sense. Sometimes a women's intuition begins early, it seems." She smiled a wise and careful smile that disarmed much of the tension in the room.

Wladus's half-gagged scream disarmed the rest as the focus shifted back to her.

"Áine, scrub your arm, my heart. We'll need your capable little hands to free the baby."

Áine nodded and dashed to the hearth. She gritted her teeth against the scalding heat of the water, but she knew that it must be as hot as she could stand to keep infection from opening a path to evil in the body. *I guess I get to free two babies today.* She turned back to Tesn with wide green eyes.

"Tell me what to do, mother."

It was nothing like freeing the seal pup. Tesn guided her verbally as Áine slid her oiled hand inside Wladus's body. She felt the soft crown of the head and gently pushed it back until she could slip her own slim hand into the womb. She felt the cord, letting her strange, double sense of being both the child and herself guide her to the right place. She closed her green eyes and slowly, so terribly slowly, loosened the birth cord until she could twist it free of the child's head.

She let go and pulled her hand from the woman as soon as she felt that the baby had bloodflow again. Her hand was covered in blood and sticky fluids and a fresh rush of blood followed its removal from the womb. Áine went to rinse it off as Tesn had the women lift Wladus to crouch so she might push again.

Áine leaned against the hearth and watched. There was a lot of blood now, but births always had a lot of blood. The baby came, Tesn gently pulling the child free and hanging him upside-down as she expertly cleared the fluids from his tiny nose with her other hand. The boy's first cry rang out through the lodge and broke the silence. The women laughed and patted their friend as Áine came forward with a sharp knife and soft cloth. The wisewoman and her assistant bathed the baby. He had the thick white cream coating his skin that newborns sometimes got when the birth was long or difficult.

Wladus slowly stopped bleeding as she drank down the special tea Tesn prepared for her. She was helped onto the bed they'd brought in for her and tucked in with a heavy quilt. Her son's appetite whet with a little honey on his tongue, he settled in and drank his first meal with barely a complaint.

Deicws, Wladus's husband, came in and greeted his wife with a broad smile. His first child was a son and a tiny perfect babe at that. He gave a necklace of beautiful shell beads to Tesn in thanks.

"We've lost the two before this, early in her time. Thank you for saving my son." His front teeth were crooked when he smiled behind his thick beard.

"It be my assistant you'll want to thank. It was her intuition and her small hands that saved your son's life," Tesn said, taking the necklace. Áine knew they'd trade it in a bigger village for supplies. A wisewoman carried only what she needed and had no use for baubles.

Deicws turned to the strange girl. If not for her large green eyes, he'd have wondered more if she were not a changeling or one of the Fair Folk what with her pale white skin and blood-red hair. She had a strangely brave and confident demeanor as well, rare in a girl so young.

"I thank you, Wise One's apprentice." He nodded solemnly to her.

Áine nodded to him as well, smiling at the appreciation and glowing with pride that Tesn approved of what she'd done.

They slept on the cot, Tesn rising at dawn to check on the sleeping mother and baby. Áine, bleary-eyed, sat up as her mother returned to the bed.

"I felt his pain, I felt her pain. How is that, Tesn?" she whispered.

"I don't know, my heart." Tesn had been thinking on that very thing since the others had left them. "I think perhaps it was the selkie's gift." She kissed the top of Áine's head and drew her in close.

That made sense to Áine's young mind. She was special, after all, so it was fitting that the selkie would give her such a gift. "I'll make sure to use it well then," she said seriously.

"What is our rule, love?" Tesn smiled into her child's hair.

"Do no harm." Áine said as she sank down sleepily in her foster mother's arms. "Mother?"

"Yes dearest?"

"I think they should name him Moelrhon, after the seal." Áine smiled and slipped into sleep.

Eight

The rain had let up early that morning, but the ground shifted and soaked through Áine's shoes, giving her the sensation of walking on a wet blanket. Tesn, leaning heavily on her walking staff, wore a blank expression broken only by tiny smiles everytime Áine glanced back. Though the season turned toward spring, the days were still short and darkness came before they'd reached the next village.

Áine set about making a fire as best she could from the drier wood she found under the spreading oaks while Tesn rolled out an oiled cloth that would protect their bodies from the worst of the wet ground. The fire smoked and gave off little heat, barely enough to heat water for tea.

The wisewoman and her young apprentice ate a cold dinner of hard bread and little cakes of fruit and fat. After Áine stoked the fire as best she could, they curled up together and fell into a fitful sleep.

Áine woke abruptly from a dream of cobwebs and fire to the dim grey light of false dawn and a huge wolf stalking the edge of their camp. She jumped to her feet, scrabbling for her staff.

The huge beast, gaunt with hunger and scarred from a hard life, growled deep. His jaws dripped foul-smelling foam and his body twitched, eyes rheumy and full of promised death.

"Áine," Tesn's voice came from beside her ankle as the old woman rose very slowly to kneeling. "He's sick, be careful. If we show him strength, he might leave."

Áine nodded, not taking her eyes from the wolf. The creature growled again and leapt straight for her. She swung the staff but it was caught by the wolf. He ripped it from her grasp, sending her tumbling sideways, almost into the smoldering fire.

The wolf twisted with a snarl and darted for Tesn.

Áine, with adolescent bravery, grabbed a smoking brand from the fire and threw herself between the charging wolf and her mother. The brand smashed into the wolf's face with a sickening crunch. The huge creature screamed and thrashed away, disappearing into the dark woods.

Áine half-crouched, shivering. It took her a moment to realize the pain in her hand and she released the charred branch with a tiny cry. Her skin was blackened and red from gripping the burning wood so tightly. Tesn's cool fingers wrapped around her wrist, steadying her. She poured a little water over Áine's hand.

"You are lucky, love. Is but a slight burn. I think it likely you gave that wolf far worse, my brave, beautiful child." The old woman shook her head.

Áine took a couple deep breaths. "I don't think I'll be able to get back to sleep," she said.

Tesn chuckled. "I, also. It's light enough. Walking off the tension will be good for us both, I think."

They arrived in a little village along the coast of Cantref Gowen near midday to find a wedding celebration in full swing. The wisewoman was greeted with much respect and kindness, though the chief and others looked at her young companion with the normal mix of curiosity and suspicion.

Bowls full of savory goose and mushrooms, Áine and Tesn settled a little apart from the main group. Áine ate slowly, watching the newly married couple. Something within her stirred as she saw the husband lift little tidbits and feed them to his new wife. There was a mystery there, lingering between the two young people. Something Áine desperately wanted to touch, to understand. They looked both shy and content at the same time.

Áine turned to Tesn. "Is it always so at weddings?"

Tesn, seeing the young couple, smiled sadly. "No, love, not always. Marriage is first a contract, usually to bind two families together or bring in fresh wealth and goods. That the two people care for each other is a good sign, but often that, too, comes with time. In a small village like this, it is more likely. The more important the family involved, the less likely such affection will exist before the marriage, for it is less likely the two would even know each other beforehand."

Áine digested this information as she chewed. "What about wisewomen? We are freer than the village women, no? Can we marry who we wish?" She watched the couple, imagining a dark youth looking at her with such tenderness.

As her body had started awkward changes this last year, so had her mind it seemed. She found herself self-consciously brushing down her hair when around handsome youths her own age. This annoyed her; people always looked on her strangely, and she didn't want to care even a bit what anyone besides Tesn thought.

"Áine, love." The sorrow in Tesn's voice made Áine turn her head. The old woman's dark eyes looked at her, full of deep compassion. "Wisewomen do not marry. A wife belongs to her husband, a wisewoman belongs to all men, all people. We do not settle or raise families, though we do occasionally have children. The boys are fostered, the girls raised to follow our path as I have raised you."

"I see. But if we do not marry, how do we have children?" Áine bit her lip. She knew the basics of how babies were made, but she'd not seen an unmarried woman give birth in all her thirteen years.

"Ah, that. You are a little young yet, my love, but just as there are many kinds of injury, not all of them physical, so, too, are there many ways to bring healing. In a few years, I'll show you what I mean. There is joy in this healing too, you'll see."

Áine turned and looked back at the young couple. The woman bent her wreathed head close to hear something her husband murmured to her and then laughed, radiating joy. *But what if that's what I want?* She shoved the uncomfortable feeling aside.

Tesn knew best, and anyway, Áine thought bitterly, who would want a girl marked by the fey as she was? She put her back to the happy scene and stared off over the rooftops into a deep-blue sky.

Nine

Áine put her back to the wind and pulled her cloak tighter against the autumn wind. She slipped the cloak pin back into it, knowing that nothing short of five more brooches could hold the cloak tight to her body in this wind. At least the soaking drizzle they'd walked through since morning had finally given way to a cloudy but drier afternoon.

Tesn, leaning heavily on her staff, plodded ahead of Áine on the slight path they followed along the cliffs overlooking the sea. Áine shook her head. Here she was struggling with the wind and cold, and Tesn, who had a good extra forty years in age over Áine, was moving along as though today were a sunny stroll in the loveliest day of summer. It didn't help that Áine hadn't quite gotten her land legs back after the rough two-day sea voyage.

Quit being such a lame goose, she admonished herself. *Two days travel across the great bay is hardly a sea journey. You came further on the back of a seal when you were tiny.*

She sighed. They'd landed at the tip of Cantref Llynwg, for Tesn wanted to travel up to Arfon for the winter. The boat had been Áine's idea. Tesn was getting too old for so much walking, despite what her adoptive mother said about wisewomen and immortal legs.

The whole journey worried Áine. It had started last spring when Tesn gave Áine a red belt signifying her graduation from apprentice to full wisewoman status. At twenty-one, she was thrilled to achieve what she'd studied her whole life to become. However, instead of staying on their usual circuit of the southern cantrefi, Tesn had begun to migrate north along the coast.

It was a wet and uneasy summer. Everywhere they went people were sick with coughs and lung fevers, the damp getting into the livestock as well. Áine's unique gift of knowing the pain in others tired her and their travel wasn't nearly as quick as Tesn might have liked.

As the fall harvests approached and they'd only reached Cantref Cered, Tesn had finally told Áine that she feared she'd not too much longer to live in this life. She wanted to travel to Arfon where she had been born. Tesn had never gone back since a wisewoman took her as apprentice. She wished to return and see if her family lived. If so, Tesn wished to finish out her twilight years there. She wanted Áine to come with her and take a lover that she might have a daughter to apprentice someday.

"Your first shall be a girl. I've had the true dreaming of it," Tesn had said to Áine.

Áine knew they'd never make Arfon by winter on foot, not with Tesn's slowing pace and the horrible weather that seemed to persist through all seasons this year. So she'd engaged a fisherman to ferry them across the wide mouth of Cymru to the shore of Llynwg. He could not sail them up around the point and to Arfon due to the strong currents that flowed past Llynwg's coast and the Gefell, the river that ran down to the sea from the great woods of Llynwg, Eifon, and Arfon, was too swollen with rain to navigate with any ease. But the boat had saved them weeks of walking, for all Áine's seasickness.

The cold wind caught at her cloak again and wormed its way inside, pulling her back to the present. She stretched her long legs and caught up to her mentor.

"Tesn, the boatman said there was a village nearby; perhaps we can stay the night there before we move north?" She was cold and tired and welcomed the thought of a warm night indoors at a real hearth.

Tesn looked at her foster daughter and smiled. "That's a good plan, child. We'll turn a bit east then and see. We've got to find the river anyway." Her eyes were dark and bright as always but she also was glad at the idea of a warm hearth. She put on a strong show for Áine, but her bones ached and her chest hurt with every damp, cold breath.

It was nearing full dark by the time they spotted the village. Long lean hounds rushed out to greet them with bony wagging tails as they crossed between the buildings into the light of torches, looking for a central hall. Two men stepped from the largest building to greet them with a small, middle-aged woman on their heels.

"I greet you." Tesn said, holding open her cloak so that her red belt and undyed clothing would name her profession and status. Áine behind her did the same, shivering as the damp air cut through the aging wool of her gown.

"Wisewomen, we greet you. I am Meiler ap Eynon, and this is my sister, Morfyl." The shorter of the two men spoke, introducing himself and the tiny woman beside him. The other man turned out to be little more than a youth of perhaps fifteen who stood awkwardly by with a strangely hopeful look on his face. Áine felt a tingle in her blood. Something was wrong here.

"It seems the gods have answered our prayers with not one wisewoman, but two. We are so grateful that you've come." Morfyl stepped forward past her brother. "Our grandfather is ill and nothing seems to ease his pain." Her brown eyes were deeply lined and exhausted shadows darkened her lids.

Áine looked at Tesn and suppressed a sigh. Such was the life of a wisewoman. As Tesn loved to put it, the gods guided their feet as they would, unknown need pulling them from one place to another.

"Take us inside, child. We'll happily see what might be done." Tesn smiled her comforting smile at the little group.

They stepped into the hall and found that a bed had been set up near the roaring hearth. The two long tables were pushed aside to the far wall and there was a small group of men and women gathered on benches around the venerable man who lay amidst the piled furs and woolen blankets on the bed.

Tesn tsked and turned to Morfyl. "We'll need the room cleared of folk while we talk to your grandfather. Too many cooks spoil the food."

Morfyl nodded. "May we stay?" She motioned to her brother and then to herself.

Tesn nodded. Áine undid her oversized cloak and then removed the heavy pack. She set it down against a bench and carefully removed the top layer of folded spare clothing to get at the waterproofed and oiled leather healing kit beneath. Unfolding the pouches on the table, she carefully checked each for dampness before turning to Tesn and nodding. They were ready.

The old man in the bed watched them with clear eyes, waiting to be introduced. He could already tell they were wisewomen from the red belts and plain dress. His eyes widened as Áine approached the bed, taking in her blood-red hair and pale skin. She was used to it and smiled calmly at the little group.

"Grandfather, these are wisewomen, come to help you." Morfyl smiled at him, the love in her gaze making her suddenly appear a decade younger.

"I see that. Wise Ones, I greet you." He tried to sit up straighter and had to take a couple of heaving breaths, the strain clear in his face. "I am Ynyr ap Eynon. The elder Eynon, not my son, rest his spirit well. You've met my grandchildren here, and I think my great-grandson as well." Áine realized he must be referring to the youth who had greeted them with the others.

"How old are you, Ynyr?" she asked as she looked at his deeply lined face.

He laughed though it died in a fit of heaving and left him lying back again on the pillows. "I'm not certain, though I think I've nearly eighty years."

"And she thought I was old." Tesn smiled. The smile died in her eyes as she returned to business. She asked him a series of the standard questions. Where does it hurt, what does it feel like to cough or to piss, how was his appetite, and other questions.

Ynyr had some symptoms that could be attributed to old age. His bones ached when it was damp or cold, his appetite was gone completely, and he had trouble sleeping some nights while others he could barely keep himself awake. His mind was sharp and able, however.

The new symptoms had come on late this summer. Where before he'd been able to keep down food, he often felt a burning in his throat and belly after eating even the thinnest of sops. There'd been a little blood in his urine, though it was infrequent. He'd lost weight as well. Though he'd never been a heavy man, he'd gotten hearty in his old age as inactivity and the doting love of his grandchildren kept him fed and happy.

There were other signs as well, obvious to the wisewomen. He smelled of sickness and age but it was tinged also with the metallic scent of true illness. His eyes were yellowed, which could be age or something worse, and his gums and tongue were very pale.

"Do you sweat at night? Even if you are chilled?" Áine asked.

"Aye. What does that mean?" He looked at her.

Tesn shook her head. "We don't know yet. We'll need to do a full examination, if you don't object."

"I don't at all." He managed a somewhat brave and leering smile. "It'll be a nice change to be handled by a woman not related to me."

Áine smiled back as she washed her hands in the water Morfyl had heated for them. She appreciated the man showing a good face for his grandchildren. *He knows he's old and close to death anyway. I think he can already guess we'll be able to do naught but ease his pain.*

Tesn washed as well and they pulled the coverings off the old man with the help of his granddaughter. Meiler stood by and Áine appreciated that he refrained from pacing, though he couldn't help but stare at her with a worried, questioning look from time to time. Their love and concern for the old man touched her heart and she looked at Tesn with a pain of her own love.

Let her live 'til eighty. As if hearing her thoughts, the wise woman looked up at Áine with her deep-set dark gaze and gave her a tiny reassuring smile that flickered for a moment like a spark in the darkness.

"Go on, loves, leave the women and I now." Ynyr motioned to his grandchildren. They looked as though they'd protest, especially Meiler, who glanced again at Áine, but instead, after a long moment, they both nodded and gave in to his will as they met his ancient, clear eyes with their own troubled ones. Morfyl pulled her brother out and they closed the door behind them against the autumn damp and chill.

Ynyr was painfully thin under the covers. He looked old and vulnerable with only a thin linen shift covering him from wrist to knee.

Tesn looked at Áine and said softly, "It's time."

Áine nodded and took a deep breath. She noticed all her own aches and pains and carefully catalogued them so that they'd not mar her diagnosis. She leaned over Ynyr.

"Are you a Fair One come to guide me beyond the veil?" he asked as she reached for his hand.

It was not the first time Áine had been asked that question and she sighed. "No, grandfather. I'm only a mortal healer come to ease your pain. Now hush and let me work." She softened her chiding tone with another smile.

Her long white fingers closed around his thin hand. A wave of sickness washed through her. Her joints ached and her lungs hurt. While her vision was clear enough, her eyes stung from the light of the fire and little lamps of fat and wax. There were a few bedsores along his buttocks and behind his knees he'd not said a word about. Though they felt clean and free of infection, she recognized the pain of old wounds that wouldn't heal. Áine noticed and catalogued these as well, wondering how he lived with such pain. He swallowed and Áine felt the pain of that in her own throat, fire leaping from her belly to race up to her mouth and then back down again. Her saliva was thin and tasted of ash and copper.

Taking another deep breath, Áine pushed herself deeper. There she felt the little lumps of sickness. It was in his throat, in his lungs, and down in his stomach as well. She let go of his hand with a small, sorrowful cry.

Ynyr met her eyes and seemed to deflate as a look both calm and accepting stole over his thin face.

Áine pushed back the sudden burn of tears. "I'm sorry, grandfather. You've got the wasting sickness."

"Sorry, child? I've lived a long time and seen my children's children have children. I held only faint hope anyway that it might be something easy. But you don't live this long on hope." Ynyr gave her a wan smile.

Tesn began to pile the blankets back on him. Áine shook herself and turned to help. No one spoke for a while as the fire popped and crackled in the hearth.

"We can ease your pain, Ynyr, though it could speed your passing to do so," Tesn said.

He nodded. "I understand. Fetch my grandchildren in so they know the fairy's magic hasn't eaten me."

Áine gave an exaggerated sigh and made a face at him but went to the door. She opened it, unsurprised to find Meiler and Morfyl standing with the youth in the cold outside. She beckoned to them all.

They came in and moved quickly to their grandfather's bed. Áine and Tesn pulled back and let the old man speak to his offspring. He told them what the wisewomen had found, though not the mysterious process of it, and the option Tesn had laid out for them. Meiler, upon hearing it, cried out and shook his head.

"There must be something else to be done," he said as he turned with pained eyes to the wisewomen.

"Meiler, dear one, I am old. I hurt. It is time I moved beyond the veil and left this life to the young and able. Would you deny the chance to pass without pain in the company of those closest to my heart?" Ynyr asked.

His courage touched Áine. She'd witnessed the passing of more than she'd like in her life thus far, but few had the strength to face it so bravely. She put her hand on Tesn's shoulder and squeezed gently. Tesn looked up at her adopted daughter and raised her own small dark hand to rest on Áine's own.

The little group talked quietly at Ynyr's bedside for a few moments more and then Morfyl turned to the patient pair.

"What do you need?" she asked with a resigned look.

Áine brewed an infusion of fennel, mint, comfrey, and mullein to ease the pain in his lungs. She added a generous amount of clover honey to the brew and helped Yfyr drink it down sip by painful sip. His breathing eased slowly and he smiled at her.

Tesn took the two large stones brought to her by Meiler's son who was called Ynyr Vach, or Ynyr the smaller, which Ynyr the older thought was a fine joke when looking at his tall and hale grandson. She bathed the stones with warm water and said a small prayer of healing over them. Then she brought them to the bedside and motioned for everyone else to stand away.

Ynyr watched with interest. "I'd heard of this wisewoman's magic, though I've never seen it done in my lifetime."

Tesn nodded. "Aye, 'tis a dying art. We grow fewer in number every generation, but not all old knowledge is lost to us yet." She turned to his grandchildren. "Áine and I will use these stones to draw the pain from his body. Please, it takes much concentration, give us space, if you will."

Áine moved to the other side of the bed and took one of the stones from Tesn. With coordinated and practiced gestures, each woman took a hand of the old man into her own and laid her free hand onto the warm clean stones.

Áine visualized the man's pain as a living thing, crawling like a shadow over his body and through his blood. She pulled on the shadow, willing it to follow her will and come free of his weakened body toward the strength of the stone. She lost track of the time as she fed the pain measure by measure into the stone under her hand. She didn't stop until she felt the stone begin to crack under her palm. Then, with another careful breath, she pulled gently away and released her patient.

Looking across the bed she saw that Tesn was already done. Pulling pain was a hard task and Tesn's age was telling in her lack of stamina for a prolonged healing these days. Tesn smiled at her and then sat down heavily on the hearth.

"Wrap the stones in white cloth and bury them outside or toss them into the river, if running water is close enough. We'll all need food; healing takes a lot from patient and healer," she said to the nervously waiting group.

Morfyl gave herself a little shake and nodded. "Of course. Come, Vach, help me with the stones."

Ynyr closed his eyes and relaxed into sleep as the stones were removed, wrapped, and buried by the great-grandson outside the hall. Tesn and Áine were served a thick stew before the two grandchildren returned to their bedside vigil.

Tesn dozed beside the fire and Áine wrapped a now-dry cloak around her shoulders. She looked toward the bed and saw that while Meiler dozed as well, Ynyr's eyes were wide open and he was staring at her. She moved to stand beside Morfyl.

"Thank you, pengoch," he said, calling her "red-hair", something which only children had done in her youth.

"For what, grandfather? We've only done as we've been allowed. I'm sorry that we could not do more." Áine laid a hand without thinking on Morfyl's shoulder, trying to comfort the sad woman. She felt the woman stiffen under her touch and pulled her hand away.

"No, I'm sorry," Morfyl said suddenly as she shifted to look up at the tall fair-skinned, green-eyed healer. "Please, I don't mean to give offense."

"No offense is taken, Morfyl." Áine looked sadly down at her. "You think you're the first to not wish my touch or to be suspicious of my origin? Would it help ease your fears if I touched something wrought of cold iron?"

"Please, that isn't necessary. Forgive me, this is a hard night." Morfyl held a hand out to Áine and didn't flinch as the woman took it with her own pale fingers.

"She's a gift, come to see me beyond the veil, and no mistake." This time when Ynyr laughed it was just a hoarse, soft sound and caused him only a little pain. He felt light and free, as though only the smallest of threads held him to his body. It was a good feeling after so long living with pain. "Wake Meiler, there. I think I'm about ready to leave."

Áine moved away again as Morfyl reached across and shook her brother awake. Ynyr took a hand of each in his own and spoke in quiet tones of his pride and love. He asked that when they saw his other great-grandchild the following summer to request she name her first son after their father and his son Eynon, rest him well. Then he lay back into the pillows and looked again at Áine. She touched Tesn's shoulder and they both rose to come to the foot of the bed.

"Thank you. I'm ready now." Ynyr smiled and closed his eyes.

The little group stayed nearly unmoving until he issued a final and shuddering breath. Morfyl, who'd managed to stave off weeping thus far, gave a small cry and threw herself down over her grandfather's body as her own small shoulders shook with sorrow. Meiler looked up at the wisewomen, his dark eyes reddened and wet with tears.

"I'll prepare herbs for his bath," Tesn said softly.

Meiler just nodded and looked back down, placing a hand on his sister. Áine blinked hard to contain her own tears. The last thing she needed was to weep here and now. She busied herself with helping Tesn. Tomorrow, perhaps, on the road, there would be time for sorrow and loss.

They set off early the next morning, though they'd hardly slept the night before. Áine had protested, but Tesn was set on leaving that morning. She meant to make the river by afternoon and from there they could turn north and, she hoped, make Clun Cadair by nightfall on the day following. Áine hated the idea of camping out in the cold and rain on the moors but knew from the stubborn calm in Tesn's face that there was little she could to do deter her companion.

They made good time, the rain holding off until near evening. The river was narrow and fast, swollen with rain. They found a small wind-stunted cluster of trees a small distance from the bank and made camp. There was no dry wood for a fire and so they spent a damp night huddled together under the oiled skins of their little tent.

Áine dreamed. She dreamt often, but only on occasion did she have vivid and strange dreams beyond the usual half-remembered images of everyday life. That night, hugging Tesn close for warmth, she had one of her stronger visions.

She stood alone in a forest, the trees towering above her with long strands of silvered moss hanging like banners from the branches high overhead. To her right and then to her left, out of the wood emerged two long-legged hounds. Their eyes were the warm brown of wood in firelight and their coats deep black. She looked down and saw herself standing on a growing number of pure white stones. When she looked back up, Tesn stood a little way ahead of her in the trees. The old woman smiled at her and then suddenly sank out of sight. There was water everywhere and Áine couldn't breathe.

She woke in the light of false dawn, gasping. Tesn slept beside her, alive and oblivious to Áine's sudden panic. Áine shook her head at herself. She was no child to be wallowing in a night terror so. She curled back down to wait for the true dawn.

Tesn had a small cough in the morning but shrugged off Áine's concern, pointing out that if they made good enough time, they'd be in a large warm holding by nightfall. Clun Cadair was, after all, the seat of the Chief of Llynwg. The rain began again in earnest as they packed away their shelter and broke their fast with a cold meal of hard bread and boiled eggs given to them the day before by a sorrowful Morfyl.

The river swelled further as the day grew older. Áine glanced at it nervously from time to time, recalling her dream. Tesn marched stubbornly onward, hiding her cough within the hood of her cloak as best she was able.

Ahead, near a bend in the river but beyond where the women could see, the river had grown so full of debris from its headwaters in the forest that it had dammed itself. Two large broken tree trunks were wedged in the steep banks at the bend, piling up more debris behind them. The wind and rain grew fierce as the day progressed and it was hard to tell how late it was since the great black clouds hid the sun from sight.

Áine glanced again at the river and then back to her companion as they neared a bend. Tesn smiled at her.

"This bend means we're nearing the forest. I think we'd be able to see it if not for this bothersome rain." Tesn hunched her shoulders.

"It's getting late, mother. I think we'd best find a camp and wait 'til light again. It's hard to see with this storm." Áine was cold, wet, and tired. The ground beneath her boots was growing slicker by the moment and she thought she'd never have dry feet again.

"We can't be far now, love. I've no mind to sleep outside in this wet; I'd rather walk for that at least warms my blood." Tesn said. Their heads were bent close so the wind could not tear away their words.

With a mighty crack heard by both women, the trees blocking the river lost the fight. A huge flood of branches and water spilled down to the bend and broke over the banks.

The water hit Áine at about waist height. She'd barely time to scream a warning as she looked up before she was swept away from Tesn's reaching hand.

The pack and her cloak dragged her under. She couldn't breathe. She grabbed at the cloak and managed to tear it over her head. It was swept immediately away. The swirling current bobbed her to the surface for one precious moment and she gasped for air as something snagged the pack still slung over her shoulders and pulled her down again.

Áine struggled under the water to shed the heavy pack. She twisted and suddenly felt it come free as one of the straps snapped.

She rose to the surface again and tried to open her eyes. There was water everywhere and no sign of Tesn. She saw something large and dark spinning toward her and ducked down reflexively. Something struck her head with a sharp pain and then there was only darkness.

Ten

At Clun Cadair, Emyr pulled on clothing as Idrys flopped on the bed and let his tongue loll. He pulled the coverlet over the bed and shooed the hound down.

"Quit drooling in my sheets." Emyr smiled, knowing full well that it had been he drooling all night and Idrys who'd tolerated it.

The two emerged into the hall and waved to a rumpled-looking Urien and Llew. Llew's wife, Caron, smiled from the hearth where she stirred a pot of oat porridge. Emyr snagged a bowl from the stack on the hearth and nodded thanks to Caron as the pretty woman ladled his breakfast.

"There's honey and a preserve of water elder and blackberry on the table. Fresh milk too." Caron ducked her head and blushed at his smile.

Emyr thanked her and sat down with his men. Idrys flopped down on the rushes beside the table. He'd break his own fast later since he didn't care for porridge even when he was in human form. Emyr always remembered to cut cold meat from the cellar before they went about the day's duties.

"Some storm, eh?" Llew said as he spooned a generous portion of preserve into his bowl.

Emyr opted for honey. "Aye. The rain seems to have let up. I think we should ride out and make sure the shepherds' crofts are still intact, especially near the river."

Idrys lifted his head and gave a small yip of approval. Emyr turned his head and smiled at his brother.

"I'll get the horses saddled." Urien swallowed the remainder of his food in three wolf-like gulps, wiped his bearded chin with his sleeve, and stood up. All three young men had felt cooped in by the rain in the last week and were eager for adventure.

They rode out as the morning light grew toward the promise of a sunlit day. The river looked as though it had crashed over its banks in multiple places as they cantered over the moor. Emyr was glad that the holding was far enough from the swollen waters to not risk flooding. They didn't try to ford, instead choosing to check on the crofts on the near side due to the still-raging current.

They reached the first croft quickly and found Tuder and Hywel letting out the flock of sheep. Their flock was the larger of the long-wooled, white-faced sheep. The men hailed the shepherds and asked how the night had passed.

"Oh, you can see by the silt marks the river fair tried to down us, but fell a few feet short, didn't it." Hywel gave them a good-natured grin through his thick beard.

"Glad to hear it." Emyr nodded. The sheep eyed Idrys nervously and the sheep dogs kept their distance, remaining between the lean hound and the flock. Dogs and sheep didn't care for Idrys, though horses and cats paid him no more mind than they would a man.

They rode on down along the river, letting their horses stretch their legs. The sun peeked from between high, fluffy clouds and though the air held its autumn chill, the day sparkled with promise.

Idrys found the women first and set up a warning howl that drew the men past the bend in the river. Emyr dismounted and dropped his reins to ground-tie his mount. The others followed suit and they all made their way cautiously through a field of broken branches and other debris.

Underneath a heavy, snapped-off trunk, Emyr found the wisewoman. Her old face was swollen from the water, her eyes clouded over with death's veil and staring into nothing. The upper half of her body was clear enough that he could see the undyed wool of her dress girthed by the signature red belt of her station, her cloak tangled and obscuring one arm.

"Govannon's balls, a wisewoman." Llew came up beside him and shook his blond head.

"We should dig her out, give her a burial," Urien said.

Emyr nodded and was about to reply when he heard Idrys give a sharp bark. "Work on that, I'll go see what Cy wants." He picked his way over the silt and branches until he could see Idrys further down river standing near a dark lump.

The lump turned out to be another wisewoman, this one young and fair of skin. Her eyes were closed and as he reached her he thought he saw movement in her chest. Emyr pushed Idrys away.

"Go on, brother," he said, "Go use those oversized paws to help dig out the other." Idrys gave the dog equivalent of a shrug by dipping his head low and wagging his tail before turning and bounding off toward the other men.

Emyr bent and gently lifted the woman's head. He felt the knot at the back of it and saw the thin trickle of blood that flowed away into the silty soil. She was filthy, but alive. He pulled his cloak off and started to move the woman onto it. Maybe his mother could revive her if the head injury wasn't too serious.

Warm hands touched Áine's face and she murmured for them to leave her in the dark. But it was too late; pain found her hiding place and brought her into the light. With it came memory and she opened her eyes as she cried Tesn's name.

Emyr froze as the woman opened her eyes and said a word he could barely make out as a name through the raw pain of her cry. Her eyes were the brightest green he'd ever encountered, like sunlight through summer leaves. They were large and striking in her broad face. He couldn't make out the exact color of her hair through the mud and tangles. He thought perhaps a reddish brown.

"Sah, sah, Wise One. You're safe now. I'm going to help you, you're hurt," Emyr said as he tried to soothe her.

Áine stared up at the handsome youth. He looked to be about her age, clean-shaven with dark, curling hair that fell just below his shoulders and warm brown eyes. She could read nothing but kindness in the lines of his face and relaxed a little.

Her head hurt, as well as her right leg. *Tesn always says to take stock before acting. Think, you.* Áine sighed and let her body talk to her for a moment. Her head wound was superficial. She probably had a concussion, but it was hard to tell. Since it was daylight, if it were going to kill her, it would have done so when she was unconscious. Her right leg and ankle were another matter.

"I think," she said carefully, "my leg might be broken, and the ankle is definitely strained or bruised. Please, where is Tesn?"

"Was she your companion?" Emyr said but the sudden shadowed look in his eyes told her all she needed to know.

Áine stared through him as all her hope and joy at being alive fled her, leaving a hollow shell for grief to fill.

"Where?" she said very softly.

"She was trapped under a log; my men are digging her out now. We meant to give her a burial. You're lucky to have lived," he said the last to try to comfort her, knowing there was little he could do as her expression turned from hopeful to one of grim pain.

Áine struggled to rise and Emyr wisely didn't stop her. He helped her instead and draped his cloak around her damp and muddy shoulders. With him as her crutch they hobbled back toward the old woman.

Áine's first tears fell as they neared the bend and she could hear the men hacking at the trunk with the little hatchets. The tears dripped off her chin and soaked into the muddy collar of her ruined dress at first. She stumbled and fell to one knee, taking Emyr down with her.

"I'm sorry," she said and a tear fell from her nose to the earth where it bounced before laying still. She gasped and moved to cover it with her hand but Emyr was quicker.

He picked up the perfect pearl and stared at it as Áine scrubbed at her face with her free arm. She looked at him with worried, cautious eyes. He gave her a small smile and slipped the pearl into his belt pouch.

I spend half the day as a hound, Emyr thought, *who am I to judge a wisewoman whose tears turn to pearls when they touch the earth?* He'd have to mention it to Idrys, however, and see what his brother thought of it all.

They made their careful way and found that Emyr's companions and the hound had nearly freed Tesn. Urien and Llew looked up at the bedraggled pair. Emyr's trousers and tunic were smeared with mud, his knees and boots caked from their stumble.

Áine cried aloud with wordless grief and, tearing free of Emyr's strong arm, half crawled the last few feet to Tesn's side on her own.

"Tesn," she said over and over as she pulled the dead woman's hand from the mud and held it to her chest. Áine tried to call upon any power in her body, but found no response. Death was a pain she could not touch and Tesn had long since passed beyond.

"Not like this, mother. You weren't supposed to leave me like this. Mother!" She choked on her tears as they spilled onto the dead woman's dress and some onto the ground where they turned to tiny pearls. She didn't care if anyone noticed for it didn't matter now if they named her Other or outcast or thought she was fey. Besides, one of them already knew.

Urien and Llew looked at the tall woman for a moment and then turned back to pull the tree trunk free. They'd hacked enough branches loose to provide places to grip. Emyr pulled Áine away as the other two men lifted and pivoted the tree away from the dead woman. Urien gallantly offered up his cloak to wrap her body in. They lifted Tesn to the back of the calmest mare. Áine's pearl tears slipped unnoticed into the wet silt.

Áine looked at Emyr as he gently wrapped his cloak back around her and lifted her to his own horse. She sat staring out into the sunlit day with a grey, bleak expression, her green eyes dull with pain.

It was a long walk back to the holding. Llew walked as well out of respect for the others, though his horse danced at the end of the reins wanting to have its head again for the return to the stable.

Hafwyn, sitting in the courtyard spinning and carding wool with Caron and Melita, spied the men first with her sharp eyes. She saw them walking with a lone rider and that Urien's horse carried a bundled burden.

"I think we'd best get the herbs and heat some water. It looks like they might have found some refugees of the storm." She set aside her spindle and rose.

"Not one of the shepherds?" Caron rose as well, upsetting her pile of wool.

"I cannot say for sure." Hafwyn turned and walked to the hall as the other two gathered up their projects and made to follow her.

A few minutes later the sad group rode into Clun Cadair. Emyr helped Áine down from his horse as Urien and Llew carefully lowered her adopted mother's body. Áine leaned against Emyr as a beautiful middle-aged woman in a purple dress with a band of simple red and yellow embroidery decorating her neck and cuffs emerged from the hall. Her long dark hair was braided and pinned up with bone combs carved to look like birds diving. Áine recognized something kindred in the woman with the man upon whom she was currently leaning.

"I greet you, wisewoman. I am Hafwyn wreic Brychan. Be welcome to Clun Cadair," Hafwyn said and Emyr flushed as he realized he'd not even introduced himself to the young woman.

Hafwyn looked at the bundle that Urien held and realized it was a woman. She stepped quickly closer and saw the look of death on the ancient, wrinkled face beneath the muddy and tangled white braids.

"My mother," Áine choked out. She shivered against Emyr's warm strength.

"I'm sorry. We'll see her bathed and prepare her pyre. You must also bathe and do something about your injuries, yes?" Hafwyn recognized the lost, distracted look on Áine's face and motioned for Emyr to bring her inside.

Caron and Melita were filling the copper tub in Hafwyn's room. Áine barely protested as Emyr gently pressed her onto a bench and left the women alone.

"I did not get his name," Áine said as Hafwyn helped her pull her torn dress over her head. She hissed with pain as the dress pulled on her hair which in turn caused her head wound to smart anew.

"Nor have you given yours," Hafwyn said gently. "He's Emyr ap Brychan, my son, and chief of Cantref Llynwg now that his father has passed on."

"So young," Áine said, and then she flushed as she processed the rest of what Hafwyn had said. "I am Áine. And she." Áine paused and swallowed hard. "She, that is, outside, she's my mother, Tesn."

"Áine is not a usual name in Cymru, is it?" Hafwyn said keenly.

"No, it isn't," Áine replied.

Hafwyn pressed her no further; instead, she and Melita helped the young woman into the steaming bath. Áine sighed as the heat restored a measure of feeling to her flesh she hadn't cared was missing. The water stung the various scrapes and cuts, especially when Melita used a horn cup to dump water over her tangled hair and the oozing lump on the back of her skull.

Both the older women exchanged a look as Áine's hair came clean under their ministrations. They used a soap of lavender and tea rose. The bath water looked as though they'd filled it with mud, which technically they had. The woman under their hands, however, was revealed to be unusually fair of skin with strikingly red hair that flowed like dark blood over their hands and the back of the copper basin.

Hafwyn's eyes narrowed as the red and white coloring was not lost on her. She'd heard her son's descriptions of the Fair Lady who'd cursed them, however, and knew Áine's coloring, while striking, didn't quite live up to their fearful, reverent recounting. Besides, Idrys had told of the Lady's ability to heal with a touch, so surely if she were one of the Others this girl would have closed her own scrapes and healed her numerous bruises. She was certainly a mystery, this wisewoman with a name and the green eyes of the Isles.

A small gasp of pain escaped Áine's lips as the women helped her from the bath. Her ankle was swollen and the bruising, now revealed out of the filth, was quite awful.

"Is it broken?" Melita asked, looking at Hafwyn.

"I'm not sure," Áine answered her. "If you'll help me to sit, I can feel it out and see." She leaned heavily on Hafwyn.

"Melita, fetch her one of Caron's gown's, she taller than I. And bring my bag of herbs from the garden workroom." Hafwyn sat Áine on the bench again and helped her dry off with a soft white linen cloth.

"Thank you," Áine said, flushing though she wasn't sure why. Even in her haze of grief, she hadn't missed the looks the women exchanged. She was so used to the questions and suspicions that she was grateful the woman was saving them for another time.

Then she remembered Emyr and her pearl tear. *They'll have plenty of questions, won't they? And I'm not sure how to answer.* She sighed. She'd deal with all that later.

Now, first her leg, and then... Áine took a shuddering breath and shoved the wave of sorrow away. Then she'd burn her mother and build the cairn to bury her properly. She wished that they'd thought to look for her pack, but she remembered it breaking in the flood and knew chances were faint that they'd have found it anyway.

Áine let her mind sink into her body. There was the pain of many scrapes and bruises, all of which she acknowledged and filed away. She felt her head, a dizzying throb under the weight of her drying hair. Then she moved to the pain in her leg.

It was two injuries, she realized. Her calf was bruised down to the bone, though thankfully the bone itself was unbroken if sore. Her ankle had been twisted somehow in the torrent and she felt fluid in the joint that was irritating and inflaming the rest. Nothing would heal that but a tight binding and a week or two off her leg.

She opened her eyes and looked up at Hafwyn. "Nothing's broken, though the ankle is twisted and angry. I'll need tight binding and I'm afraid I can't travel for a week or two."

"Of course not. You're welcome here, wise one, as long as you wish to stay. Winter brings many ills and we'd be glad of your gifts." Hafwyn smiled and her tone made it clear that she meant what she said fully.

Áine realized with a start that in her distraction she'd forgotten to make a show of prodding the injuries and had instead, to all appearances, just sat quietly for a few moments before pronouncing her diagnosis. She shook her head at her clumsiness. Tesn would chide her for her foolish trust.

The sucking hollow loss hit her like a fist as her heart jumped from her chest and into her throat again. *Tesn won't be chiding me for anything, not anymore. I'd commit a hundred careless acts to hear her voice again.* Áine fiercely scrubbed at her eyes with her palms as Melita returned to the room.

The serving woman carried a soft woolen gown of deep blue with broad bands of red and yellow embroidery at the collar and down the sleeves. There were delicate bronze clasps at the cuffs and small bronze buttons decorating the front. It was beautiful and Áine sighed. She wasn't supposed to wear dyed or decorated clothing. Wisewomen, Tesn had taught her, always travel with only what they need and give up the trappings of comfort for knowledge. This allowed them a freedom women rarely enjoyed and they trusted the Gods to provide and the world to yield up a few of her mysteries. The only color she'd worn her whole life was the red belt that denoted the wisewomen's profession.

And where did that get us? Áine shivered. *Tesn is dead and I'm alone.* She looked up at Hafwyn. "Thank you," she said again, hating her slow mind.

The women helped her dress. Melita had scraped the mud from her red belt and offered it to her as well. Áine hesitated and then pulled the familiar leather around her hips and looped the trailing end through the simple bronze ring.

"We've no gowns of undyed wool, Wise One, I'm sorry. We'll make you one as soon as we're able," Melita said, licking her lips nervously and looking away from Áine's startling green gaze.

"I might be able to salvage mine, though I fear I've lost all our gear in that flood." She hesitated and dropped her eyes down to her lap. "My gear," she said softly.

Caron entered the room and noted the silent tension among the three women. Hafwyn stood by the filthy bath watching their guest who stared down at her folded pale hands. Melita was also standing, looking lost for once instead of her normal capable bustling self.

"I've got bindings and an assortment of herbs, plus an ointment for cuts, if it's needed," she said, taking in the fair skin and fresh-blood color of Áine's drying hair.

Áine nodded and set about binding her ankle up with Melita's capable assistance. The older woman gave herself a shake and returned to some measure of her usual self once given a task.

Gethin, now too old to spend much time with the flocks, though still strong enough for work, as he'd point out many times a day if questioned, came in with Urien to remove the copper tub.

Hafwyn helped Áine out into the hall where Caron had returned to fixing the midday meal of a simple bone broth thickened with soaked barley and a handful of small onions from the holding's garden.

It was late autumn. The flocks were already coming in from the moors and going to the small crofts that lay within the radius of a half-day's ride from the holding. Within a week or so, those who would winter in Clun Cadair from the mostly seasonal fishing villages down near the sea would straggle home to their now boarded and dormant dwellings within the berm.

Áine sat gratefully beside the hearth at the long table and accepted a bowl of rich broth. She sipped at it though to her it had no taste. Hafwyn and Melita sat across from her and spooned their own meal silently.

To break the awkward silence and distract from her lack of appetite, Áine asked them questions. "The holding seems empty. I saw boarded houses on the way in."

"Aye," Hafwyn replied. "The farming folk mostly will stay out for the winter, though some come in to the holding. The trappers will come home, as will our fishermen and their families. In a fortnight's time, perhaps less, Clun Cadair will be full enough."

Áine nodded. They were a little different in the south, where farming was more common and the land more clearly divided. There were other things different here as well.

"Your son, his men, they do not carry swords. Do you not worry about attack? You are not so far from the sea and that great wood must harbor some who bear ill will."

"We've good relations with Arfon and Eifon to the north and east. The current flows quickly past our coastline with few places to land. The northmen prefer easier and richer points to plunder. Our men are quick with a knife or a bow, though we've had no banditry since my husband's time." Hafwyn smiled. "We're peaceful folk here."

Áine was glad to hear it. She'd be traveling on her own, after all. *Going where?* she thought bitterly. Then she shook herself mentally and took a deep breath. *Tesn did for decades before you came, did she not? Why should you be different and give up the life she's taught you?* She balled her hands into fists below the table and closed her eyes. The women cleared her half-eaten meal and wisely left her in silence beside the fire.

Although he wasn't sure of his motivations, Emyr avoided the hall until the preparations for the wisewoman's pyre and cairn were complete. He tapped the belt pouch from time to time as he considered the mysterious green-eyed girl and her pearl tears.

She'd seemed mortal and human enough in her pain and her injuries. Oh, he acknowledged that if he hadn't seen the true fey up close, she might have disturbed him more with her strange tears. Perhaps she, too, was cursed. He shivered at the thought, both wishing it were true and wondering what he should do if so. A curse could be dangerous, and he didn't wish to bring any harm to his people. But turning her away for something she could not help was hardly compassionate either. Emyr struggled with his thoughts and lost himself to the easy work of chopping wood and collecting stones.

Caron brought out a bolt of clean sunbleached linen in which to wrap the dead woman. Emyr folded Tesn's arms and with Llew's solemn help gently encased the woman from head to foot in the clean cloth. Emyr scraped the mud from her bright red belt and coiled it carefully. He set it then on her chest and Llew helped him move her out into the courtyard and onto the waiting pyre.

It was late afternoon, the sun beginning to drop. Emyr knew from the tingle in his blood that sunset was coming quickly. He sighed and stepped into the hall.

His mother and Melita were keeping quiet vigil with their guest. Áine sat with her head bowed over her hands, which lay folded on the table. She wore one of Caron's gowns, the sleeves a little short on her long pale arms. Her hair was loose and spilled forward in a soft cascade of burnished scarlet. The color was so very near the remembered color of Seren's locks that he gasped and heard Idrys, who'd come in behind him, growl softly deep in his black furred throat.

At the sound Áine raised her head and the spell of memory was broken. Though her skin looked pale enough in the fire and lamplight, it was not iridescent with its own inner glow. Her face was striking, but not beautiful. Her nose was straight, and her lips full, almost petulant, even with the deep lines of sorrow marking her broad face. Her mouth was offset by a stubborn chin that bore a faint crooked scar. Her eyes were not swirling silver but instead that new leaf-green, which he remembered from earlier being marked with specks of gold like sunlight on leaves. Those eyes were now full of shadows and pain, too human in their reflective suffering.

Only her hair, straight and red as precious gems in the dancing light, only her hair was like the woman of the Fair Folk.

Emyr put his hand down to quiet Idrys and forced himself to smile and walk forward naturally. *What care I if she's some sort of halfblood? The stories say it's possible. She's a wisewoman and clearly human enough for grief and injury. She's not Seren, that's all that matters.*

Idrys kept his distance, circling the group and watching as his brother told them that the pyre was set and ready. Hafwyn tactfully suggested they sit and keep vigil 'til dark set in fully. Idrys heard Áine agree.

He sniffed the air, parsing her scent from the woodsmoke. She smelled of his mother's soap, lavender and tea rose, and something else besides. She had a scent almost like spiced wine, sweet and strange at once under the other threads of smell. She smelled human enough, the metallic taint of blood from her scabbing scratches adding in yet another layer. He sighed and turned to head to his room. The tingling in his blood was growing stronger. Soon enough he'd meet her as a man and could take her measure then. His brother seemed to like her well enough, though his face, too, was troubled.

Áine hobbled outside with the help of Melita. Emyr and his tall black hound had disappeared into one of the rooms off the back of the hall. Hafwyn brought a bench out for her and sat beside her, keeping vigil as Urien and Llew lit torches around the square to stave off the deepening gloom.

Áine felt like wood or perhaps stone. Dead and heavy. She could feel her heartbeat and cursed it softly under her breath. When the tears came, silent and thick, she made sure each was caught in her lap or her sleeves.

She looked up finally, rubbing her palms into her sore and reddened eyes. It was full dark and a little group had assembled. Hafwyn noticed her looking around and whispered introductions as each approached.

"That's Gethin there. He's our master of flocks." She nodded at the older man who stood a little distance from the pyre with his graying head bowed in respect. "And you already know Urien ap Daffyd and Llew ap Evadi," Hafwyn said, naming the men.

Urien was the shorter, stockier man with the thick umber beard. Llew was slender and tall, and fairer, though still more tan than Áine, with gold hair and a clean shaven face. Áine had met Melita virch Badi and Caron wreic Llew now by name, and so Hafwyn did not point them out again.

A small family appeared out of the darkness. Hafwyn named them all for Áine as well. The oldest was Madoc ap Madog whom all called Moel, the Bald, for his smooth pate. He was as old as Tesn had been and walked with a slight limp.

His son was Adaf, an unassuming man of middle years with his dark hair just starting to thin and worn loose about the shoulders. His wife and two young children followed. She was called Maderun and looked at her feet more than ahead. She was younger than her husband by a good decade if Áine reckoned it properly.

Maderun's daughters, Gwir, who was four, and Geneth, seven, clung to their mother's skirt and stared alternately between the pyre with its white-wrapped burden and Áine. Another handful of men and women filtered in, all passed their middling years. Áine lost track of names as her eyes fixed on the pyre and memories floated in and out of her vision, sharp behind bleak eyes.

Finally Emyr emerged, having washed the mud from his skin and changed clothing. He walked out into the square and nodded to Áine. She leaned heavily on Hafwyn and rose to her feet.

"This is…" She choked on her heart and paused to breathe again. "This is Tesn. She was my mother and my teacher. I've traveled near the length and breadth of Cymru learning by her side." She paused again as the tide of memories lifted her voice from her for a long moment. "She was the most generous, kind, loving, and patient woman ever to serve the people. I don't…I don't know what I'll do without her."

Áine crumpled then, falling against Hafwyn as a cry of pure anguish tore from her sore throat. She knew she should say the prayers to ease the passing of another. It's what Tesn would have done. *Damn her and damn what she'd have done. She can't do it, can she?* Áine stood there as Emyr walked forward to set the pyre aflame. She watched as the fire caught and consumed.

She turned to Hafwyn and asked for her small knife. The woman looked a question at her but did not ask it aloud and instead pulled the small blade from her belt.

Áine let go of her and limped toward the pyre. She gripped her hair in a tight fist and hacked into with the little knife. It came free in her hand, clean and soft and red as blood. Wisps of hair floated around her chin as she tossed the flowing handful onto the fire.

She stepped back and leaned against Hafwyn again. Hafwyn kept a tight arm around the taller woman's shoulders until finally Áine turned her face away from the growing heat and bent to weep into the shoulder of a stranger.

Eleven

They gave Áine the extra room off the central hall that was reserved for guests. She fell almost immediately into an exhausted slumber. Melita and Hafwyn made sure that her fire was well banked with coals and then slipped from the room as their guest's sobs died slowly into sleep.

"Poor thing," Melita said to Hafwyn as they walked into the main hall.

"Aye," Hafwyn said. "But the only thing that heals grief is time."

"Which she'll have in abundance here, I suppose." Idrys leaned against the long table with his still booted feet resting on the stone of the hearth. Emyr was sprawled on the rushes with a raised head and alert eyes that shifted between his mother and his twin.

"I meant it when I said she was welcome here as long she'd like to stay," Hafwyn said firmly.

Melita looked between the two and gracefully excused herself saying she was going to go check in and perhaps have supper with Llew and Caron if they'd no further need of her here. Idrys watched the older woman leave with a calm gaze and then turned back to his mother as she came to sit on the wide stone hearth.

"There's cold meat and fresh bread, if you want supper," Idrys offered.

"Nay, thanks love." Hafwyn sighed heavily. Emyr sat up and put his head in her lap. She smiled down at her other son and stroked his silken ears. "Too much sorrow today for eating, I think."

"Moel's fit to raise a fuss, I think," Idrys said.

"About Áine? Did he say somewhat to you?"

"He's not spoken exactly, though he did ask me how long our guest might choose to reside here."

"That's the chief's business and not his own, isn't it?" Hafwyn tipped her head to the side and considered. "She's not one of the Folk, I don't think."

"No." Idrys's mouth set in a line and he stared into the fire. "She's not, or at least not entirely. Her eyes are all wrong, and her skin more milk than moonlight. But that hair…" He stopped and shook himself, then looked back at her. "She might be ill luck, her. And if that woman was the mother that birthed her, I'll eat my horse, saddle and all."

"There are many kinds of mother, Idrys." Hafwyn reached out and laid her hand on his knee.

"Hush mother. Idrys is dead." His look darkened as he returned his gaze to the flames.

Emyr gave a growl of protest and rammed his narrow head into Idrys's thigh. His twin relented and abandoned a portion of his sad and bitter thoughts as he scratched his brother's head in the same way that Emyr often scratched his during the day.

"We'll see how it goes. Mayhap she'll not care to stay past when her leg is healed up anyhow. And," he raised a hand to forestall his mother's next comment, "I'll make sure she's accorded everything a wisewoman should be and when she chooses to leave, we'll outfit her." Idrys looked down into his brother's liquid brown eyes. "Satisfied, brother?"

Emyr licked his leg and wagged his tail. He appreciated how hard it was for Idrys to fill his shoes, to pretend that he was his twin while his own identity died away. Emyr was more natural as the chief. He liked to argue the finer points of cantref law and custom while sitting around with his men or riding out to help shore up a wall, till a field, or hunt down wayward flocks.

Idrys was confined to darkness, though he rode out at night often enough with only Emyr to accompany him. While he could drink with his friends, a thing Emyr envied, Idrys had little contact with the outer settlements other than the dealings that took place at suppers or in the feasting after dark on holidays.

Emyr knew too that Áine's resemblance to the Fair Folk, faint enough though it was, would sting Idrys more as well. His twin still blamed himself for their fate and on very dark, very bad nights Idrys had a time or two confessed he still dreamed of the moon-pale Lady and her warm bower as only a man trapped in the deep of winter can yearn for a summer's day in the light.

Seren. Though she'd cursed them out of pique at being unable to separate the two, she'd still managed to come between them. It was a wound that Emyr longed to heal but could see no clear path.

Time, his mother counseled. *Time, indeed. Seven years of slow healing ripped open by one blood-haired woman.* He gave a very un-doglike sigh and sank down into the rushes at his brother's feet.

Áine dreamed of waves and small white birds and she wasn't sure at first where she was when she awoke. Her leg hurt and the bed she lay in smelled strange. She wondered if they'd reached Clun Cadair and turned over to feel for Tesn's warmth.

The events of the day flooded into her memory with a sharp, cold pain. She curled into a ball and felt the tears threaten to rise. She took several careful breaths and sat up slowly.

Her crudely shorn hair hung at odd lengths around her face, reminding her of her inadequate gestures the night before. She was wearing only a light linen shift and recalled Melita and Hafwyn helping her undress the night before.

Grimly, she took stock of her body. Her leg throbbed, though perhaps a little less than the day previous. Her head felt sore, but better for the comfortable, warm rest she'd gotten. Her shoulders ached and the biggest scrape on her hip had scabbed and pulled tight so that it protested with a sharp pain as she moved and stretched. She was alive and going to mend, it seemed.

And what good is that? I've got nothing. No Tesn to guide me, no healing kit, no pack, no clothes of my own, nothing. She shivered.

She had her skills still, if grief didn't dull her intellect. And worse come to worse, she could always cry somewhere in private and trade the pearls for goods. Áine smiled ruefully at that thought. It was something Tesn had told her once, counseling her ward that if desperate times struck, she should be not faint to use whatever means she could to continue her service to the people of Cymru.

All right, you silly nit. You can lie here feeling sorry for yourself or you can try to be useful. Tesn would have your ear off if she saw you laying about when there might be work.

Áine shifted and painfully pulled her legs over the side of the bed. The dress she'd borrowed the day before lay folded on a bench near the casement. She limped over to the bench and struggled into the gown. She tidied the bed as best she could and then hobbled to the door.

Leaning heavily against it she steeled herself to face the people she could now hear moving about in the hall. She ran one hand through her mangled locks and shrugging, pulled the door open.

Emyr, Llew, and Urien had ridden out at first light to finish their circuit of the wintering crofts and to check on the progress of those who would be returning to their homes this week with goods for taxes and trade. Emyr had glanced at Áine's door but decided she'd like as not stay in today anyway, what with her grief weighing so hard on her slender shoulders.

Caron was in the hall with Melita and Hafwyn. They were boiling down a vat of berries for preserves over the cooking hearth while Melita pounded out the week's bread. Hafwyn sat calmly on a bench against the wall with her spinning in hand. She was smiling as Áine emerged but quickly turned her head to nod to her guest.

"Sleep well, did you?" Hafwyn asked.

The other two women stared silently at the pale young woman. Áine's hair hung in uneven lengths around her face which was still red-eyed and pinched with sorrow. She filled out Caron's borrowed gown nicely, but her shoulders were hunched and her gait halting as she limped to the table and sat with a heavy sigh.

"Aye, thank you." Áine gave a wan smile to Caron who quickly left off stirring the berries to fetch the plate of bread and cheese and pears she'd laid by at Hafwyn's bidding for their guest.

"My son is riding out toward the river today to check on the crofts. He's going to keep an eye out for your pack. Meanwhile, I've got a lovely bolt of thick bleached linen, which I hope will suit you for a dress?" Hafwyn smiled warmly at the girl. She understood the pain of grief and felt a depth of compassion and good will toward the young wisewoman that surprised her.

Áine picked at a chunk of bread and nodded, flushing. "Please, put me to work. I need something to do or else…" She trailed off and stared into her plate.

Caron and Melita looked at each other and then at Hafwyn. Her gentle dark eyes lowered in her own remembered pain for a moment. She knew the refuge in being busy that hard work could provide.

"Can you use a drop spindle? I've also got a goodly amount of herbs to categorize and preserve from the holding's gardens, though I think you're best kept off your feet until that leg can heal." Hafwyn smiled, banishing her own sad thoughts.

"Aye to the first and I'd be happy to share all I know about the creation of potions, tinctures, and salves. I've lost all my own, but I've been well trained, I assure you, for all my youthful years." Áine looked up at her, grateful.

The rest of the crofts survived the storm unscathed; not even one sheep was lost in the wind and rain. Idrys flushed a healthy buck from a little patch of scrub brush and the men found themselves in a merry chase across the moor. Llew's arrow brought the deer down and the men were in fine spirits as they returned to the holding with fresh meat to share.

"Urien, mind ducking in to Moel and his son's? I'm sure they'd like to share in the meat tonight in the hall." Emyr curried down his chestnut mare as the men finished putting up the horses.

Urien nodded and left Llew and Emyr to finish butchering the deer in the courtyard. Emyr skinned it carefully with expert skill while Llew carved up a green branch for a spit.

They both carefully stood in a way that shielded their gazes from the dark burnt smear on the hard-packed earth where the pyre had been the night before. Though much of the charcoal and ash had been carried to the cairn in the trees just beyond the holding's berm, the stain remained and would until the winter rains washed it clean.

"I wonder how Áine is today," Llew said after a moment. Caron, his wife, had come out to give him a kiss in greeting and then dashed off to fetch herbs to rub the meat with and roots to bake in the fire beside it. To one side of the hall was a small covered structure with a slate roof and a deep fire pit dug into the earth and lined with large, flat stones. Beyond lay the smokehouse.

"How do you think she is?" Emyr shrugged.

"I think that often women don't mind a little comfort in their sorrow," Llew said with a bright grin.

Emyr resisted throwing a piece of offal at him and instead tossed it to the three waiting hounds that sat patiently at the edge of the yard.

Idrys sat near the hall, keeping his distance from the other dogs. He didn't care for raw meat, hound form or no.

"She's just lost her mother, you lecherous oaf." Emyr glared at Llew.

"True. But she's a Wise One, you know. They're supposed to be free to wander and love as they would. And no man should deny to them anything, or so my mother always taught me." He shrugged. "Besides, it might do you both some good to put a few smiles back on your face. Little enough does these days."

Emyr froze for a moment and then relaxed as he realized that the "both" in Llew's statement referred to him and Áine, not himself and his brother. It hurt his heart to lie to his closest friends, but he feared the hurt that might come if they knew he and Idrys were cursed. Better to not test a friendship so, in his mind.

And if the likes of old Moel was suspicious of Áine's origins because of something so small as blood-red hair and pale skin, how much more would he be if he knew the truth of his chief? Emyr remembered then the pearl and wondered if there would ever be a good time to bring that up. Probably not today nor for another handful of days. Best let the woman grieve before he tormented her with questions.

"Emyr?" Llew watched a curious series of emotions cross his friend's tanned, handsome face.

"Sorry, Llew. I was thinking."

"Don't hurt yourself," Llew muttered as he turned away to prepare the fire pit.

Emyr smiled as he heard Idrys snort behind him.

"Nay, Urien. She's got the look of a fey witch and I've no mind to sup with her like. They beguile you, the fairies, and trick from you what you hold most dear." Madoc Moel shook his smooth bald head at the stocky tanner.

"Father," Adaf said in a resigned tone, "I'm sure Hafwyn and Emyr would hardly have extended their hospitality if she were truly so. Besides, the grief I saw last night looked human enough."

"Oh, that's a trick, you can be sure. Red and white, red and white, don't we all know the stories?" The old man folded his arms. "She was even wearing red and white when they brought her in."

"She was wearing mostly mud. What red there was would be her own blood and her wisewoman's belt." Urien rolled his eyes to the gods. He knew that when Moel took something into his thick, shining head it was like a hound and a bone.

"More tricks," Moel said.

"Fine, father. We'll go and bring you back a plate, if Emyr's generosity extends to those who refuse it so soundly." Adaf threw up his hands. He wasn't going to pass up fresh meat and Caron's fine cooking because of his stubborn father.

"I'll not go, neither." Maderun said softly from the hearth. "And neither will our girls. She's fey touched, that woman. Not good to have around children."

"You as well, wife?" Adaf shook his head. "I fear my house has gone a bit touched themselves, Urien." His two daughters looked up from where they were sorting apples into crates of bruised and clean, their round and cheerful faces fascinated at the fighting among their elders. "Urien, my wife and I will be there tonight with our children. Tell Emyr."

Urien wisely took his dismissal and left the house to the sound of Adaf bickering with his normally silent wife. Urien himself was a very practical sort. He gave little credence to stories, though they could fill a long cold night.

He'd seen Áine's pain and it was as real as the horror and loss they'd all felt when Emyr returned those years ago without his twin and a winter later when Brychan suddenly died. A broken heart, they'd said, but Urien thought it was small wonder the man's heart had given out when he'd scarce touched food or wandered far from his bed that last season.

He guessed that Emyr blamed himself for it all. His friend would on occasion confess as much when the three were deep in their cups on a late night. Though determinedly cheerful and kind during the day, Emyr changed a bit at night. Urien figured in the dark there were fewer distractions to keep the demons of his memory and grief at bay. He was used to his moody friend and lord.

Urien shook his head again as he made his way between the mostly empty homes to the courtyard. Áine was no fairy lady. If the stories were true the Fair Folk were supposed to be passing fair indeed. The anguish-wracked guest was odd looking, perhaps striking at best. Oh, her body was nice enough, though perhaps a little too muscled and thin from all the walking a wisewoman did, but she was hardly the definition of unearthly loveliness.

"Emyr!" Urien called as he emerged from between the stone houses. "Adaf will be joining us with his wife and daughters."

"And not Moel?" Emyr's dark eyes narrowed. "Because of our guest?"

Urien sighed. "Aye. He thinks she's a fey touched witch out to trick us all."

"Áine?" Emyr said. His incredulous look faded as he remembered the pearl. "Well, she's strange indeed. But wisewomen always have mysteries to them, do they not?"

Urien shrugged and moved away to help Llew with readying the pit.

Emyr finished his butchering and folded the skin for Urien who would scrape and tan it for them. He rinsed his hands at the well and went inside the hall, Idrys following at his heels.

Áine sat at the large table near the hearth, sorting small bundles of dried herbs and talking in a hushed tone with his mother. He was surprised, a little, to see her up and working. She'd been so distraught the night before, he figured she would have wanted to lie in bed and rest with her sorrow. *Like your father? Great good it did him.* Emyr shoved aside the sudden bitter thought.

Idrys walked over the hearth and flopped down beside his mother. Melita sat further down the table, a rough dress shaped out before her in a bolt of thickly woven white linen.

"Emyr." Hafwyn looked up and smiled. She bent as well and greeted her other son with a quick scratch of his bony head. "Caron says you've caught us a deer."

"Well, to be fair, Cy flushed it and Llew's arrow took it down. I just rode along and broke an arrow in support." He grinned.

"Cy?" Áine raised her head from her task. "You call your hound *hound*?" *I call him brother.* "Aye. It suits him well enough."

A tiny smile played at her drawn mouth. "Do you call your horse *march*?"

"Nah, I call her Cloud." He sat down on the long bench across from the women.

"Is she a grey mare then?" Áine raised an eyebrow as his quick smile and light banter momentarily banished her pain.

"Brown as a nut, I'm afraid." Emyr's grin lit his handsome face.

"Emyr, quit teasing our guest." Hafwyn's admonishment carried no sting. It was good to see her son smile and to see the young woman's response.

"Teasing her? You're the one who put her to work," Emyr replied.

"I asked, actually." Áine's smile slipped away. "It helps, a little. To be busy, I mean."

"Good," Emyr said, sad to see her smile go. His mother, or perhaps Melita, had evened up Áine's shorn hair and it hung now around her chin, partially obscuring her sorrow-lined face. "Well, I'd better change and go take care of the hounds." He excused himself.

Idrys stayed, feeling the tingle of coming night simmering in his blood. He had an hour yet before it was time. He studied Áine with dark and human eyes.

She returned to talking with his mother about this herb or that, naming them and explaining the uses and properties of each. Her voice caught on occasion, especially when she would bring up her mother's name. Her deep love and devotion to the dead wisewoman was carved plain and strong in every word, every sorrowful gesture and choking stutter.

Idrys grudgingly admired how she'd take a deep breath whenever the hollow look threatened to overtake her features and return to her chosen task with careful-minded stubbornness. *She's not a soft nor cowardly woman, that.*

He knew only too well that inactivity could allow sorrow to fester and grow. Better to move, to act, to do. *If you figure out how to outrun grief, healer, tell me.* Idrys let his head fall to the rushes with a sigh.

The meat was sliced crackling off the bones and the little group of permanent residents sat inside the hall and ate. Adaf had turned up with his silent wife and two daughters in tow, making apologies for his father who, he said, wished to stay in and have a quiet night. Though Maderun shot Áine a cautious and considering look or two, she held her peace, sitting herself and her daughters at the opposite end of the long table.

Áine barely noticed the tensions. She had only picked at her breakfast and refused a midday meal. The spiced venison smelled good and she tried for courtesy's sake to eat some. She cut it into small pieces with her knife and managed to swallow a little fresh bread as well. She'd never been one to drink much mead or spirits and even in her grief she refused it when offered in favor of fresh water from the well.

For a while no one spoke much, mostly eating. Llew told the story of the hunt, such as it was and everyone chuckled at his overdramatizing the bold sacrifice of Emyr's arrow and the graceful competence of his faithful hound.

Idrys watched, bitterly amused. There was an odd dissonance that he'd grown used to over the years in these sorts of exploits. One or the other of the twins would be praised or teased for something their day or night counterpart had done. Then each would have to gauge his response to fit well with their own differing personalities.

Ducking his head, Idrys let his dark curls cover his lack of a blush. After all, he hadn't missed the shot so wide and hunted himself up a mighty stone, as Llew put it. He'd flushed the deer in the first place.

Emyr pressed a cold nose to his twin's elbow and looked up at him with mournful eyes. *Glad that dogs can't blush, aren't you?* Idrys smiled down at his twin and put another piece of meat down onto the wooden platter on the floor for him.

"Cy seems to like cooked food," Áine said. She was seated to the right of Idrys, in the place of honor across from Hafwyn.

"Aye. Can you blame him? Caron's cooking is delicious." He smiled easily though a shadow flitted through his brown eyes.

Adaf and his little family left with Gethin at the close of the meal, each praising the stewed pears and honey Caron had thought to make as a finish to the impromptu feast. Llew and Caron excused themselves as well shortly after, leaving Urien and Idrys to help with the washing up.

Áine tried to hobble out with dishes but was quelled with a look from Hafwyn. She sighed. She wasn't used to being lame, and while she'd never wondered at the respect Tesn always garnered, Áine felt unworthy and useless.

Áine sat with Hafwyn and helped her wind the thread she'd spun onto skeins. She was tired, true, but she wanted to be bone-tired before she faced her room alone carrying her grief. The food which had tasted somewhat good to her was now a hard lump in her belly. She pushed aside the black tide of sorrow again and again, willing herself to stay calm and hollow.

Idrys joined them, pouring himself a cup of mead and propping his boots on the hearth. His black hound flopped into his normal place before the fire, half under the chief's legs.

"What do Adaf and his family do?" Áine asked to make conversation. The girls had been young and full of giggles all through dinner. Áine liked children well enough, though she'd not got on well with them as a youngster. Children could be cruel to those who seemed different from themselves.

"They help with our orchard and garden here, and the livestock we keep around full time. He's a good man," Idrys said.

He lifted a leather satchel and laid it on the bench next to him. From it he removed a delicate set of carving tools and a few pieces of clean bone. One was already slowly forming into a comb like the one Hafwyn had in her braids. He set to work with his roughened rasp to smoothing out the tines.

"Did you make your mother's?" Áine asked.

"Aye. It fills the nights. I picked it up from Llew's father before he passed last winter."

"Llew seems a good friend," Áine said, her mind wandering. She'd never known more than Tesn, never really had friends besides her adopted mother.

"Oh he is, provided one has a thick skin." Idrys smiled at her wryly.

"I never would have picked sweet Caron for him, though," Hafwyn said with a shrug. "But they say the easiest way to a man's heart is through his belly. And she had a fine gift with spices and flavors. Was our lucky day when she settled with Emyr's right-hand man."

"I always thought the quickest way to a man's heart was straight through his chest," Áine said, trying to pull another smile out of Idrys.

It worked. "And what would a wisewoman know of a man's heart?" He leaned forward toward her.

"More than I could teach a cur like you in one evening," she said and sniffed with mock indignation at his saucy tone.

To her surprise Idrys sat back and pain, deep and sudden, flickered through his face. "A cur like me, oh, indeed," he muttered. He put down his carving and rose, walking out of the hall without a backward glance. His hound rose with what she would have sworn was a sigh and followed after.

Áine shivered, unsure how she'd given such offense so quickly. She looked at Hafwyn with a question on her lips but the older woman just shook her head and said only "he's moody, my son. Takes after his father."

Áine excused herself shortly after, not wishing to face Emyr again that night. She wasn't sure what she'd said or why it had stung. It was a cold reminder that she was an outsider here, for all her strange ease around the handsome young chief. Áine knew from spending time in villages healing with her mother that adversity and loss often bred camaraderie where it might not have thrived otherwise. She wondered if she'd been too forward in her friendliness with Emyr. Perhaps she'd imagined the compassion in his gaze as he'd helped her home and cared for her after the ordeal.

Alone, she stripped off her dress and then rewrapped her ankle. The swelling was down; another week, perhaps two at most, and she'd be free of that annoyance at least. She blew out the little stone lamp and curled underneath the covers, alone with her grief.

Twelve

The second night was the hardest for her. Grief and memory tormented her with lonely dreams where she wandered lost and afraid searching for Tesn and always too far behind.

The next morning, Emyr acted as though he hadn't stormed out the night before and greeted her warmly. Áine put his moods out of her mind and set herself to being as useful as possible. Together she and Hafwyn worked to preserve and prepare a healthy stock of herbs for any ailment and the older woman found herself very impressed with the sheer depth of knowledge the young wisewoman possessed.

The third night was easier; she cried herself into an exhausted sleep and dreamed again of birds and waves. When she awoke, Áine felt ready to stop crying and face the dawning day. She carded wool and chatted with Melita who was a wealth of funny anecdotes about the various residents, permanent and not, of the holding.

Áine had questions about the young chief, but held them back. Her healer's instincts told her pain lurked there and she wasn't ready for any more of that for now.

The days passed quickly. Emyr showed her his tallfwrdd board and, with Urien's patient help, began to teach her to play. She enjoyed playing the attacker more than defending with the king, though defense did seem to carry with it a tactical advantage. The men were impressed with her agile mind and Urien joked that she'd be able to out-play Emyr in another fortnight at the pace she was learning.

"Try memorizing and categorizing all parts of a single plant for use in perhaps tens of ailments or pains, and then ask me again how I learn so easily." Áine laughed, the sound thin but growing stronger with use.

A week passed before the first group arrived for the winter. Emyr had explained how here they would house those who came to pay their taxes and have any disputes heard by the chief. Taxes would get the little holding through the winter. Most residents stayed in the small stone houses for a month or so before moving back to their own outlying homes.

If it were a bad winter, they'd stay longer. The main flocks belonging directly to the chief were all now housed within a half-day's ride and Gethin was out checking on the preparedness of his shepherds as Emyr's proxy and master of flocks.

By the end of the second week the little holding had filled to capacity with the arrival of the fisherfolk. Some stayed in the little villages by the sea, but many migrated back with their families and salted catches to pay the year's tax and visit relatives and friends. Áine had been in much larger holdings, but once the village swelled to nearly one hundred folk and family, she felt both more comfortable and strangely uneasy.

The mysterious, young wisewoman was the center of a great deal of gossip once the holding began to settle. Emyr and his men had their hands full sorting through the tithes and getting everyone settled for a winter that was already proving it would come early and hard. The rain had turned to sleet by the end of the third week and many gathered in the main hall seeking audience or diversion.

Áine was not oblivious to the whispers. She was used to speculation and faced it bravely. No one dared make open accusation of anything and she remained nearly glued to Hafwyn's side as her ankle healed.

Her main respite from the dark nights full of grief and the days full of work and the speculative glances of strangers was Emyr. No matter how busy he got, he always seemed to steal a moment or two for light conversation with Áine during the days, and she looked forward to their intense but friendly games of tallfrwdd.

Emyr was quieter at night, his smile less easy, but when Áine did manage to coax it from him, it was as though a lamp lit in the handsome man's face. She found herself looking more and more for those smiles, pushing through the day's work in anticipation of sharing a late midday meal with Emyr or a night of games and gentle teasing.

Melita had helped her sew two plain white dresses, one of thick linen, the other of finely woven undyed wool. The wisewoman made a handsome figure sitting near the hearth dressed in red and white. Her sad smiles and gentle banter did little to quiet the speculations.

Moel and his daughter-in-law lay at the foundation of it. Their version of the events after the storm dropped responsibility for the death of the old wisewoman and indeed the storm itself firmly into Áine's own lap. That the young, unwed chief seemed so friendly with her only fueled Moel's strident accusations. Many shrugged and turned away from him when he spoke, but quite a few listened, especially when the normally quiet and reserved Maderun spoke up in the old man's defense.

It came to a head on a windy night nearly a month after Áine had arrived in Clun Cadair. Old Gethin was out making the rounds of the crofts again, but Urien, Llew, and Emyr sat at the head of the main table talking with Áine and Hafwyn. Melita perched behind her large loom, humming a lullaby in the warm hall. A handful of the fisher folk sat further down the long table, playing tallfwrdd.

Moel had come into the hall that night with his son and their family. They kept to the far end of the hall, Adaf and his father conversing with one of the farmers who'd come to ask for help building an extra pen for some cattle he'd traded for in Arfon. The two young girls, joined by the young son of one of the fishermen, were playing with a leather ball on the floor with Cy.

Áine glanced their way and wondered again at how gentle the huge hound was with the young children. She smiled and looked back to her companions. Her sorrow was an older wound now, still there and throbbing but more easily ignored with each passing day. Hafwyn kept her blissfully busy, seeming to keenly understand Áine's fear of idleness.

The leather ball fetched up against her leg and she bent to pick it up. Gwir, the younger of Maderun's daughters, dashed up to her and held out her hand for Áine to return the ball. Áine smiled.

Her smile died as Maderun rose from her seat and screeched at Gwir to "get away from that woman!"

Everyone went silent in the hall and looked between the two women. Áine handed the ball back to the stunned, frightened child who backed away from her with wide eyes.

"I'd not do her any harm," Áine said carefully. "I like children."

"It's ill luck for a child to be touched by the fey. Everyone knows this," Maderun said, her voice high and thin.

"You believe me to be one of the Fair Folk, do you?" Áine's green eyes snapped with annoyance. She'd felt this coming but had hoped that the easy respect her host's family had for her would alleviate the superstitious nonsense.

Moel stood and looked at her with hard dark eyes. "Are you not? Red hair like that, and skin that looks to have never seen the sun despite the wandering you've said you've done."

"She's our guest." Idrys stood as well, towering over the still-seated wisewoman.

He was unsure how to explain that she was not fey without giving away secrets he did not care to reveal. He was the chief; his word should have been enough. He could see by the faces around him that remained full of questions that it wasn't near enough.

"Perhaps she's witched you, how would we know?" Moel said stubbornly. "We know naught about her, though I'd eat this table if that woman we buried gave birth to your guest."

Áine stood and held up a slender hand to forestall whatever reply Idrys might have made. She paused and met the gaze of every man and woman in the room, her new friends and host included. She noted even Cy watched her intently. Then she shifted her leaf-green eyes back to Moel and his family.

"Tesn," she said, "was my adopted mother. I was given to her just after my birth." Áine decided to leave out the part with the selkies.

Around her, many of the small crowd was nodding. Though unusual, it was not unheard of for a girl so young to be given to the wisewomen's path when she was not born on it. It was a powerful calling.

"I never knew my birth family," she continued. "Perhaps they thought that my unusual coloring meant I was born to the path of knowledge Tesn walked. I do not know. What I do know is that I'm a wisewoman now myself. I earned this belt and my knowledge and it would be far beyond my simple calling to dishonor my mother and teacher by breaking the cardinal rule of my profession." She paused again and raised a crimson brow. "Do. No. Harm."

Áine turned and hobbled around the table to the hearth where Caron sat dumbstruck by the tall wisewoman's beautiful anger. Áine snatched up an iron poker and held it against her own flushed cheek.

"Cold iron, Madoc ap Madog, called Moel. If you know your stories so well, you'd know that no fey or even a half-blood foundling could stand its touch." Moel flinched from her sparking green-gold gaze. "Are you satisfied? Or should I strip and rub the iron all over my skin?"

Idrys could not help but smile at that thought. His blood rose at the image of her milk-pale skin tinged pink with fury. She was glorious in her brave rage and he didn't doubt for a minute that if Moel had demanded it, she just might have torn off her white gown and done as she'd offered.

The bald man did not demand it. Instead, he looked down and mumbled a soft apology to the hall. He walked as quickly as his old limbs would allow and left the hall. Maderun gave a little curtsey and gathered her girls. They left as well. Adaf stood and shook his head.

"I'm sorry," he said to the still-seething Áine, "she's, well, they, well. You know. I'm sorry, we meant no offense." He nodded as well to his chief and followed his family out the door.

The fisher folk returned to their game and calm settled over the room. Áine dropped the poker back onto the hearth and limped to her seat. Her ankle was mostly healed, but it still stung to put her full weight on her leg as yet.

Llew broke the tension with a leering smile. "You sure you don't want to strip? I mean, it never hurts to be thorough where the tricky fey might be concerned."

Caron moved swiftly and smacked the back of his head. Idrys laughed as Llew tossed his wife a jokingly hurt look.

"He has a point," Idrys said as he looked at Áine with somewhat other than just humor in his dark eyes.

"Boys, leave the poor woman alone." Hafwyn came to Áine's rescue as she smiled at the young men. "I hope that little display will put an end to the strange looks, hmm?"

Áine sighed. "It might. I wish it were the first time I'd had to touch cold iron to prove my blood. Some days I curse my unknown parents that I'd be born so strange. But as Tesn always liked to remind me, they like as not shared the same coloring and could not have had it any easier."

The dark wave of grief crashed into the empty space anger left behind as it fled her. She shuddered and put a hand up to her suddenly damp eyes. "I'm sorry. I think I'll retire. Good night."

Thirteen

A small rash of fevers and other complaints brought on by the worsening weather over the next few days kept Áine, Melita, and Hafwyn busy. Áine was thankful that Hafwyn had such a keen interest in gardening and kept an impressive variety of herbs, roots, and flowing plants in stock. Áine dealt with the sick in a calm and friendly manner.

Emyr found himself watching her often. She had a gentle yet firm way about her whether it was prescribing a warm bath of hawthorn flower, rosemary, and peppermint for a chilblain or brewing and administering willow bark, garlic, and honey for a fever. He liked how she was calm with the adults and warm and friendly with his mother and her serving woman. He knew his mother had lost a daughter to miscarriage before giving birth to her twin sons. Perhaps Hafwyn saw something of that lost child's spirit reflected in the capable young woman.

Idrys, however, grew more distant as the week wore on. He always hated winter with the longer nights that forced him to wear his brother's skin and manner for hours longer than was his want. There was a certain freedom in being a hound. It was easier to keep busy during the day as well, running about with Emyr and seeing that everything was in order with the people. No one talked to him save his brother, and certainly no one expected a response.

The winters also meant more people, with the complaints and concerns that brought. And of course, winter brought reminder of the cold night his father had finally given up on this life and passed beyond the veil.

Áine's frequent smiles and teasing banter should have been a light in his darkening world. However, she somehow made it worse. He'd not even thought about a woman in a sexual way since Seren and had quickly if politely refused the few offers for marriage that had trickled in over the years.

Áine had reawakened his buried passion with her broad mouth, flashing eyes, and obvious strength. There was also the unspoken shared knowledge of deep anguish between them. She recognized his secret pain, though he was sure she didn't know the cause, and although neither spoke of their grief to the other, the understanding lived in every gesture and every stolen glance.

Besides that, she was becoming a very vicious and cunning tallfwrdd opponent.

Idrys did not care for his growing feelings and so he pulled away from her as well. His brother did not, Idrys knew, and sorrowed that he was the cause of the confusion that tensed her gaze when he'd refuse a game after a long day and retire to sit alone in his room with only his hound.

"You're an idiot," Emyr told him one cold morning as he hastily dressed.

He didn't even bother to explain what he was referring to, for neither had missed yet another considering and closed-off look from Áine the night before.

"She's neither inexperienced nor unwilling. But if you won't touch her, I can hardly make a move, you know." He sighed and sat beside his brother to pull on his heavy woolen stockings.

Idrys lay on the bed and dropped his narrow black head to the covers at his twin's words.

This was the hardest time for both of them, in the moments after they shifted. They usually responded to things the other had said while they had a voice. It was a strangely delayed conversation. There was no banter or teasing between the brothers, no back and forth or quick exchange of ideas. And though each could physically touch the other and often did, it was not human contact and the loss always hung immediate and present between them in the early and late hours of the day.

"How much power will we give the Lady? How much of our lives will she destroy if we let this keep us from the normal things a man wants?" Emyr did not speak her name, but Seren's curse lived between them always and needed no identifying. Idrys whined softly and dropped his head to his brother's thigh, staring up at him with sad brown eyes. "I'm sorry. I know. It's winter, it's hard for you. I feel the darkness too, you know." Emyr rose and they went side by side to face the day.

Áine was observant and finally her questions grew too many to hold in any longer. It was nearly six weeks after she'd come to Clun Cadair and she'd noted more and more that Emyr was always missing around sunset. She took the opportunity one quiet night in the hall to ask Hafwyn and Melita about it.

The women were sitting alone at the hearth, Melita and Hafwyn embroidering and Áine winding yarn. The younger woman looked up and took a deep breath.

"What happened here? With Emyr and your husband? If it is not too forward to ask," she added as the two women exchanged a sharp look.

"No, child. It is not too forward." Hafwyn sighed and set aside her stitching. "I used to have two sons. Emyr had a twin, Idrys. They were nigh inseparable, those two."

She smiled with the memory of her carefree, handsome boys. Her smile faded as she continued. "About seven years ago now, they went hunting. There was a rockslide, and only Emyr returned. I fear the pain of losing one of his sons was too much for my husband. Brychan was older than I anyway, and his heart full broke the day Emyr returned alone. He sickened that winter and could not hang on. Emyr keeps a nightly vigil for their spirits." She told the story in a rush. Her lovely brown eyes, so similar to those of her son, lowered with remembered pain.

Áine had heard whispers of tragedy and seen the sorrow that rode like a comfortable mantle over Emyr's shoulders, but she'd never heard the tale in full and so baldly spoken. She leaned forward and placed a hand over Hafwyn's own.

"Thank you," Áine said. "I'm glad I know. I can see the loss in Emyr, and it is good to finally see the source. There are days when I wish that I knew an herb to salve away the pains of grief and death, but I have no skill to heal the wounds of the heart."

Hafwyn looked into the girl's large green eyes and saw her deep sincerity and own loss painted within. A strange little smile curled her generous mouth. "Do not sell yourself short, wise one, for you may have ways beyond your own ken as yet."

Áine opened her mouth to ask her what she meant by that but whatever she might have said was lost as the outer door was thrown open and a gust of cold air followed a distraught Maderun into the hall. She ran to Áine and threw herself at the woman's feet, sobbing.

"I'm sorry, please forgive us. Just save my Gwir and Geneth. Please, wise one." She looked up with desperate eyes.

"I do not know what you mean?" Áine said as she reached down to lift the smaller woman up.

"They took sick, two days ago. Moel would not let me bring you and even Adaf thought they'd be all right, for many have had small fevers. But they're getting worse. Moel thinks you've cursed us."

"And you?" Áine said, raising a brow. Her body was tense and she hated the verbal game she played. She knew no matter the woman's answer she'd go and heal the children if she were able. But anger and remembered hurt held her still to hear the words.

"I saw you touch the cold iron, I'm satisfied. My mother always said no fairy could take the touch without burning. Please, help us." She gripped Áine's hands in her own.

Áine rose. "Of course. Now, tell me the symptoms that I can get what I need from the garden house."

"No need, Áine. Go with her; Melita and I will come along. Once you've seen them for yourself I'll fetch whatever you might need."

"Thank you. Now, Maderun, talk as we walk, shall we?" Áine paused only to grab Emyr's cloak from the peg by the door, figuring he'd hardly need it, sulking as he was in his chamber.

The women hurried across the courtyard and through the inner ring of buildings to Maderun's home. It was simple stone and wood structure with a central hearth for cooking and three small sleeping rooms portioned off by slatted walls. The girls had been brought out to the main room and their straw-ticked mattresses placed on the floor beneath them.

Moel glared at Áine as she entered behind Maderun but Adaf looked up from his seat on a small bench near his girls with relief on his face.

Áine nodded to him, ignoring his father, and bent immediately to examine the children. Both were unconscious, which did not please her. She shook each gently and found them reluctant and slow to rouse. Prying open their eyes, she noticed a rheumy fluid and slight discoloration. Their gums were pale, their breathing labored and uneven, and their skin was flushed with fever.

"Have they been coughing?" she asked.

"Aye, when they are awake, which is less and less in the past day," Adaf answered her.

"Any blood? What color is the phlegm?"

"No, no blood. No fluid at all. It's a dry cough, though sometimes they are so overtaken they vomit. What does that mean?" Maderun shifted from foot to foot, her expression a rough mix of dread and hope.

"We'll see. I think I've seen the like, years ago," Áine said. "We need to keep them isolated from other children. You all as well. Everything will have to be washed in very hot water once they're healed."

"Then they'll heal?" Adaf sighed with relief.

"Perhaps," Áine replied. She hated to dash his hopes, but she didn't wish to raise false ones either. "We have to get them breathing properly and get fluids into them as well." She looked at Melita and Hafwyn. "I need mustard seeds, ground fine, hot water, and," she paused, thinking, "cherry bark, wild lettuce, red clover flowers, coltsfoot, lavender, and that peppermint and marjoram tincture we made last week."

The two women hurried to gather what she needed as Áine knelt quietly beside the girls and let her consciousness sink into each in turn. She felt the pain in their lungs, a strange burning itch that crawled like a living thing through the thin spongy tissue. The fevers were high as their bodies rebelled against the sickness. Both children were dehydrated and exhausted, too young and weak to put up a strong fight.

She pulled back into herself as Hafwyn returned with the first basket load of the requested items.

"Adaf, go with Hafwyn and fetch the copper bath. The children need to be bathed to reduce the fever." He nodded and left.

To their surprise, Moel limped out behind them after grabbing a kitchen bucket, muttering that he'd start bringing in water.

Emyr, brought forth by his mother's light knock, returned with the others, helping Adaf carry the bath. The little house was overcrowded and Áine calmly ordered everyone out except for the women once the bath was partially filled and two kettles and a pot set to heat on the hearth.

They undressed Gwir first, since Áine was more worried about the younger daughter's condition. She did not wake or protest as they lowered her gently into the tepid bath, which Áine had steeped with mint and chamomile. They bathed her and then Maderun held her daughter's head up as Áine coaxed a strong tea of garlic oil, honey, wild lettuce, and cherry bark down her throat. They returned her to the bed and covered her to the waist with the blankets. Áine showed Melita how to carefully massage the little girl's bony chest with the peppermint and marjoram tincture.

They repeated the process with Geneth, who woke briefly and was overtaken for a moment by a deep dry coughing fit that left her weak and her skin red-purple in tone.

Maderun massaged her elder daughter's chest gently as Áine had demonstrated while the wisewoman turned to making a paste of mustard using water as hot as she could stand to touch for a count of ten. She took strips of clean linen and soaked them in the mustard paste, then laid the compress onto the chests of the girls in turn until the mix cooled and hardened.

It was a long night. They repeated the forced feeding of the honeyed tea mix and the chest massage combined with the hot mustard compress every hour or so. Geneth's fever broke before dawn, though she did not wake. Her breathing evened. It seemed to Áine they were through the worst with her at least.

Daylight was seeping in under the door and through the slatted casement when Gwir finally opened her eyes and asked for water. The sheets beneath her were soaked with sweat and Áine hugged Hafwyn with deep relief. The younger one's breathing was still too ragged for her taste, but her cough brought up a little phlegm and subsided quickly as she sipped the lukewarm tea.

Áine looked at Maderun and nodded. "I think we're out of the worst, though you'll need to keep up the tea, as much as they can drink. And a broth made with fish oil wouldn't hurt either, though they may not care for the taste much."

"Thank you, Wise One." Maderun rose and clasped Áine's hands to her chest.

"Remember, wash everything, and no visits from children or people with children for at least three more days or 'til all symptoms clear, whichever is later." Áine smiled. Her back ached and she was suddenly aware of her own exhaustion. "Now, if you don't mind, I think I'll go to bed before I'm of no use to anyone. If the fever returns or they start to cough even after a sip of tea, send for me immediately."

She turned and walked back to the hall with Hafwyn beside her. Emyr was up early as usual and greeted both as they entered.

"The children?" he asked.

"They'll live, I think, thanks to Áine." Hafwyn smiled. Her face was lined and her eyes sunk and dark with fatigue.

Áine waved a weary hand and stripped off Emyr's cloak, hanging it back on its peg.

"Have to get you one of your own, I suppose, though you're tall enough to wear that well." Emyr grinned at her.

Cy came up and pressed his head under her hand. She smiled down at the hound and scratched his ears.

The memory of her dream the night before the flood crashed into her exhausted mind with unbidden vividness. The tall black hounds, the forest, Tesn, the flood. She looked down into the face of the large dog and felt a strange recognition surge through her.

Áine pulled away and fled quickly to her room. The three left in the hall watched her go with curious faces.

"This home is overfull with a bounty of mysteries," Hafwyn said softly. "Good night, my heart. If anyone needs me before midday, come and wake me."

Fourteen

"Ha. You sad, tallow-faced assassin of joy." Áine grinned and shot Idrys a gleeful look as she moved a little blue peg and surrounded yet another of his defenders with her own men.

"Perhaps you should concede the game now and save a little pride, friend." Llew said and Urien chuckled as he refilled their cups with the fizzing honey mead.

"Hush, you. I've not lost yet." Idrys leaned over the board and considered his options as he fingered the small bone die.

Hafwyn smiled at the little group. With gentle prodding from her and not so gentle words from his twin, Idrys had finally emerged from his shell and seemed to be enjoying winter for once. She imagined it had no little to do with a certain red-haired young woman who grew more lively and comfortable by the day. As the season neared the longest night, Áine seemingly put aside her grief with more and more ease, the moments of hollow pain less frequent though no less sudden or troubling.

Áine was happy as she'd never been and part of her twisted with guilt over it. She told herself that Tesn would have wept to see her surrounded by such good people and making friends with men and women near her own age. There was no reason to feel shame in her happiness because her mentor and mother was dead. But knowing a thing with the mind and knowing it in the heart were different matters and Áine struggled with the latter.

Emyr helped. Áine had taken a couple lovers in her travels, though never for more than a night or three. Tesn had finally explained near Áine's fifteenth birthday about how Áine might choose her own lovers for a time, though never to marry or settle with. She'd shown Áine the herbs to take before and after to help prevent unwanted children and told her gently that learning the full range of pleasures of the body would only help her understanding of her fellow humans and enable her to serve their needs with greater knowledge. There were, after all, many kinds of healing.

More and more, Áine eyed the handsome young chief and wondered how forward with her wishes she'd have to get before he noticed her. She'd done a little subtle asking around and knew that as far as anyone could tell, Emyr had never taken a lover or had a sweetheart. Certainly the chief had turned down a few offers of marriage, despite being the age when men usually looked for wives.

She'd wondered if he preferred the company of men, but the look that came into his eyes on occasion when he'd help her haul wood or water or caught him looking sidelong at her over the tallfwrdd board in the long evenings told her he felt desire.

She'd started making a point to brush her hand or hip against him by apparent accident whenever she had the chance. He often blushed, though Áine noted he rarely moved away. But still, frustratingly enough, he made no comment or overt show of interest and instead he'd glance aside with that distant sorrow filling his firelit eyes. She often found herself shaking her head, wondering what secret pain it was that kept them apart.

Emyr offered to teach Áine to ride, appalled that she'd never learned.

"A wisewoman *walks*," Áine said dryly. "Occasionally we ride in carts."

"Well then, you'll have to expand your knowledge, won't you? Be a shame to leave yourself so uneducated," Emyr teased her.

"You just want to see me fall on my arse." She narrowed her green eyes.

"I don't know about him, but I'd like to see that." Llew broke in.

"All right, scoundrels. But I'll be borrowing a pair of your trousers, if you please, Emyr. I've no mind to have my skirts over my head with that shameless boy hanging around." She made a sour face at Llew and set her hands on her hips.

Emyr laughed. And so it was that on a cold but clear day, Áine had her first riding lesson on a chestnut mare called Cloud. She did not, to Llew's great disappointment, fall off. The horse liked her, staying calm and easy under Áine's gentle leg. She felt an easy rapport with the creature, letting her breathing settle in to match the mare's without thinking.

"They are marvelous creatures," Áine sighed as she dismounted back in the courtyard.

"Very." Emyr smiled at her. Her face was flushed with cold and the exertion and her eyes alight with simple joy. He remembered his first look at her lying half dead and filthy on the ground and wondered that he'd ever thought her anything but beautiful.

Áine caught the look in his eye and stepped in close, laying her own slender pale hand over his dark, calloused fingers that held Cloud's reins. Her large leaf-and-sunlight eyes spoke a silent but clear invitation.

Emyr shivered in a way that had nothing to do with the cold and looked down at her. She was inches away from him and he felt the heat of her body seeping through the cold air to warm his own. Her full breasts brushed his chest and the layers of linen and wool seemed both too much and not thick enough all at once.

He froze, torn between wanting to claim her lips with his own and wanting to pull away for fear of where that might lead and what memories it might arouse.

Idrys butted his twin in the thigh with a bony head and saved him the decision. Emyr laughed, releasing the tension, and shoved at the hound.

"It's well past midday. I think the black oaf is hungry, eh?" He turned a little too quickly and pulled Cloud behind him into the stable. "Go on, I'll take care of her."

Áine looked down at the huge black hound and gave him an exasperated look. "I certainly hope you're happy," she muttered. "Come on, mutt. Let's see what sort of acceptable food we can poach for you before you waste away of neglect."

Three days before the longest night, the holding bustled with earnest preparation for the midwinter feasting. Gethin had brought in one of the overlarge hogs he kept for routing acorns and truffles in the forest and they were all fattening the beast with table scraps for its imminent slaughter. Caron had taken over the cooking hearth and delicious smells of the food she was overseeing the preparation of filled the hall day and night.

Even the weather cooperated with the merry air of celebration. The days were generally sunny, though very cold. Small drifts of dry snow added their own sparkling decoration to the little houses.

Gwir and Geneth, now recovered from their sickness, joined the other children of the village in making winter garlands of holly and pine that the men then strung over every threshold and window.

Sunset neared and Emyr retired for his vigil with his hound. He stripped carefully in the chilly room and looked at Idrys who sat expectantly on the sheepskin rug.

"I mean to court Áine. I may not have the experience to tell, but her interest seems plain enough to read and I find myself well disposed to her." He shivered in the chill as he stood naked before his twin. "I cannot, for obvious reasons, do it without your help and consent, Idrys. I know you fear what we feel, because, well, because of Seren." He shivered again for reasons unrelated to the temperature and forged ahead. The tingling in his blood grew and he had little time to say his piece. "But Áine is as far from that cold, selfish Lady as we'll find I think. I don't want to watch her leave or choose another; I've got loneliness and sorrow in my heart enough, and so do you. Think on it, Idrys. For us. Please."

The change took him as the sun dropped below the rim of the world.

Idrys dressed quickly and then sat on the bed and took his brother's narrow furry head between his hands.

"I don't know, Emyr. My desires are what damned us. What further harm might I cause by unleashing them again?"

The hound whined and licked his brother's arm.

"All right. I'll think on it, though she's a wisewoman, and we can hardly marry her. She's going to leave someday, Emyr. Besides, what if we let down our guard and she finds out the truth? That might only invite further pain if she wisely chooses not to tie herself to ones so cursed." He rose and paced to the door.

Emyr realized with a start that he'd never told his brother about Áine's pearly tear. *She might understand better than you know, Idrys.* He resolved to speak of it the next morning.

That evening after a hurried supper, Idrys turned to carving and the women to cooking and preparations. Gethin burst into the hall and came to Idrys's side.

"Emyr! It's Dancer. She's foaling I think," Gethin said.

Idrys rose and nodded to the women as he made his way outside. Emyr raised his head and then stayed where he was next to the warm hearth. His twin hardly needed his company for the birth of a horse. Besides, the mare was all Idrys's project.

He'd taken her to be bred by the fastest stallion of the chief of Cantref Arfon the spring before, though the journey had been fraught with the danger of discovery for both twins. After seeing the proud stud, Emyr had grudgingly admitted it was worth the ride and risk. The journey had also had a somewhat cathartic effect on both, as they'd had to travel near where they'd met the Fair Lady all those fateful years ago.

After a time as the hour grew late and slowly the work was stored away, Áine decided to go and check on Emyr and the mare. Though wisewomen primarily healed people, the creed applied to all living things and Áine had many times assisted with the healings or births of four-legged creatures. *Even the care of some ducklings, once,* she remembered, smiling fondly.

She took her newly sewn grey cloak from its peg and slipped out the door, leaving Hafwyn and Melita to their quiet conversation with Cy fast asleep at their feet.

The night was cold and a light snowfall settled in silent flakes over the courtyard and buildings. She made her way quickly across to the stable and ducked in the wide door, securing it behind her.

The chief sat alone on a stool outside the expectant mare's stall, keeping vigil.

"How is she?" Áine asked, coming up alongside him and peering over the wall into the wooden box.

"In labor, I think. I sent Gethin off to bed. It could be hours, after all." Idrys glanced at her before returning his gaze to the restless mare.

Dancer shifted in her stall. Sometimes she snatched up a bite of loose hay and chewed absently only to turn in place and nose her bulging belly. Áine watched the mare for a while and then turned to Idrys.

"Her sides are sunk, it means the foal has dropped. And I think that fluid down her flanks was like as not her birth water. She should be near now."

As if on cue, the mare dropped her head and sucked in a heaving breath as she pushed. Then she returned to her ritual of spinning and chewing. The pushing grew more frequent. Something, though she could not be sure what, worried Áine. She unlatched the gate and stepped into the stall, murmuring nonsensical words to the mare in a calm tone.

She laid her hands against the sweat-slick neck of the bay mare and let her mind sink down into the body of the horse, focusing on the foal within.

The labor pains buckled her knees and she swayed, causing Idrys to rise and say her name. She ignored him, focusing deeper instead.

There. She felt the foal and realized he was facing the wrong way around. His hindquarters were firmly wedged in the birth canal and time was running low as his heart rate came slower than Áine would have liked in a horse. She pulled away and turned to Idrys.

"The foal is backwards. And I think he's stuck," Áine said.

Idrys came into the stall as well, though Dancer pinned her ears in irritation at yet another human body making her stall all the more crowded and confusing.

Though he wondered how she knew, he did not ask and instead trusted it was like as not some wisewoman's secret skill. Áine had an uncommon intellect and perceptive nature, after all.

"What can we do?" he asked instead.

"You? Not much I think. Stay with her and keep her calm. I've got to go boil water. I think I might be able to turn the foal." She smiled at him and left the barn at a half run.

She returned with clean rags and a heavy bucket of steaming water. Idrys was swearing quietly under his breath and leaning heavily against the wall of the stable with one hand pressed to his ribs and the other gripping the mare's halter.

"What happened to you?" Áine asked with a tone that said she meant more to ask what he'd managed to do wrong in the short time she'd been gone.

"Bloody creature kicked me." He flushed with embarrassment and flashed her a rueful grin.

"Good on keeping her calm," Áine said with a tiny smile. "Let me see your ribs."

Idrys waved her back, not wanting her to touch him with his brother's words and proposal so fresh in his mind. "I'm fine enough. What will you do?" He nodded at the distressed mare.

Áine took off her cloak and draped it over the stool outside the stall. She entered with the bucket and set it in a corner where it would be out of the way. She laid the rags over the gate and turned to Dancer.

"I need to reach inside her and push the foal back. I think I can turn him then so he's born properly."

"Done this before, have you?" Idrys said, his raven's-wing eyebrows meshing with worry. "Are the chances good?"

Áine answered him truthfully. "I don't know. Better than if I do nothing. And no, I've never put my arm inside a horse, though I watched Tesn do it once with a cow. And I've done it with a woman," she added.

Idrys raised an eyebrow and nodded. With a suppressed groan he came off the wall and held the mare's head with both hands.

"Keep her steady as you can," Áine said.

She hesitated but decided there was nothing for it. She untied her belt and tossed it over the wall. With a smooth motion she pulled both dress and shift over her head and shivered as the cold air of the stable raised bumps all along her skin. She didn't look at Idrys, though she heard his sharp intake of breath, instead setting her clothing over the side of the stall.

"And the nakedness is a necessary part?" Idrys swallowed.

He took in her milky skin, noting how her nipples rode high and dark on the swell of her ample breasts. The thick patch of hair at the meeting of her muscled thighs was as blood-red as the hair on her head. Her waist tucked in neatly, giving way to the gentle curve of her young hips. As she turned half away from him with a slight blush, he noted with another swallow that she'd dimples in more than just the cheeks of her face.

"There's going to be a lot of blood and ick. I only have two dresses and blood is hard to rinse clean." She looked at him through her long lashes. "I did not think a woman's flesh could distract you so," she said with a teasing tone.

He raised his eyes and his gaze hardened. "Best do it before you freeze to death."

She turned her head to hide her smile and moved slowly to stand close behind the mare.

The process was slow and strained her arm muscles horribly. She wished that she could tell the mare not to push against her so, but it was a vain desire. The bright side of it all was that by the time she managed to twist the colt around and grasp his forelegs, she was shining with sweat and felt the cold not even a little.

With a last painful push, Dancer's tired body released the foal. He slid out nearly into Áine's lap and she quickly bent and tickled his nose with straw, wiping it free of fluids.

"Hand me a rag. You can release her head; she should help now anyway," Áine said.

She toweled off the colt and withdrew, taking her bucket as the little creature fought clumsily to his feet.

Idrys held the gate for her and grinned. "He's beautiful, isn't he? He's to be the basis for my new stock someday. I aim to breed the best in Cymru perhaps."

He forgot her nakedness for a moment and stepped in close to clap her on the shoulder as he might a friend. His hand touched her bare skin as she stood looking up at him. A thrill of hot desire spiked through both of them and Áine parted her damp lips as Idrys bent his head.

They kissed, his mouth finding hers, and for a moment nothing but physical hunger reigned in his mind.

He came back to himself as she shivered, finally registering the frigid air.

"I'm sorry," Idrys said, stepping away from her. "You're going to freeze."

"Emyr." Áine reached for him with her free hand, feeling his sorrow and confusion return.

Hearing his brother's name helped ground him. Idrys, grasping at a clean rag, thrust it between them. Áine took it and quickly rubbed herself clean. Idrys turned his back and watched as his beautiful bay colt drank its first meal while Dancer cleaned up the afterbirth.

"Do women eat their birth sack?" he asked without thinking.

Áine laughed in surprise at the strange question and looked behind her as she dressed. Safely garbed and much warmer she came to stand beside him again.

"Nay. We burn or bury it." She remembered that, of course, he'd never seen a birth; men weren't allowed generally until long after the babe was out. She touched his arm and looked up into his face as he turned to her.

"I feel it too, you know," Áine said softly. "Guilt at being happy when the one I loved is dead and beyond such things. But I think your twin would want you to find joy and comfort where you might, as I believe my mother would have wished for me."

Idrys's full lips twisted in a half-bitter smile. Emyr had said as much that very morning, though of course Áine could not know that.

Think on it, Idrys. For us. Please.

He shook his head. "It's too deep, this sorrow, Áine. I don't know what to do." His eyes, warm and dark, stared into her own, full of want and loss. She reached and cupped his stubbled chin.

"Shh, I know what might be done." She slipped her hand around and caught a handful of his dark curls to pull his head down for another kiss.

He winced as she pressed against his bruised side but soon his aches were forgotten as they sank to the rush-covered stone floor. In the flickering light of the lamps Gethin had hung around for the birth, they coupled. Due to the cold they removed little clothing, clutching each other close for both warmth and comfort. Idrys clung to Áine, whispering her name over and over like a litany against his fears.

They lay tangled for long moments after their passion was spent, breathing and each enjoying the warmth of the other. Idrys finally shivered as the cold air raised bumps along his exposed flesh. He rolled to his knees next to Áine.

"Thank you," he said as he touched her cheek with the back of his hand.

"And you." A satisfied and gentle glow suffused her face and she sighed.

They cleaned up and extinguished all but one lamp. Áine left the bucket and dirty rags with the intent to return in the morning and tidy up.

The combination of hard labor and pleasure worked their magic in her body and she was bone-weary. She glanced at her lover as they moved across the square and entered the hall. It was empty, though a lamp had been left burning on the table for them. She blew it out and walked with Idrys to her door.

He bent his head and kissed her again. "Good night, Áine."

She didn't press him to stay with her, knowing there would be time and time for that. *Small steps,* she thought.

"Good night, Emyr." In the dark she missed his wince.

Idrys crept into his room to find his brother sprawled across the bed. He pulled his boots off and sat heavily, knowing he should undress but too tired to care. He shoved Emyr aside and crawled under the covers.

Emyr pressed a cold nose against his brother's neck and let out a small huffing breath.

"Emyr?" Idrys said into the dark.

The hound raised his head and licked his twin's cheek in response.

"I've thought on it. You're right. We can court Áine, if you like. And we should tell her, if she chooses to stay, about us. It's only fair. Though if we intend to wed someday, we should be careful of letting her too close."

If it's not too late for that already, he thought with a sigh. He tried to imagine wanting a warm, female smile that wasn't Áine's and couldn't conjure it.

Emyr gave out a great bark of joy that hurt Idrys's ears and excitedly covered his brother's face with wet puppy kisses.

Idrys shoved him again laughing. "Sleep you. Good gods, man." He fell asleep quickly and, for once, the woman he dreamed of was not Seren.

Fifteen

Emyr slipped out into the hall with a tired and sore Idrys creeping behind him. Melita was up and building the cooking fire. There was no sign of Caron or any of the others yet, and given Idrys's late night in the barn with Áine, his twin knew she would likely sleep later.

He tapped on his mother's door and heard her bid him enter. She was awake, as he'd guessed she might be, and combing out her hair before the little hearth.

"Good morning, mother," Emyr said.

She smiled at her sons as Idrys flopped down onto the rug at her feet. "Good morning. You've somewhat on your mind?"

Emyr sat on the edge of her bed and nodded. "Aye. We mean to court Áine. Idrys and I thought it best to speak with you first, however, since we know you'd like us to wed."

Hafwyn set her comb in her lap and carefully folded her hands. "Well. Anyone can see plain as sunlight that she's fallen for you." She looked down at Idrys. "You say we?"

The hound raised his head and clearly nodded. He realized he should have told Emyr what had transpired the night before, and perhaps also mentioned his bruised ribs since Áine would likely ask. It was an oversight he didn't usually make, but the night had left him drained and strangely happy. He'd speak to Emyr about it first thing that evening.

Hafwyn nodded slowly. "She's not the most politic of choices for a lover, mind. But her skills and knowledge are powerful things and it would strengthen our standing to have her dwelling here year round. Love is rare enough in life. She is a wisewoman, however, and will likely move on someday. And you must wed, eventually, which Áine may not take well to, though I think she'll understand." Despite these warnings, Hafwyn had to smile at the joy that lit Emyr's dark eyes. "Have you decided if you'll trust her with your, well, with this." She gestured between the twins.

Emyr thought of Áine's tears and nodded. "If she agrees to stay on here, we both agree she must be told. For ill or other."

Hafwyn sighed and wished there were a clear and easier path for her sons. *Let them keep this small happiness,* she prayed.

Áine rose later than she'd intended and dressed quickly. She emerged into the hall and found it bustling with the usual winter talk and industry as the night of the feast drew nearer. She nodded to Hafwyn and smiled at Caron.

"Is Emyr about?" she asked as she snagged an apple from a bowl on the long table.

"He's out in the stable I think." Melita had come in from the rear door with an armload of wood.

"Showing off his new colt, I imagine." Áine grinned. "I'll be back to help in a moment." She pulled her cloak off its pin and ducked out the door and into the bright cold day.

"Did I miss something?" Caron looked from Hafwyn to Melita.

"If you did, so did we all, dear." Hafwyn smiled and shook her head.

Áine found Emyr and his hound leaning over the stall watching the little bay colt and Dancer. Urien was there as well.

"Morning, Áine," Urien said. He glanced at Emyr and read his strange expression. "I've got work to do, no more time to gawk over even this handsome little fellow. Good day."

Áine watched him leave with a tiny smile playing over her lips. She stepped in close to Emyr and grinned up at him. "I guess we're not so subtle, are we?" Her long white fingers twined with his.

Emyr started in surprise at her bold touch and saw her eyes darken with confusion as she pulled back a little.

"Áine," he said, reaching for her hand again. He glanced at his brother who had dropped down beside him and now sat with tongue lolling out leaving a trail of steam in the cold air. *What didn't you tell me, Idrys?* Emyr sighed.

"I'm sorry." Áine said, looking down at their hands. "I thought, well, I'd thought we'd made our feelings clear enough last night." She flushed as she looked back up into his face.

Emyr stared down at her as revelation dawned on him. He shifted his gaze and glared at his brother as a small pain of jealousy pricked his heart. *You impish little wretch! You slept with her and didn't think to mention it?* He sighed.

"No, don't be sorry. This is new to me. I'm a bit rough around the details, I'm afraid." Emyr stepped in close and cupped her strong chin with his free hand. He kissed her then and it was sweet and soft.

Áine smiled up at him. "How are your ribs?"

Confusion flickered through his eyes. "Well enough." He squeezed her hand and inwardly wondered what else his brother hadn't said. Emyr and Idrys were used to smoothing over each other's omissions as small things sometimes slipped through the cracks in their imperfect and delayed communication.

Áine did not miss the flicker in his eyes. Suspicion prompted her to take a deep breath and let her consciousness sink into his body through their joined hands. She steadied herself mentally for the expected pain of his bruises and found nothing of the sort. Emyr had only the usual aches and pains found in an active human body and no trace that he'd been kicked by a distraught mare the night before. She pulled away from him, ducking her head to hide her own thoughts.

"I'm glad to hear it. I woke late; I should probably go make some use of myself before Hafwyn thinks I've turned lazy, shouldn't I." She stood on tiptoes and kissed his cheek before spinning and leaving the stable.

"You," Emyr said to his twin, "you and I are going to have a long talk later."

It was past the midday meal and the dark was coming on quickly before Áine had a chance to speak quietly with Hafwyn in the hall. Caron had left to help inventory the foodstuffs brought by a late-arriving family and Melita was dozing at her loom with her back propped against the wall. Everyone was out or busy with preparations for the longest night.

"Hafwyn," Áine said as she settled beside where the older woman sat mending stockings. "Tell me about your sons."

Hafwyn shot her a sharp look. "My son? Emyr?"

Áine shook her head. "I know it might hurt to speak of the dead, but I want to know what his brother was like, what Emyr was like, well, before."

Hafwyn studied her in a way that only fed the growing seed of doubt and impossible consideration in Áine.

After what seemed to be a very long time she spoke, "Idrys was like his father and his brother. Impulsive, passionate, given to moods that would pass as quickly as a summer storm. He had a good heart like his brother though. Emyr tempered him, I think. They were nigh inseparable." She smiled at the bittersweet memories. "Emyr, well, you know Emyr. You've spent as much time with my son these last few months as anyone." She looked keenly at Áine and the younger woman flushed.

"Do you, do you mind?" Áine asked. Her heartbeat sped up.

"Mind? Goodness, no. You're a wisewoman, Áine. And my son a man well grown. Both of you are free by age and custom to find joy where you will."

Áine's smile split her face, though a strange shadow of thought lived still in her green eyes. "Thank you, Hafwyn." She rose and left the hall again.

Hafwyn watched her go and guessed at the girl's thoughts. Áine was clever and used to unorthodox thinking, plus she'd had more experience with the world's mysteries through her own work as a wisewoman.

If they don't tell her, she's of a mind to sort it out on her own, I think. The woman shook her head with a smile.

Áine left the hall and pulled her cloak tight against the sunny chill of the afternoon. She spied Urien and Llew chopping wood by the smoke house and made her way toward them. Garlands hung over every door and casement now, lending green and red cheer to the grey and white of the landscape.

"Llew, Urien." Áine nodded at them as she framed her thoughts. She was unsure she understood her own suspicions but decided to follow her healer's instincts and go where the mounting evidence led her.

"You've been friends with Emyr for long time, no?" she asked.

Llew straightened and wiped his forehead on his sleeve. "Aye, since we were children."

"Were you around when, well, when he lost his twin?" She stepped in closer and lowered her voice.

Llew and Urien exchanged a glance. They'd wondered when she might ask questions since it seemed she was growing close to their chief and friend.

Urien answered her. "Aye. Bad business, that. He's never been the same since."

It was the simple truth. The Emyr who had left had been a happy and kind youth with none of his brother's brooding or impulsive tendencies. He'd returned hollow with grief and the healing of time had only damped the pain, not banished it. He was prone these days to all sorts of odd or rash actions, like riding out hunting at night or passionately arguing a decision he'd made himself earlier in the day.

"He changed? How?"

Llew explained some of it and added, "Grief and that nasty bump his head took, most likely. There weren't ever two men closer than Idrys and Emyr in heart."

"Bump on the head?" Áine recalled Hafwyn's tale and wondered that she'd failed to mention her son being injured before.

"In the slide that killed his brother," Urien said. "He forgot himself for near two months before he recovered and came home. Lucky a kindly hermit found him and healed him up."

Pieces of the puzzle settled into place in Áine's mind. She stared at the inner pattern and found it made a sort of impossible sense. Her dream of the two black hounds returned to her mind again and she fit that in as well and wondered at it.

"You could always ask Emyr yourself, if you'd like," Llew said after she remained silent for too long. "Sometimes a man will tell a woman he cares for things that he wouldn't speak to another man."

She gave herself a small shake and winked at him. "So if I'd like your secrets I should pry at Caron, eh?"

"Oh, aye. That little lady has skinned me cleaner of secrets than bones picked over by wolves." He chuckled good-naturedly.

Áine grinned and thanked them both. She turned and saw Emyr walking into the hall with his hound on his heels. It was very nearly sunset. She needed only one more piece to confirm her thoughts and, if she were correct, she'd have to wait until dark. She shook her head at her impossible thoughts, but now that it was all coming together she couldn't find another shape that fit so well.

"You slept with her? And didn't think to mention it?"

Time was shorter than Emyr would have liked since his day had been filled with the usual tasks surrounding a feast day and the winter tax collections. He sank down to the bed and pulled his stockings off. "Though I suppose expecting you to make up your mind about anything without some rash act associated would be expecting the sky to turn green, wouldn't it?" He shook his head.

Idrys stood on the sheepskin rug and hung his head. He knew he should have mentioned it, but Emyr had covered well enough.

The tingling in his blood rose to fever pitch and Emyr knew there were only moments left. He thought belatedly of the pearl tear and realized it would have to wait until morning.

Idrys had just pulled his tunic over his head when the soft knock came at the door. He picked up his belt and glanced at his brother.

"Come in?" he called.

Áine entered, closing the door behind her.

Idrys's heart sped up and he smiled. He'd never dreamed that anything would ease the relentless pain of guilt and loss he carried with him always, but today he felt differently. He felt as though some part of him that had been out of place for years had finally settled back down where it belonged and taken with it the sharpest edge of his troubles.

She moved toward him, a white-and-red vision with a strange smile on her face. "How are your ribs?" she asked.

"Didn't you ask me this earlier?" he said, raising a raven's-wing brow at her.

"I'm a healer, we worry." She shrugged lightly and stepped in close to him. Her hands came up and wound around his neck. He sighed with pleasure and bent to kiss her.

Áine let her mind sink into his body as she'd done earlier that day. This time she felt the throbbing bruises on his ribs, though none were broken and it only hurt when he forgot and breathed too deeply.

She pulled slightly away from him with a gasp and her smile fled. In its place there was only an intent searching knowledge in her leaf-and-sunlight eyes.

"Idrys?" she said softly, making his name both a plea and statement in one.

A painful shuddering ran through him and he gripped her close with a small strangled cry, burying his head in her sweetly scented red hair. She knew then her suspicions for truth, though she did not understand the full story as yet. She was in love not with a man with strange and shifting moods, but with two men, one dark and brooding and tormented with unspoken guilt, the other sad and kind and full of compassion for his twin's pained spirit.

Áine turned her head and looked at Emyr who stood staring up at her with all too human eyes. She wondered that she'd not noted how the hound's eyes matched his master's so well before.

"Emyr," she said to the hound and he nodded his head in an incongruous gesture. "Sit," she said to them both. "Tell me the story, please?"

Idrys sat with her on the bed and told her the events of those horrible days in fits and starts, glancing often at his silent twin. His telling was slightly different than Emyr might have spoken had he a human tongue, for Idrys's guilt weighed heavily on the words, but the basic story remained unchanged.

To Emyr's surprise, his brother shared with Áine what he'd withheld from their parents and spoke of his shame and desire for Seren. At the end of the tale, he stopped abruptly and looked at her with hollow and dark eyes.

Áine slipped her hands over his. "Idrys, I do not think your mother or your brother blame you. You were both so young. Seren manipulated you, played on your passions and inexperience."

"What is done cannot be undone," he said as he dropped his gaze to their joined hands.

"I'll have you both, if," Áine paused and took a deep, steadying breath, "if you'll both have me?"

Emyr rose from his place and pressed his head into her thigh as Idrys threw back his head and laughed.

"Are you crazy, woman?" He shook his head at her mildly annoyed look, remembering his own standoffish and moody actions. "Áine, Áine, it was not for lack of love that I've resisted you but fear of inviting further pain. I'm sorry for it. Emyr is right, I think, perhaps it is time to let go the past at least a little. Though," he added more solemnly, "I've small practice at it and can't promise it'll go with ease."

Áine smiled at him and her own heart pricked with a shadow of grief. "We've all had loss, Idrys."

She wished Tesn could have met these strange young men. It would be just the sort of mysterious story her mother would love. Áine knew she'd have to tell them of her own obscure origins and the selkie eventually. She realized that Emyr had never asked her about the tear and wondered if he'd even mentioned it to his twin. She guessed somehow he hadn't.

There was time and time for that later, however. She responded to Idrys's heated looked with her own passion and crawled into his embrace.

Emyr sighed very heavily and gave a small whine. Idrys looked up from the bed and grinned. "Dawn will come soon enough. Do you want me to let you into the hall?"

Emyr shook his narrow head and flopped down with another sigh onto the carpet. He'd lived enough moments vicariously through his twin that he was willing to survive a few more if it meant a preview of Áine's lovely form.

"I don't mind if you stay," Áine said, "though while I might love the man, I think I'd rather not have the hound in my bed." She looked at him with worried eyes, not wishing to offend.

Emyr looked at her and nodded again. He understood completely though his exile stung as a painful reminder of his cast-off humanity. He lay on the rug and found himself looking forward to the dawn for the first time in many years.

Though many glances were cast at the closed door, no one disturbed the chief. Hafwyn made sure of that, murmuring excuses and smiling every time she looked toward her sons' quarters. When Caron politely asked if

Emyr might wish for supper, Hafwyn made the younger woman blush by mentioning that there were many kinds of hunger.

And many kinds of healing, she reminded herself with another small smile.

Áine fell asleep with her head pillowed on Idrys's warm broad shoulder and found herself caught in a strange dream.

She stood in a familiar clearing with the two black hounds on one side and the twins standing on the other. Idrys and Emyr stared only at each other and did not seem to hear her calling their names. She found she could not move.

Before her a tall white stone loomed and out from behind it emerged a woman. Her body was draped with white cloth but her face was bare and her features shifted between the selkie's broad face and Tesn's wrinkled smile.

"Mother?" Áine said softly, paralyzed with grief and confusion.

"Do you love them, daughter?" Tesn/selkie asked.

Áine felt the weight of the question and paused, knowing somehow that there was more than just a dream in this. She looked at the twins who stared through her, unseeing and lost. Her heart ached with the desire to soothe that despairing look forever from their handsome faces.

"Yes," Áine said, "though I know I cannot stay."

"You can free them, Áine, free them and perhaps then stay. What man could refuse to wed a woman who'd saved him?" Tesn/selkie said. "But you must come to the Ilswyn before the end of the longest night. And you must not speak of where or why you go to anyone."

"What? Why not? And where is this Ilswyn?" Áine asked. She looked again at the twins before returning the implacable gaze of the shifting dream woman.

"Because it is thus done with magic, my heart. You must go now. Follow the owl, she'll show you to the gate."

The dream began to unravel and Áine could feel Idrys's breathing warmth beside her in the bed.

"Wait!" she cried but the dream dissolved leaving only the faint memory of Tesn whispering *I love you* as Áine awoke in the cold dark room.

Idrys slept on beside her and did little more than shift as she rose and dressed quickly. She wondered at her own mind being made up so quickly, but she'd failed to heed a dream such as that before when it had warned her of the flood and she'd no wish to ignore such a gift again. If she were wrong she'd lose only a little time and get some exercise.

Emyr raised his narrow head and looked at her with eyes that reflected the dying firelight in their curious depths.

"Shh, love," she said to him, "I'll return. Tell Idrys. I promise I'll return, just wait for me if you can." She bent and kissed his bony head, breathing deep of his soft scent.

She eased open the door and walked into the hall. It took only a few moments to pull on her boots and cloak.

Áine slipped out of Clun Cadair in the light of false dawn. She looked up and saw the dark form of a bird circling to the north and east. She set her shoulders and though she took many a backward glance at the sleeping village that had become home these past few months, she put her feet on the path her heart bid her and moved off into the snowy morning.

Part Two

Sixteen

Áine swung her arms to warm her numbed hands as the sun climbed sluggishly into a sky pockmarked by clouds. Looking back she could no longer see the settlement and in front of her the wall of the forest loomed. The strange urgency and certainty she'd felt upon waking from the vivid dream faded away with daylight and left her chilled and wondering what she'd been thinking.

Her stomach reminded her she'd not eaten the night before and she cursed her stupidity in not even grabbing a few provisions or so much as a belt pouch on her way out. She shook her head and pulled the hood of her cloak tighter. She'd get to the trees and then turn back if an obvious path or sign had not presented itself. This was madness anyway.

You can free them.

It echoed through her mind and she sighed as she set one numb foot in front of the other in the crackling and frosted grass.

The trees, which had seemed so close before, grew very slowly larger until at last, as the sun played hide-and-seek among the clouds, Áine reached the straggling edge of the wood. It was not the unbroken and imposing wall it had seemed from afar.

The woods provided a little relief from the insidious icy wind that had crept beneath her dress and up her sleeves all morning. She walked inside the edge and looked around, waiting for inspiration to strike her.

The trees were all nearly bare, standing dark against the sky. A few little birds with black-capped heads flitted among the branches. The forest floor was dark with leaf mold and a few of the shadowed branches retained a light decoration of dry snow.

Áine stood inside the trees until her feet hurt with cold and her limbs started to stiffen with the lack of activity. She snorted finally, laughing at herself. She'd half-expected some sort of magical path to open in front of her.

"Áine, you're an idiot," she said aloud. On the up side of things, she'd have a nice long walk to decide on a believable reason for wandering off in winter by herself with only the clothes on her back. She turned and started to walk out of the trees toward home as she shook off her disappointment.

It was only a dream.

The soft rush of wings stopped her. She looked up and saw a large white owl with scarlet eyes land on a branch just above her head. A mixture of excitement and confusion swept through her. The owl barely rested once she saw it before lifting off again and winging through the dark branches. Áine turned and went after it.

I'm too cold to be dreaming still, she thought and a pang of guilt went through her. She'd almost turned back, nearly given up. She vowed to herself no matter what happened next, she'd not turn back so easily again.

You can free them.

The promise led her on. The owl stayed ahead, just in sight. Áine broke into an easy run, the pace helping to warm her body as she clutched her skirts and cloak tightly to herself. Deeper into the forest she went, following her pale guide. Low branches threatened to catch her hair and her arms and face were scratched by brush and brambles. Áine kept up her pace, pushing aside these small annoyances.

She recalled the other part of what her dream mother had told her. She must reach the Ilswyn before the end of the longest night. She had no idea how far there was yet to go and her uncertainty helped lend energy to her pace.

Darkness forced her to a walk. The owl hopped from branch to branch above her as she, frustrated, picked her way through the wood. Her guide's feathers shone with iridescent light, allowing Áine to keep an eye on the owl while also navigating the wood. She'd become nearly immune to the cold, the chill so deep in her bones that she only noticed it when she rubbed her hands together or slapped her thighs to bring the blood into them again.

Soon, exhausted and freezing, Áine stumbled more than walked, her eyes fixed on the owl. Hunger and thirst rode her but she gripped in her mind the promise her dream had given her.

She would not give in so easily again, not this soon. She had only to recall the pain and guilt in Idrys's eyes as he'd told her their story, to remember how many nights he'd pulled away from his loved ones or drank himself to sleep. She recalled Emyr's deep sorrow for a twin he could not touch nor speak with, his pain at his inability to ease the suffering of another anymore than he could ease his own.

Áine remembered and pushed herself onward.

She nearly ran into the standing stones. The owl came to rest on one of the large white stones that loomed out of the deep of night just ahead of her. Áine stopped abruptly and leaned into a stone. She closed her eyes for a moment. These had to be a sign, a marker of some sort. She opened her eyes, sniffing the air. Wood smoke and ripe apples.

The owl hopped down from the stone and transformed in midair. A slender and beautiful young woman stood before Áine. She was white of hair and complexion with violet eyes and wore a simple yellow gown sewn about with little green leaves.

"Áine, I greet you. I am Blodeuedd." The woman smiled.

"I greet you, Blodeuedd. I seek the Ilswyn." Áine's voice came out as a hoarse whisper and she licked her chapped lips.

"Follow me." The woman offered a warm hand and twined her fingers in Áine's own cold ones. With her other hand, she called a ball of light into being from the air.

They walked hand in hand between the standing stones that lined a path like silent soldiers keeping watch. The air was very still. As the women passed between the final stones, Áine gasped.

Winter was left behind and she saw grass beneath her feet in the pale golden light of Blodeuedd's fairy lamp. A warm, summery breeze danced around her, bringing the smells of apples, smoke, and fresh blooms with it.

Blodeuedd led the amazed woman through an orchard and toward a little thatched house. The trees were in fruit and flower both at once.

"What is this place?" Áine said. She'd started shivering again in the warm air and her feet and hands ached as feeling returned. She could feel the tiny scratches and scrapes and speaking made her wince.

Blodeuedd let go of her hand and opened the door to the house. "This is the Ilswyn." She beckoned her guest inside.

The inside of the little hut was well appointed with neat shelves lining one wall, many skins and pillows covering the floor, and a large stone hearth warming the space. Áine sank down gratefully onto a thick sheepskin and rubbed her stinging feet. Blodeuedd set a kettle on the hearth to heat and dished out a bowl of cooked apples and nuts from the pot steaming on the fire.

After the first couple bites burned her tongue, Áine sat back and blew on her food to cool it. "What is the Ilswyn?" she asked. "Where am I now? How will I find Seren? Is she here?"

Blodeuedd laughed softly. "Those are many different questions, but I will do my best to answer them for you."

"Thank you, I do not mean to be rude." Áine flushed and ducked her head.

Blodeuedd settled down to lean against the hearth. "I take no offense. Eat and listen. The Lady you seek, Seren, is not here." She held up a hand as Áine's face fell. "The Ilswyn is a gateway, a place within Cymru-that-is that touches upon Cymru-that-could-be. Seren dwells in the land of Cymru-that-could-be, though her home, like many of the Fair Folk, also touches upon your world."

"I can go through the gate and find her?" Áine said around a mouthful of hot spiced apples.

"Yes. I will show you the way once you've eaten and rested. We must go before dawn; this side of the gate is only open when the veils grow thin."

"Why," Áine hesitated but curiosity claimed her, "why are you helping me? How did you know me?"

Blodeuedd laughed, a soft sound like the breeze through a field of wildflowers. "Those are different questions again, are they not? I knew you because the wind whispered that you'd need of me. No one finds the Ilswyn without my help. I hear the desires of those with greatest need and come for them." Her eyes grew dark and sad as the mirth abruptly left her fine features. "As for the other question, well. I help because I am bound to help. I must guide all who have the will."

Áine thought about this for a moment. "But," she paused, "I was turning back. I would have given up if you'd not appeared."

Blodeuedd regarded her for a very long moment, head cocked slightly like a bird's. Finally she spoke. "This is true. But you turned back not for desire but for belief."

Áine laughed and it sounded bitter even to her. "Strange coming from one who loves two men cursed by a fey Lady and stranger still from a woman whose tears turn to pearls when they touch the earth. I should have believed."

"Nonsense." Blodeuedd's sharp tone surprised Áine. "You were raised by a human, given none of the gifts that are your birthright and left to wonder your whole life about where you fit and why."

"My birthright? Am I truly one of the Folk then?" She closed her eyes, remembering Tesn's stories, remembering the selkie.

She'd never really believed, even with her odd gift of knowing the pain of others. Wisewomen were supposed to have access to mysteries long lost to ordinary men and women. Besides, she could touch cold iron, a thing no fey was supposed to stand.

"You are, and are not. Most likely your mother found a changeling man and lay with him, for I think you are not even truly half-blooded."

"But it means I might have a father somewhere."

She'd never given it much thought. Tesn had always been enough and after there was only grief and then the love of the twins and Hafwyn's calm mothering. She sighed. She'd avoided thinking too much about the future, what would happen when she took to the road again as a wisewoman. She didn't want to leave the security she'd found in Clun Cadair.

A thought pricked her like a thorn. *Am I doing this because I only want to stay? Because if I free the twins everyone there will have to accept me? They will accept me? It will not change what I am, will it?*

Blodeuedd's bitter laugh brought her back to the conversation and she shoved her own uncomfortable thoughts away. "Ha! Much care fey fathers have for their daughters. If he is out there somewhere, perhaps wandering the Isle, judging by your emerald eyes, he's like as not never wondered after you." Blodeuedd's bitter laugh brought her back to the conversation and Áine shoved her own uncomfortable thoughts away.

"What is your story?" Áine asked, looking at her with the intuitive eye of the healer and reading deep pain in the beautiful woman's ageless face.

"Too long and too short." Blodeuedd shrugged. "I wanted somewhat other than my father wished for me and betrayed another to follow my heart. It went unwell for all involved."

Áine nodded and wisely chose not to press the woman any further. Her body had warmed and she took the cup of tea Blodeuedd offered with a nod of her head. Her limbs were heavy with exhaustion and she sighed, wishing only to sleep but knowing there was still a journey ahead with an end she could not foretell. She ate a second bowl of the apple and nut mash and finished her tea.

Then Blodeuedd stood and offered her hand. Áine took the woman's slender pale fingers in her own and rose. Her host handed her a water skin and a cloth sack that revealed itself to be half-full of bread and apples when Áine looked inside. She thanked Blodeuedd who waved it off and walked out into the warm night.

The women walked to the far end of the valley. The night's black faded to grey as they reached a single wide slab of pure white marble rising out of the valley into the sky far above their heads. Blodeuedd stepped up to the stone and rapped on it three times. A doorway opened and mist swirled out from it to rub against the women.

"This is where I leave you, Áine." Blodeuedd turned to her and, leaning forward, kissed her cheek in farewell.

"How will I know where to go?" Áine said, hating the uncertainty that gripped her.

"You asked why I chose to come to you even when you turned away," Blodeuedd answered. "I came because your heart was strong. Follow your heart, Áine. If you want what you've come for enough, you cannot fail. Such might not be true in Cymru-that-is, but such things are the very foundation of Cymru-that-could-be. Follow that if all else fails you."

"Thank you, Blodeuedd. I will not forget what you've told me." Áine turned to the doorway.

She paused again, staring into the shifting mists beyond. *I've fought off a starving wolf with nothing but a firebrand, I've wrestled cattle, spoken with selkie, saved men's lives, survived a flood, and uncovered a secret kept for seven years. What is one more step forward?*

Áine took a deep breath and walked across the threshold.

Seventeen

Áine walked straight through the shimmering fog that phosphoresced around her skirt and cloak and hands as she moved. She could not tell how much time had passed before she stepped out of the mist and onto a soft, grassy knoll. Dawn had broken here and the sun's light fell welcoming and warm on her cheeks. She closed her green eyes for a long moment.

When she awoke she found herself sprawled on the thick grass, her head pillowed on her arms and the sun dipping down now into the other side of the heavens. Her limbs were still heavy with sleep as she shifted to sit. She sipped water from her flask as she looked around herself more fully than her earlier exhaustion had permitted.

Áine stood in a clearing. All about her trees bloomed with pink, blue, and white blossoms. The forest floor was free of brush and carpeted with the thick green grass dotted with bright patches of tiny purple and yellow flowers. Birds sang merrily, unseen in the thick foliage above her. Joyful laughter bubbled up in her throat and she grinned at the beauty around her as a child might.

The mirth died away as she realized she had no idea where to go. Standing, Áine looked around for some sign of a path or perhaps another magically manifesting guide. Each direction looked as good as another for there was no doorway behind her anymore, only forest.

"An unaimed arrow never misses." She recalled Emyr, no, Idrys telling her one evening as he and Llew joked and told stories.

Áine smiled at the memory and chose to go east, for that was the direction of the rising sun and the direction of beginnings. She walked until the night's gloom deepened such that she could not see her way. She stopped and sat, tearing free a hunk of bread from a loaf in the pack Blodeuedd had gifted to her. As she chewed she thought about what to do next.

The ground was soft and the air summer-warm, but even after her enervating journey of the day and night before, she was no longer fatigued. She blamed her collapse and sleep that morning for she'd now wasted a whole day. She thought of the owl woman and wished she could make a light as Blodeuedd had.

Sparkling light started to collect at her fingertips. Áine hissed and closed her fist. The light disappeared instantly. Tentatively, Áine held out her palm and thought of the fairy lamp, wishing for it again.

Golden light gathered just above her hand into a shining sphere that illuminated the woods around her with gentle shadows and limned the branches in its glittering light.

"Thank you," Áine whispered into the empty air. She'd be doing Tesn's instruction a disservice to do otherwise. A wisewoman met mystery and power with proper reverence, lest she inadvertently give harm.

She arose, the fairy lamp floating just ahead of her, and continued on her journey into the wood.

Eventually she came to a bubbling brook and followed along it until she reached a large clearing. The sky spread out overhead, full of unfamiliar stars. In the clearing stood a little stone hut. There was no chimney, but soft golden light filtered out through a narrow window and from underneath the sturdy oak door.

Áine hesitated a few feet from the door. She could continue, or she could knock. Perhaps the resident within might know where she could find Seren. She took a deep breath, banished her fairy lamp with a thought, and rapped softly on the door.

It swung open to reveal a tall and lovely woman of the Fair Folk. Her smooth face and cold silvery eyes regarded Áine silently. She did not offer greeting so, after a moment, Áine spoke.

"Lady, I greet you. I am Áine." She offered a tentative smile.

Her heart had dropped when she'd seen the woman, for the Lady fit the twins' description of Seren perfectly. However, she refused to let hope push aside reason. The Fair Folk were all supposed to share the moonlit skin and blood-red hair; it was, after all, what marked the fey of Cymru. There was little reason to think she'd come upon the one she'd sought.

"Áine." The Lady gave a half-smile in return though it did not touch her swirling silver eyes. "What is it you wish, halfling?"

Áine started at the word and did not miss the flash of amused satisfaction in the woman's eyes. "I've come seeking a lady called Seren. Have you heard of her or know where she might be found?" Annoyance made Áine's tone sharper than she would have wanted for courtesy's sake, but the woman's strange manner bothered her.

"I have heard of her, and I know where she might be found," the Lady said. She paused and looked Áine over, her gaze taking in the frayed hem of the young woman's dress and the cloth sack slung over her shoulder. "You have traveled far. Come inside."

The invitation surprised Áine. Though she wanted the information the Lady said she had, Áine hardly wanted to seem rude by pressing that she was in a hurry. So she stepped into the hut and closed the door behind her.

A bronze brazier lent a lovely warmth to the little room. The home was furnished much as Blodeuedd's home had been, though without a hearth. Instead a wide and comfortable bed piled high with furs and quilts adorned the far wall.

The Lady motioned for Áine to sit and settled herself onto the edge of the bed. Áine sank down onto the skins near the brazier, feeling awkward and travel-stained compared to the clean and calm grace of the fey woman.

"Please, Lady, I do not mean offense, but I must keep going. If you could but point the way, I will leave you in peace. Is the Lady Seren near by?" Áine asked.

Something about the home seemed so familiar but she pushed it aside as weariness playing tricks. She'd never been here, she knew that much.

"She is quite near. Why do you seek her?" The Lady's full, sensuous mouth quirked in another condescending half-smile.

Suspicion tickled Áine's mind and she leaned forward, choosing her words carefully. "I seek her because she has gravely wronged the men I love and I wish to put it right."

The Lady's smile died and she jerked up straight, her lips tightening into a line of crimson on her moon-pale face. "Wronged?" she said. "Is that how their story goes?"

Áine stood in a single motion, ignoring the protest in her tired thighs. "Seren," she said, her suspicion blooming into certainty. She could see it now, the cold, terrible beauty that Idrys had described.

The women faced each other over the bronze brazier and neither spoke for a long moment. Áine's heart pounded against her ribs as one emotion after another flashed through her.

She wasn't sure what to think, much less to say. It seemed almost unreal to be standing before the cause of her lovers' grief. To be standing before the woman whom the twins had loved first. She'd never thought about what she might feel because she'd thought this meeting further away. Her mind finally settled on simmering anger and desperate hope.

You can free them.

Áine swallowed. "You can free them, Seren," she said.

Seren shrugged, her anger gone from her features as quickly as it had arisen.

"Perhaps. But why should I? I offered your princes what mortal men only dream about and they turned away. They made their choice. If they were so unhappy, why have they not come themselves to beg my forgiveness?"

Áine knew the true answer to this but it was one she could hardly tell Seren. *Idrys is not sure he could refuse you a second time, since he nearly failed the first. And Emyr is afraid of what he might swear to free his brother from his guilt. No, it had to be someone over whom the Lady would hold no sway. And perhaps it had to be someone a little fey themselves, to navigate this realm. It had to be me.* She'd worked out this much on her long walk.

"I came because I love them," she said simply.

"Both?" Seren narrowed her eyes.

"Both. They are different, truly I would not have known their secret if they weren't, and I love each for himself." Áine had anticipated this question as well.

"And you wish me to end the curse?" Seren said. Her expression smoothed again and her beauty became an unreadable mask that hid all thoughts.

"I do. Please, they've suffered enough. They meant no offense to you, they were but children and..."

"Enough." Seren said, cutting off Áine's pleading. "I'll break the curse."

"What?" Áine couldn't help herself. Shock wiped her mind for a moment. *That easily?* She wondered. Then she saw the hint of the cruel smile on the other woman's lips. *No, it won't be, will it.*

"I'll break the curse. Don't look so amazed, child. I find it insulting." Seren sat down on the bed again.

"What must I do?" Áine said, suspicion returning in the wake of her surprise.

"Well, at least you're not completely stupid," Seren said.

"Not completely." Áine bit the tip of her tongue to keep in the rest of her response. It would not do to anger the Lady now, not when she had come so far.

"Quit glowering over me and sit, halfling."

She sat. Seren waited until Áine nearly shook with impatience before she spoke again. "Now, curses are specific things. For it to be broken, I would want certain items. You'll collect them for me."

"Will I be able to do so before the twins grow old and die in Cymru- that-is?" Áine asked. She knew the stories and sensed that somehow there was a trick in Seren's words, though she could not see the whole of it.

"Yes, provided you can complete the tasks I set for you at all. I would not ask if it were not possible with a little ingenuity and dedication." Seren toyed idly with a small blue stone ring on one of her fingers as she watched Áine's face.

"What must I do?" Áine repeated.

"*Follow your heart,*" Blodeuedd's words whispered in her memory.

"Five tasks. Each will bring to me a part for the charm that you might use to break the curse."

"Can all five be completed in Cymru-that-could be?"

There was a flash of something in Seren's eyes as she answered, "All but the last."

"Where is that task then?"

"Cymru-that-is." Seren shifted and held up her hand to forestall Áine's next question. "Enough for tonight. The hour is late and I would rest. I will set you the first task in the morning. Press me further and I might decide to sleep in," she added sharply.

Áine sighed and stood up. "Good night then, Seren."

"No need to sleep outside, child. You may stay with me." Seren stroked the furs beneath her.

Áine shivered as she considered the Lady's thinly veiled invitation. To sleep in the bed where her lovers had lost their innocence, to rest touching the instrument of their pain, to think it brought anger roaring back into her. She was disgusted with her own sudden and strange desire and shoved that aside in place of the cold rage.

Understanding as clear as the chiming of a bell came to her. She saw before her the root of the twins' confusion and loss and what they'd had to refuse. A rebuke hovered on the tip of her tongue but she realized also in that moment of clarity how inhuman Seren truly was. *She doesn't see human desire as we feel it, only as a toy to be played with and set aside.* Pity touched Áine's heart for the Fair Lady, mixing with the anger into churning lump in her stomach.

"Thank you, but I'll wait outside." Áine turned away from Seren and left before the Lady could say more.

Eighteen

Áine dreamed. She soared over the forest and circled a holding. She angled her strong white wings to drift lower. Below she recognized Clun Cadair and dropped lower still until she came to rest on the edge of the meat shed. The air was cold and an icy breeze ruffled her plumage. Emyr stood just beneath her but did not look up. The tall black hound at his side, however, turned and stared toward the roof. *Idrys.*

She awoke then with the howl of a hunting hound ringing in her mind and found herself curled up at the base of a blossoming cherry. It took her a few moments to recall where she was and why.

Áine stood and folded her cloak, tucking it away into the cloth sack after she pulled an apple out for her breakfast. She noted that the loaf of bread she'd torn a piece from the night before seemed to be whole and undamaged again. Silently she thanked Blodeuedd for yet another kindness.

Áine walked to the deep pool below the waterfall that cascaded and sang beside Seren's home. Kneeling, she sipped some water and scrubbed at her face with her wet hands. She dried her cheeks on a sleeve and stood up to find Seren watching her from beside the pond.

"Morning," Áine said with a politeness she did not feel.

"Sleep well, I hope?" Seren said in a tone that made it clear she also felt the question a formality only.

Áine bit into her apple and merely nodded. Not wanting to have to throw the core away in these woods, Áine tucked it back into her cloth sack. She could bury it later, when the cold silver gaze of the Lady wasn't watching every motion.

"I am ready for my first task," she said after a few more moments when it became clear that Seren wasn't going to open the topic.

"Indeed." Seren folded her arms. She was dressed in a deep-blue gown with a lighter blue underdress peeking out at her sleeves and throat. Intricate embroidery in varying shades of red decorated the neck, hem, and sleeves as well as the cloth sash she had tied low around her hips. Tiny glittering stones were sewn into the collar and cuffs and her blood-red hair fell loose to curl gently at her waist.

Áine sighed, unconsciously smoothing down the front of her own undyed woolen dress.

"Well, halfling, to make the charm I will first need two white stones from a beach to the north and east of here."

"Any two white stones from that beach? And are they perfectly white or blemished somehow?" Áine asked, wondering at the simple sounding task.

"Nay. They must be two perfectly white stones exactly alike. And there are only two on that beach that are so." Seren shook her head, not entirely hiding her disappointment that the girl had thought to ask. "When you have found them, return to me and I will give you further instructions."

"But," Áine started. Seren smiled and disappeared between breaths, one moment there and the next gone as though she'd never been.

"Don's tits," Áine muttered. Then she flushed. Tesn always told her swearing just brought on trouble from the Gods. Emyr would laugh. She wondered what Idrys would have said and then smiled to herself as she recalled him muttering far stronger curses. Her heart hurt and she rubbed at her chest as though she could ease the ache somehow.

Áine shook herself. Standing around feeling lonely wouldn't help anyone. She slipped her bag over her shoulder and secured the strap between her breasts and then set out through the wood, traveling to the north and the east in search of a beach with white stones.

The forest gave way after a time to gently rolling hills. The tall grass caressed Áine's waist as she walked. The breeze brought her the faint scent of brine, drawing her ever further east toward an ocean she could not yet hear or see.

Colorful birds darted among the stalks of grass and grasshoppers, voles, and mice scurried from the disturbance of her passing feet. One mouse paused, and Áine saw it had tiny human hands instead of feet, with beady, scarlet eyes. She bent low to look more closely, but the odd creature disappeared back into the grass. Áine shook her head and moved on, watching this strange world with curious eyes.

The sun rose high overhead and though the day was warm, its light never quite reached the bright oppression of true summer. Áine paused around midday and sat down to rest for a moment in a patch of bright blue wildflowers. She drank water from her flask and then opened the cloth sack to get bread and another apple. Remembering her plan to bury her apple core, she removed her cloak from the pack and looked within. There was no sign of the remains of her breakfast.

It then occurred to Áine for the first time that she'd felt no urge to relieve her bladder either, not since that morning when she'd left Clun Cadair. She'd been so tired and chilled on the journey to the Islwyn and then exhausted and amazed after that it hadn't even occurred to her to attend to such a natural function. She considered but cast aside the notion that she might be dehydrated or sick. She felt fine; if a little weary of walking.

"Well," she said aloud, "that simplifies life for the moment, doesn't it?"

Áine gave her head a little shake as she realized she was half-waiting for an answer. She sat on the bed of flowers and ate her midday meal, enjoying the play of sunlight on the glossy blue petals that shivered in the light breeze. A little family of swallows danced in a daring spiral around her, circling closer and closer until their nerve broke and they skimmed away like tiny feather ships on the rolling meadow.

Áine washed down her last bite of bread with a swallow of water and smiled as the birds left her. Her smile dropped away abruptly as the emptiness of the landscape struck her. She tucked her apple core away in her sack and laid her cloak back on top. Then she stood and turned slowly in a circle as she considered the strange feeling that had come over her so suddenly.

She was alone.

Though she searched her memory, she could not find a time when she had been without the company of another human for any real space of time. She'd spent time gathering herbs or food of course, a few hours on her own here and there. But she'd never gone far from a village without Tesn. And after Tesn's passing, Áine had been surrounded by people. Though she'd felt alone and lost at first, they'd still been there, loud and very present.

Life buzzed around her: insects, birds, little skittering furry bodies, and the hush of wind through living plants. But there was nothing human here and she felt an emptiness spread out around her, unnatural and vast.

Tears rose unbidden to burn behind the eyelids she closed to shut them in.

"Áine, stop it. This isn't helping anything. You have work to do. You hardly need your hand held to collect a couple of bloody rocks," she whispered the words aloud to herself as she scrubbed at her eyes with the cuffs of her dress.

The sun was making its way past zenith in the shimmering sky when the smell of brine rode the breeze to Áine's nose. The hush of wind in the grass gave way to the rhythmic rush of waves as she quickened her pace toward the sea. Áine broke the brow of a hill to see the grey-green expanse of the ocean. Below her lay a little cove, the beach covered in stones of grey, white, and black.

Picking her way carefully down the hill, Áine slid the last few feet down a tide-cut bank to the beach. She unslung her pack and left it hanging from a clot of low-growing shrubs by the embankment, out of the reach of the sea spray or the tide.

Áine sighed as she examined the beach. It was perhaps three times the length of a man and half again as deep. Seaweed and bits of driftwood marked a ragged tide line reaching nearly to the top of the beach. At least the tide was on its way out which gave her time even as it revealed more of the beach. Every fifth stone looked white. She shook her head.

"Two pure white stones exactly alike," she muttered. "At least that rules out some of these."

Tesn had often told her that the only way to conquer large tasks was to start.

Áine straightened and stretched. The sun had sunk quite low but she looked on her growing pile of white stones as progress. Using driftwood, she'd cordoned off an area to start in and begun sorting all the unblemished white stones out into her cloak which she'd tied into a makeshift pouch. She was thankful that there were few perfectly white rocks to choose from, though four were large enough that she'd had to lift them and set them aside rather than carry them.

As she searched, she'd decided on a method to start ruling stones out. She'd place the ones she'd found two by two into a spiral and try to get a better idea of which might match up. Sighing, Áine looked out over the beach. She wasn't even done by a third, and night was coming on, bringing with it the tide.

With a start she realized she'd broken one of the rules of being near the sea; never put your back to the waves. She knew the tide was far out now with the waves' rush receding. Áine turned to the ocean and squinted into the setting sun.

She didn't know whether to laugh or cry. There, at the low tide line stood three large, white stones. They were half her height and easily as big around as she. Áine looked down at her makeshift pouch full of white stones and shook her head.

"It can't be that," she said aloud, "Don's tits, is it so simple?"

Áine carefully set down her pouch behind the high-tide line and brushed off her skirt. She walked down the beach, the wet stones slippery with seaweed that clung to her feet.

The water lapped against the far edge of the stones and dug into the silty areas between them in little eddies. She examined each stone. They were laid out in a perfect line with each the same distance apart. No sea life grew on the stones and she could find no blemish on any of the exposed surfaces.

Áine pushed on the right-most stone and managed to rock it in its base. She bent and wrapped her arms around it, then pressed upward from her thighs to lift the rock. It shifted with a sucking sound but she couldn't yank it free. With a growl, Áine released the stone and walked toward the top of the beach.

She stripped off her dress and boots and laid them near where she'd hooked her pack. Then she found a somewhat flat length of driftwood and walked back down to the stones.

The breeze off the ocean made her shiver, but Áine thought having a dry dress and shoes was more important than avoiding a little discomfort. The tide had turned and she would quickly run out of time to get these stones free.

Áine dug into the silt and gravel at the base of the first stone. Water rushed in, chilling her feet. She ignored this and kept digging. Water swirled around her ankles before she thought she might have freed the stone enough to lift again. This time, her shoulders and thighs screaming at the effort, she pulled the stone free from its silted cradle and managed to waddle up the beach to the tide line. Áine dropped the stone far less carefully than she would have liked and sat down hard.

Her hands hurt and she sucked the grit from a wound on her left pointing finger where the nail had half broken away. Spitting out her mouthful of blood and dirt, Áine stared down the beach. One stone down, two left. She rose and clenched her teeth.

The second stone was mercifully less entrenched than its sister had been. The waves brought the water up to her knees and she resisted their pull back into the sea. With the second stone down safely at the beachhead, Áine took a moment to call a ball of light. She grinned wildly as it worked a second time, the globe flickering above her head. It moved as she moved, casting strange shadows and lending iridescent patterns to the waves.

The tide had stolen Áine's digging stick while she carried the second stone. She found a new one but even with her light, she couldn't see what she was doing with the dark water swirling in, some waves up to her waist now. She'd forgotten how quickly tides rose.

Áine blinked back tears and tossed her stick away. She thrust her arms down into the water, snorting through the waves that crested over her head as she worked to dig free the stone. She tested it and finally it popped loose, growing heavier as she lifted it from the water.

She barely remembered how she got to the top of the beach. Her feet had long since gone numb and her shoulders and legs were one mass of pain. The sharpest pain came from the ankle she'd injured in the flood those months ago. Áine dropped the stone beside its sisters and stumbled to where she'd left her gown. Wet, gritty fingers dragged it over her head and she crawled up the embankment into the grass.

Her dreams gave her feathers and she flew far away from discomfort toward the warm pulse of her own heart.

Hafwyn stood in the doorway and watched her sons as Emyr saddled a horse in the courtyard. Idrys stood nearby, his black body tense as he watched an owl that rested in the eaves of the barn. The morning air just after dawn was still, the occasional bleat of sheep all that broke the silence. Hafwyn shivered. New leaves had started to green the forest beyond Clun

Cadair but still her sons spent their days ranging restlessly across the cantref, searching for Áine.

No matter how their mother argued with them, they both seemed as determined as the other that Áine would return to them, that she was out there to be found. Hafwyn had tried to gently raise the idea that perhaps the curse had been too much for Áine to bear. But even sensible Emyr was convinced that Áine wouldn't run from such a thing.

"Not her," he'd said, a grim echo of his brother's words the night before.

"Good luck, my sons," Hafwyn whispered as Emyr waved to her and turned his horse toward the woods, Idrys a shadow racing ahead.

She folded her arms tight over her own conflicted heart. Áine had been like the daughter she'd lost, and she'd brought joy back into Idrys. But she was also a wisewoman, a woman outside ordinary society. Wisewomen had freedom other women didn't, but they had obligations that came with that freedom that precluded a hearth and children. A chief should not marry for love alone, but for the good of the cantref and the people.

Hafwyn sighed as the barn owl stretched its wings and took flight toward the woods. Idrys's smile warmed her memory and shamed her thoughts. She was the mother of a chief, this was true. But she was a mother first.

It had only been a few months. If Áine returned, Hafwyn would welcome her back.

Nineteen

Tiny yellow larks singing on bent stalks of grass woke Áine. She sat up slowly in the early morning light and groaned. Her muscles had stiffened in the night as she slept on the cold ground. She stretched her arms and looked at her hands. They were red with chill and bits of dying skin clung to abrasions along her palms.

Her feet hadn't fared much better. Áine stumbled down to the retreating sea and rinsed the dried blood from her bruised feet in the waves. None of the cuts was more than a surface wound. The pain in her ankle worried her more.

Áine massaged the old injury as she turned to contemplate her three prizes. She shook her head. Breakfast, then she'd examine the stones. Pulling an apple and a loaf of bread from her pack, Áine sank down into the grass again.

She felt better for having eaten. The sun rose higher as she chewed the last bite of apple, swallowed, took a deep breath.

Áine wasn't sure if she wanted two of the large white stones to be the two she sought. She could lift them, that she knew. But it hadn't been the shortest journey from Seren's cottage to the shore and Áine didn't trust this place nor Seren enough to leave one stone behind. If she could determine which were alike, she'd have to devise a way to bring them both at once.

"Too many ifs," she muttered.

Áine rose and put her apple core back into the pack and then removed the coil of her red belt. She slid down to the white stones and measured the girth of the first with the dyed leather. The second and third both measured the same. Áine tried the length, but all three were the same. She put on her belt and then, ignoring the stabbing pain in her leg, carried each stone up into the grass, shoving them up the embankment to where she could examine the rocks without fear they'd chip.

Áine resisted the urge to kick the third rock in frustration. Each was exactly alike another as far as her methods could tell. Tesn had always told her that the fey cannot tell a direct lie. Seren had said only two white stones are exactly alike on this beach, but Áine now had three. She sank down into the grass and stretched her sore leg.

"Think, silly girl," she said aloud, "two of these have to have something different from the third."

She'd found them all in a line, well below the high-tide mark, so that was the same. It came to her suddenly. The second stone had been less deeply buried in the silt and gravel. Thank the gods she'd preserved their order as she'd moved them. She hoped that something so simple could be the answer. But it was all she had to go on. Now she only had to get them to Seren.

"Only," Áine snorted and, sighing, rose to her feet. On a wild hope she held her palm out toward the first of the stones. "Rise!" She willed it with a cry.

Nothing happened. Áine shoved down disappointment's bitter seed and shrugged. It had been worth a try. Now she needed to get serious and find a way to move the stones. Áine had no intention of leaving one behind for later; she didn't trust Seren half so far. No, she'd have to bring both at once.

Áine contemplated carrying them herself, one after another, going a little ways and then returning for the second stone and repeating until she reached the cottage. But the deep ache in her healing leg warned her that such a feat might be more folly than sense. And her feet were swollen and bruised badly enough that her boots refused to settle onto them, even loosely laced.

The rocks weren't so heavy that she couldn't pull them if she had a way to make a sled that would work over meadow. She recalled the fishermen who sometimes used long poles with a basket strung between to bring fish up the shore from the sea.

Áine looked around. There was plenty of long grass she could weave into a crude platform, but she had no axe with which to make poles. She slid down to the beach and searched among the driftwood piled at the high-tide line until she found two sticks that she could use. They both had branches coming off them that Áine painstakingly removed with the edge of a broken rock. One pole was nearly perfect, the thickness of her arm and not too waterlogged. The other was only half as thick but Áine hoped that, since it was greener wood, the spring in it would lend it strength and prevent it from snapping.

She took her makeshift cutting tool up into the grass after laying the poles alongside her chosen stones. Áine took a deep breath, said a small prayer to whatever gods might hear her in Cymru-that-could-be, and started cutting lengths of the meadow grass.

The sun lit the waves aflame as Áine carried a final bundle of grass to her workspace. She stood and watched the water as she took a long drink from her waterskin and ate another apple. Áine washed her sore, chapped hands in the sea and then called her ball of light. She had a long night of weaving ahead of her.

The grass was tough and stubborn in her hands. Áine grit her teeth and continued braiding and twisting, braiding and twisting. She needed a platform with sides to hold the stones as well as rope to help her drag the poles. When her hands became so sore that tears leaked unbidden from her eyes, Áine rose and walked down to the ocean again. Tucking her skirt up in her belt, she bent and held her fingers beneath the cold water. Phosphorescence danced around her fingers, mirroring the strange stars filling the sky above.

Loneliness pressed in on her heart and Áine bit back a sob. She would not be so weak, not now. She'd found the stones, she only had to transport them. Idrys would not give up, but it wasn't his haunted, determined dark eyes she recalled in that moment. Instead the memory of Emyr's wide smile and kind touch warmed her. Her hands and feet numbed by the ocean, Áine turned from the waves with a half-smile and went back to her task.

"I can free them," she whispered into the night wind as it curled off the sea.

Áine finished sometime in the night and fell asleep curled in her cloak until the yellow birds and a warm sun woke her for the second time. She quickly ate part of a loaf of bread before she returned to her work. The poles were now bound with the grass rope in what she hoped was a platform sturdy enough for the stones.

Áine half-lifted, half-dragged the first stone onto her sled and tied it in with the makeshift net she'd constructed. She tested the sled with only the one stone. The stone shifted in its bindings but nothing snapped and the two tips of the poles slid across the grass well enough when she tugged.

Shaking her head, Áine took a deep breath. With a little luck, this might work.

Her luck held. With the second stone secure in its netting and cushioned from the other stone with her excess rope, Áine pulled her own haphazard harness on. She made a pad with her cloak to help keep the coarse rope from hurting her chest too much as she strung the largest strands around her shoulders and across her breasts. With another muttered prayer, Áine set out toward Seren's home.

Her journey to the sea had taken half a day. Burdened with the sled and stones, Áine's return took far longer. Her poles seemed to find each and every irregularity in the meadow and every hill posed a new test of her will.

Her back itched, her legs throbbed, her chest burned. Sticky wisps of red hair clung to her cheeks and annoyed her eyes with every breeze.

It was late afternoon by the time Áine spotted the dark line of the forest in the distance ahead of her. She fought down a premature cry of triumph and pushed forward.

The forest was open enough that her poles only caught every ten steps instead of three. Áine had stopped, cursing under her breath, to free her sled from a hawthorn bush when she heard a cry. The cries continued, off to her left and out of sight, sounding very much like a young boy in deep distress.

Áine hesitated, wondering if this might be some trick of the fey Lady. The cries continued, echoing into the growing gloom. If this is a trick, Áine thought, but if it isn't? She knew she was bound by her wisewoman's rank to help those in need if she was able.

With another muttered curse, Áine made up her mind and slipped out of her harness. She unfolded her cloak and flung it over the hawthorn to mark where her sled rested in case she wandered too far. Then she set out toward the cries.

Movement caught her eye before too long and Áine called a ball of light. It was not a child but a raven. A large thorn bush, its branches blue in the soft light, trapped the bird in its long black and purple thorns. The raven's movements only entangled and injured it further.

Áine approached slowly, speaking soft reassurances. The bird twisted its head and looked at her with dark, distressed eyes, its beak hanging open as it panted.

"Shush raven, I'm going to help you. Good raven, easy now." Áine knelt beside the bushes, careful of her own skin near the long thorns. The raven was a juvenile, judging from its size. Áine saw large purple berries growing full and ripe among the thorns and shook her head at the greedy creature.

She pulled her sleeves back to her sore shoulders and started to break the thorns and bend back the brambles. The raven resumed its pointless thrashing and Áine spoke to it sharply.

"You're making it worse, silly bird. Hush now. Let me free you."

To her surprise, the raven stopped its movements immediately and stayed still as she worked. Áine shook her head and decided she was the silly one to be surprised by anything in this Cymru-that-could-be. It was almost amusing how in this world she stood out for being too human, where in Cyrmu-that-is she was the oddity. Almost.

Áine pulled the raven free and carefully checked among its feathers for embedded thorns. "You're a lucky one, these thorns are tough enough that they didn't break and stick in you. I hope you've learned your lesson about this fruit." She smiled at the raven as it hopped from one foot to the other, its beak ruffling its feathers as though searching for thorns as well.

She jerked back in shock as the raven's coat swirled and faded and a young boy with glassy black eyes and richly dark skin the same blue-black as the raven's feathers appeared in its place. He cocked his head at her and bent in a half-bow.

"You saved me, Lady," he said, "I would give you a boon."

Áine recovered enough to find her voice. "My name is Áine, and I'm a wisewoman. I am bound to help the living if I'm able. Your life and health are boon enough."

The boy-raven laughed and the sound rang through the wood like the harsh cry of the bird he'd been until recently. "Áine. I greet you. I am Bran, king of the ravens, and your kindness will someday be repaid."

Áine doubted very much that this inquisitive-looking child before her was any sort of king, but she'd some experience with children and thought there was little harm in holding her tongue on the matter.

"Thank you, King Bran. Could you point the path to the Lady Seren's house for me? That would be quite a help, for the hour grows late and I've a task to finish." Áine rose to her feet and pulled her sleeves down over her scratched arms.

Bran straightened up and pointed. A glittering strand extended from his hand and wove its way through the trees. "Seren's home lies there; the wisping strand will guide you. Why does she task you? Have you angered her?"

Áine looked down into his black eyes and shrugged. *Not yet*, she thought, but said, "She has cursed the ones I love; I work now to free them."

"Seren does not easily release what she has. Good luck, Áine, follow your heart." With those words, Bran turned into a raven again and rose with a joyous cry through the trees and away into the darkening night.

Áine walked back to her sled, turning the boy-raven's words over in her head. They echoed Blodeuedd's advice. Follow her heart. She refolded her cloak and picked up the poles. The thin, silvery line of the wisping strand drifted ahead, leading the way toward Seren.

The aches in her body blended into one complaint and she'd lost track of how many times she'd had to stop and free her sled from branches or brush by the time the glowing windows of Seren's home shone in front of her. Áine dragged the stones into the clearing. She pulled off the harness and stumbled down to the pool. The cool water was the sweetest thing she'd ever tasted and soothed her throat, hot face, and stinging hands.

Áine rose and looked around. It was full dark and likely deep into the night. Seren did not come out to greet her and Áine sighed. She was exhausted. The stones and Seren could wait until morning. Áine wrapped her cloak around herself and curled up next to her sled.

"Halfling." Seren's falsely sweet voice woke Áine.

She opened her eyes to full daylight and squinted up at the Lady. Seren wore a bright-green dress and tiny white flowers woven into the rippling cascade of her blood-red hair.

Áine self-consciously brought a hand to her own ragged and dirty locks, then pushed aside her feelings. She might look a mess, but unless she was mistaken, Seren's expression looked most displeased.

Áine smiled and sat up. "I have brought you two white stones, exactly alike." *I hope.*

"I see as much," Seren said and Áine's smile grew wider at her tone. "Let us find out if they are the stones I requested."

Seren stood stiffly by while Áine rose and pulled the stones free of their netting. Áine motioned, not trusting her voice. The Lady walked around the stones and considered them from all angles. Then she stepped forward and rapped on the first rock.

The woods rang with the clear chiming tone of the purest bell Áine had ever heard. She shivered, gooseflesh rising along her arms and neck. The stone split neatly down the middle, cracking to reveal a small iridescent gem in its heart. Seren plucked the gem free and raised a perfect red eyebrow at Áine.

"The first stone is correct. Let us see if the second holds its match."

Áine held her breath, thinking of the third stone she'd left near the beach. Would she have to go back for it? Would it still be there? She wrapped her arms around herself and prayed.

Áine couldn't stop the cry of joy that escaped her throat as the second stone's voice rang through the wood and it too split to reveal an iridescent gem at its heart.

Seren's face looked pinched as she turned to Áine. She didn't smile so much as pull her lips back from her perfect teeth. "You have completed the first task. I suppose you have no wish to rest before you start the second?"

Áine wanted to rest. She wanted to sleep for a fortnight, preferably in a soft bed with a hot meal or ten in her belly. But a task sooner started was one sooner finished, and she doubted there was a hot meal or soft bed to be had here. Seren might have offered such before, but her displeasure at Áine's accomplishment had likely revoked such a thing, though Áine told herself she'd refuse it again in any case. She hoped.

She realized she'd been silently staring at the Lady. "Yes, Lady," she said, licking dry lips. "What must I do?" No more rocks, she prayed.

Seren considered her for a moment and then her lips twisted into a far more genuine and unpleasant smile. "Very well, Áine, you must travel to see the fairy smith, Trahaearn and ask him to forge two clasps."

"That is all?" Áine said and kicked herself for voicing it aloud. "I mean, any specific clasps? Must they also be exactly alike?"

Seren shrugged. "Tell him they are to break a curse, and he will know the clasps I want." She turned away from Áine and started to disrobe. "Go on now," she paused and looked over her shoulder, "unless you'd like to join me in a swim?"

Áine shook her head. "No, thank you. Which way is this smith?"

"Find the mountain to the east. Between two twining holly trees lies a door. It will lead you to Trahaearn." The green dress slipped over Seren's head, revealing her shapely hips and unblemished moon-pale skin.

Áine rubbed her hands with their cracked nails and numerous scratches against her dress, which was more grey and brown than white now. She muttered her thanks and fled into the woods, heading toward the rising sun.

Twenty

Áine stopped at the straggling edge of the trees and stared. Ahead of her, though the exact distance was hard to tell in the fading light, rose a towering expanse of stone. The forest died out around her and gave way to a rocky expanse that rose slowly to meet the base of the mountain.

Áine found a tree whose roots grew in a way so as to create a comfortable cradle for her tired body and sank down to eat her dinner. Her pack still contained apples and bread and she silently gave thanks for the kindness of Blodeuedd. Her belly full and her heart aching, Áine slid down until her head rested on her arms and slept.

Her dreams pulled her away toward the twins, close and real enough that she could smell the wood smoke and feel the cold autumn wind on her dreaming skin.

Emyr stood at the door of the great hall, holding it open for his brother to enter in hound form. The two went quickly into their room and Emyr started stripping out of his clothing, annoyance in every bone in his body.

"Can't you feel it? You're pushing the time too near, Idrys. What if you change while I'm not there? Or someone sees you? Or..." He had no time to finish as the change took him and his body flowed down into that of a hound while Idrys's dark shape grew and turned to that of a man.

"I'm sorry, brother, but I had to stay out as long as I could. I had to keeping looking." Idrys shook himself as though he were a hound still.

Emyr stared up at him from the pile of his clothing for a long moment and then looked away. Idrys sighed and started to dress.

Autumn was turning to winter. Emyr's duties kept him from the daily search for a sign or word of Áine, but Idrys as a hound had no such restrictions. Day after day he ran as far as he dared in every direction, though his hope at what he might find grew thin.

He barely touched his dinner, speaking little to Urien or Llew or Caron. They left him alone. The chief had grown more and more withdrawn as the months passed and there was no word of the wisewoman or her fate. During the day his eyes would wander from a familiar face and stare toward the trees or out across the moor. At night he was even more withdrawn, sitting on the low wall under a torch at the edge of the berm outside town, carving absently as he watched the path from Clun Cadair.

A white owl that rested sometimes in the eaves of the barn flew overhead and disappeared into the night. Idrys looked up from his carving and watched her ghostly flight. He rubbed the tiny horse taking shape in his hands and thought of the strong young foal that Áine had helped to save. He couldn't bear to see the colt these days and Emyr had thankfully sent the mare and her foal off to be cared for by one of their herders.

Unbidden, the image of Áine's smiling face danced before his mind. How alive she'd been that night with her green eyes warm and happy, her skin flushed with triumph. Her soft, pale skin. She'd given herself so freely into his arms, wanting nothing from him that he wouldn't wish to give. Her gentle laugh had pushed away so much of the darkness that clung to his heart. The black night suddenly seemed warmer for the spark of his memory.

Idrys choked and stopped himself from crying out her name, just. For a moment she'd felt so near he could smell the clean scent of her hair, feel her breath on his cheek. He set the mostly carved horse down on the burm and rose. There was no Áine there, nothing but the sounds of the settlement behind him and the wind playing in the foliage of the woods ahead.

"Áine, love. Come home."

The owl swept down in a hush of white feathers and plucked the little horse from the stones beside him. Idrys watched as she disappeared again. He smiled and turned toward home to find Emyr.

Áine was out there, the owl was a sign. He would trust his heart and he hoped his brother would believe as well. They spoke so little to each other these days, the distance growing even as Áine's presence had closed it. But Idrys would speak, and Emyr could listen and perhaps share his own thoughts come daylight.

The owl winged across the land, down through the dark forest and toward the dawn, carrying the little wooden horse.

Áine woke and wished she hadn't. Her leg muscles had stiffened even more this night than the last and she groaned. Her neck hurt as well and her arms felt like wood. She'd slept with her head on them and her left hand had fallen asleep. She sat up slowly and stretched her toes out.

"Oh." Áine uncurled her left hand, ignoring the needles of pain. There was something clutched within it.

She stared down at a little wooden carving of a horse. It wasn't polished and its legs were mere suggestions in the wood; however, she recognized the style of it. For a moment she was frozen with surprise. Áine jumped to her feet, casting her eyes wildly about.

"Idrys!" she shouted, "Idrys. Please, Idrys."

The woods stilled around her in answer for a moment and then the birdsong swelled again as a morning breeze ruffled the leaves. She turned and looked out toward the mountain, trying to remember her dreams. It was hopeless; she could only recall a forest canopy and a cold wind carrying something light and white upon it. Áine sighed. She wondered how her foal was doing. Did Idrys look on the colt and wonder how she was? He'd made this carving, that she was certain of. But how it came to her sleeping hand she could not fathom.

"This world is too strange for me," Áine said, "I never thought I'd wish for a world where I'm the oddest thing in it."

She tucked the little horse into her pack and took out her breakfast. As she walked toward the mountain she fought down images of the twins. Idrys's lips on her own, the gentle touch of Emyr's hand as he adjusted her stirrup for her first riding lesson. The wooden horse in her pack lent her strength and she trudged toward the mountain with renewed determination.

The mountain was further than it looked but after hours of walking under a warm summer sun, Áine reached where the monolith left the ground. It looked to be a giant tower of solid stone the width of many houses that rose into the sky far above her head. Birds circled its crown, forming dark wheeling shapes. Áine skirted the base, searching for holly trees.

They were easy enough to find. Two old holly trees grew together out of a hollow at the base of the mountain, next to a burbling spring. The trunks leaned in, the branches above with their dark-green, sharp leaves forming the mantle of a doorway. She could only see solid stone beyond, however.

"Another fey riddle, I suppose," Áine said, mostly to hear the sound of a human voice. "I have a feeling I'll be well and weary of these by the time the tasks are finished."

She examined the stone between the holly trees. It was rough and composed of many small flecks of black, grey, and white, some of which glinted in the afternoon sun. Seren had said this was the door that would lead Áine to the fairy smith. It had to be the door, and Áine once again cursed under her breath that she hadn't thought to stay and ask better questions. Seren, Áine was sure, had known exactly the sort of unnerving effect her naked skin would have.

Knew it would remind me of her and the twins before I met them, remind me how they learned the joys of flesh.

Áine sat back on her heels and sighed. She hadn't come this far to be stumped by yet more stone.

It's a door, so why not knock? The thought was ridiculous and Áine smiled. Well, she wondered, why not? Tesn had always told her that there was rarely anything to lose in trying.

The stone rang with a strange hollow tone as she beat her fist on the door with more force than she'd meant. "Please," she whispered and then cried louder, "please, open this door."

Horrible grinding echoed from within the mountain. Tiny pebbles jumped from the crags of the stone above and danced down in shower onto the leaves of the holly trees. The rock between the holly trunks cracked and fell apart. Áine brushed at the dust and peered within, a desperate hope awakening in her belly.

"Who wakes me from my slumber?" From the gloom within came a voice as graveled as the debris under Áine's feet.

Áine jerked back, then gathered her courage. She stepped into the doorway and nearly fell as the floor cut away abruptly into a flight of stairs. She laid a hand against the rough wall and walked carefully down until her feet rested on flatter ground. Hesitating there, she considered and called a little ball of light.

The light revealed that she was in a large hall. The ceiling lay in shadow beyond the reach of her glow, but Áine could make out tables against the near wall and a huge hearth across the cavernous room. The room was very cold and smelled of dust and ash. She saw no one.

"I am Áine, I greet you," she called out, shivering.

"No need to shout, girl." Part of the thick chimney peeled away and revealed itself to be a man unlike any Áine had ever encountered.

He was twice her height with skin that looked more like stone or bark than flesh. He lumbered into the brighter light and peered at her with rheumy eyes. From this close, she could see the wiry grey brush of his beard beneath a pocked, bulbous nose.

"Forgive me," she stammered. "I do not mean to disturb you, but I seek the Trahaearn who lives beneath this mountain."

He made a harrumphing noise and shrugged his massive shoulders. Áine realized that some of what she'd thought might be skin was actually a hide apron sewn around with pockets and loops for tools. Charcoal smeared it and dust trickled like water off his shoulders as he moved.

"I am Trahaearn. What do you want, girl?"

Better to make this true. "I need you to forge two clasps, the kind used in making a thing that breaks a curse. Please," she added, "I am willing to do whatever you ask in return." Áine swallowed hard. Who knew what a giant might ask for, but she was quickly learning that little in Cymru-that-could-be came free. *That is not so different from Cymru-that-is,* she thought and her heart agreed.

Trahaearn clutched his belly and began to laugh. It boomed through the cavern and made little tools long resting under their layers of dust rattle and dance on the tables. Áine raised her chin and stared up at the shaking smith. Annoyance overrode all remaining fear and she stepped toward a table and slammed her fist down hard on the surface, biting back a wince as her sore fingers protested.

The fairy smith choked down his last bellow and sniffed. His eyes were brighter when he looked back down at her and he smiled, revealing teeth like old bone between grey lips.

"Well, girl. You wish to break a curse, do you? I laugh because this thing you wish is prevented by another curse entirely." He chuckled again and Áine realized it held no true mirth. Then he called out in a language she couldn't understand and torches on the walls flared to life.

Áine blinked and stared down at her dirty feet until her eyes adjusted. She could feel Trahaearn's warm breath above her as his huge boots drew close. She looked up again.

He raised arms as thick as her waist and held his hands in front of her face for inspection. Áine gasped. His fingers were thick and curled in a painful and unnatural way. The swollen joints oozed from chapped sores. His nails were broken back to the quicks and grit filled every crack and hollow in his skin. His thumbs looked to be dislocated as well.

"Stupid girl. Don't cry because no one told you my hands can't hold a spoon much less a forging hammer." He dropped his hands and turned away. "Go home."

Áine was crying. She'd never seen hands so destroyed; she could only imagine that the pain must be unbearable. *Perhaps not as unbearable as knowing you're a smith who will never forge again.* Only semiconscious of her action, she reached to her waist for her healer's pouch and patted herself, confused for a moment, when it was not there.

"What happened to your hands?" Áine said, taking a step toward Trahaearn.

He did not turn back to her but spoke instead to the cold hearth. "I don't suppose someone sane and biddable would have sought me out here, would they? Well, girl, go to the third table down there and tell me the thing you find wrapped in cloth-of-gold."

Áine obeyed, wondering on her own sanity and supposing that, in fact, perhaps she was indeed neither sane nor biddable. She sneezed twice as she brushed away years or perhaps centuries of accumulated dust from the table. A cloth-wrapped bundle lay in a heap beneath the mess. Áine was unsure if this was cloth-of-gold since it held little color any more, but she lifted it and turned toward the hearth. The bundle was the length of her forearm but light in her hand.

"Unwrap it," the fairy smith ordered, his back still to her.

Áine leaned away from the soiled cloth as she pulled it apart. Dust and grit billowed around her hands as she turned the bundle around and around to undo the swaddling and it took a moment for her eyes to make out what she held even as her hand gripped something smooth and cold. In her hand was a dagger, forged with more skill than any she'd seen before.

She dropped the cloth and examined the dagger, surprised to find a thing of iron in a Fairy place. The hilt was laid out with bronze and copper, its grip black and subtly textured. The pommel was crafted from jade, or coral perhaps, a delicate wing carved in filigree to look like the bridge of a haircomb. She touched a finger to the edge of the blade and was surprised to find it dull. She looked over at Trahaearn and saw that he'd turned and now watched her.

"The Daughter of the Wind commissioned that knife. It is the culmination of my skill, worked so that the iron would never touch the fey hand that wields it and light enough that a woman might slip it into her braid. It was not until I'd finished that I realized what I'd made. Once sharpened, that knife would be capable of killing any fey. The Wind's daughter is petty, her ire easily raised. To give her a weapon such as this, well, I could not agree." He stopped his story, staring at the knife and Áine wondered if he'd forgotten her presence in his reverie.

"She cursed you," Áine guessed.

His head jerked up. "The fey do have a fondness for cursing. She willed that I grow as ugly as my mountain and filled my hands with twisting agony so that I might never hold a hammer again." He sighed. "Put the knife away. I would help you if I could, please know that, girl. If you are cursed, the one who sent you here would likely know my circumstance. You've been set up to fail from the start I fear."

Áine set the knife on the table and walked toward the fairy smith. "Aye, I've been set up, I know this. But there must be a way. Please. I have to free the men I love."

"I cannot forge," Trahearn cried as he advanced on Áine. She backed away at the bleak sorrow in his face. Her feet bumped against the steps. "Go, stupid girl. Go find another way. What you seek is not here. There is nothing here but broken things and bad thoughts."

She backed up the stairs as he shouted at her; she backed away until the warm afternoon sun touched her back and she felt the fallen stones of the doorway beneath her cold toes.

"Trahaearn," she began, holding out her hands in supplication.

"I do not know that name. I am nothing. Get out!" With a final yell, the smith shoved Áine through the doorway.

She fell onto the sparse grass and scattered stones as with a grinding rumble the fallen pieces of the door lifted up and reformed into a solid wall of rock once more. Áine sat for a moment in shock and then rose. She beat her fists on the door, calling out for the smith. Her hands bruised, then bled before she stepped away, heaving.

"Calm, Áine, review your options," she told herself.

The options looked bleak. The sun was nearly set, the mountain throwing a long shadow across the barren landscape. She couldn't return to Seren, not without those clasps. She had no idea how she might break the curse without the clasps and though she hated to trust Seren even a little, she couldn't see her way through this without the Lady's help.

"I cannot go back, and I cannot go forward." Áine sighed. She was tired, dirty, and hungry. She turned to the bubbling spring and washed her face and aching hands in the cool water. She rinsed and refilled her waterskin and pulled out a loaf of Blodeuedd's bread for her supper. Then, sinking down to rest her back against the sun-warmed stone of Trahaearn's mountain, Áine stared into the sky as unfamiliar stars spread their blanket over the unfamiliar land.

"When there is so much to do, getting a little sleep always does a trick." Tesn's face wrinkled with friendly mirth.

Áine looked around her but shadows obscured the world just outside a little circle within which she and Tesn sat. "Am I dreaming?" she asked. She felt a leap of joy at seeing her mother, but her limbs wouldn't move, wouldn't obey her demand that she rise and throw her arms about the smiling old woman.

"Of course you are, love. We have a little time. Tell me the remedy for pain of the joints." Tesn reached forward and patted Áine's leaden arm.

At her touch Áine's heart throbbed painfully and she blinked hard to hold in the hot tears that threatened. *I miss you,* she wanted to say, *I'm lost mother and very alone.* The warm compassion in Tesn's eyes made speaking the words aloud unnecessary and Áine smiled back through the haze of her grief as she considered her mother's question.

"Oil from evening primrose or kelp would help rebuild cartilage and bone, taken orally. A tea of nettle or hawthorn would assist in circulation, as would rubbing the joints with an oil of marjoram and rosemary. I'd use a poultice of comfrey or cabbage to help draw out swelling." It felt good to recite these things. She'd learned them as a child and speaking her knowledge aloud gave her confidence. *I am still a wisewoman, whatever else might come.*

"Always, love, always." Tesn nodded. "Remember your gifts, stay true to your heart."

The circle started to fade, the gloom closing in. Áine's eyes didn't want to stay open. "Wait, mother, please."

Áine woke to a weak predawn light and pain in her shoulders from where she'd slept crammed against the stone. Her nose was stuffed and her throat ached as though sorrow dammed it in a twisting knot. She took deep gulping breaths as her mind scrabbled to retain all the details of her dream. Every wrinkle in Tesn's face, every impression of kindness and warmth. She thought then of Trahaearn's swollen, cracked hands and recalled her initial response of reaching for her healer's bag.

Áine stood and stretched, surprised at how rested she felt despite the nagging aches from sleeping on hard ground propped against a rock. She cast her mind back to her walk the day before, trying to recall what plants she might have passed. All the ones she thought of were either not useful or a long walk away.

The woods were a dark smear across the western sky over the rocky moor. There'd been hawthorn there, she knew, and perhaps licorice root. She'd seen no lavender, no marjoram, no devil's root or peppermint. Nothing she could even begin to use out here on the moor. Just sparse grass, wild wheat and sticky crabgrasses, and rock. Plenty of rock.

Remember your gifts.

Rock! Áine started as though coming awake for a second time. She'd used rock to remove pain but rarely while traveling with Tesn. It was an old art and as hard on the healer as the patient. Áine recalled the last time with a pang. They'd taken the burden from an old man, leaving his family to say goodbye for as the pain passed, so did he.

I thought I understood their pain then. Aiee, I wish I still had so little understanding of grief.

Áine shook her head and retrieved her pack from the ground. She almost laughed at the irony of what she needed now. "Two strong stones. I'll never be free of bloody rocks."

She forced herself to drink more water and eat two apples along with half a loaf of bread. She'd need strength if her plan were to work at all. Áine wasn't certain that pain caused by a curse could be lifted in this way, but trying was still better than weeping and wringing her skirts in defeat.

It was midmorning before she felt prepared. She stood in front of the holly trees and tapped again on the stone door.

"Trahaearn. Please, hear me," she cried with more confidence than she truly felt. "I am a wisewoman, a healer. If I can lift the pain from your hands so that you might forge again, will you grant me my clasps?"

For many long breaths nothing happened and Áine started to despair again. Then a deep rumble shook the mountain and the doorway crumbled as it had the afternoon before.

"Stubborn girl." Cold air and flickering torchlight greeted her with his graveled call.

Áine chose to interpret it as an invitation and walked back down the stairs and underneath the mountain.

Twenty-one

Trahaearn heard her out in silence, his craggy head bowed over his barrel chest. Áine laid the two rounded rocks she'd chosen from the moor on the nearest table and brushed off a bench to sit on.

"If you can do this thing, as you say, then yes, I will forge the clasps you need." At his words the hope smoldering in her eyes lit aflame.

"Thank you," she said, then hesitated and continued. "This is not permanent. I do not know how long the pain and swelling will stay away if I succeed."

"To live without it, even for a little while, to craft something of beauty again, these things are worth much to me." He raised his head. "Don't diminish my own hope, girl, for it's you that brought it to me."

Áine stretched her neck, looking down and away from him. "Let us begin."

Trahaearn lowered himself to sit on the great bench opposite her and laid his right hand across the table with a puff of dust. Áine gently rested her own hand on his skin. The warmth of him surprised her; his skin felt like fine leather with rough lines hatched through it like scars. With a deep breath Áine let her mind sink beneath his skin.

The heart of the fairy smith beat with a deep, slow rhythm. Áine felt her own heart racing in comparison, her body rebelling against the calm strength of the man she touched. Beyond that throbbing pulse laid a terrible chill its steady power could not touch. Áine pushed herself toward that chill, down into his hand.

Pain assaulted her. It twisted as a snake twists, coiling and uncoiling as the curse's venom filled the joints of his hand with unceasing torment.

Áine did not hear herself cry out, did not see her blank-eyed terror. Deep inside Trahaearn's hand, she wrestled with the pain, its existence an affront to everything she stood for as a healer. She would not suffer this; the snake must be forced out. She resisted her own gifts enough to feel the hard stone beneath her other hand. Bit by bit she tugged at the pain, dragging it out of his twisted fist and into the uncaring rock. The serpent of pain within uncurled and sank away coil by coil.

Áine came back to herself as the stone under her hand cracked with a strange sound. Her face was gaunt with exhaustion and she had to lick her lips several times before she felt she could speak. She lifted her eyes from the cracked stone and her own pale hand to Trahaearn. He'd removed his hand from under her own and she'd not even felt it.

"Thank you, girl," he whispered, his eyes wet but far more clear than they'd been before, the rheumy film all but gone and their pupil-less, golden depths visible now. His right hand was straight and perfect with long, strong fingers and clean nails.

His hand's the size of my head, Áine thought. She was exhausted, but she couldn't leave the work unfinished.

"Give me your other hand," she managed as she shoved the broken stone from the table. The second stone seemed far heavier than it had before as she slid it toward herself, but Áine refused to think too much about her weak and sluggish body. She had worked a miracle and wouldn't leave it half-done.

Trahaearn pulled his gaze away from his newly made hand. Desire and doubt warred in his craggy features and he chewed at the corner of his moustache with his old bone teeth.

"You don't look well, girl," he said. "You didn't mention there'd be a cost to yourself for it."

"No," Áine said, more sharply than she meant. "But what in life comes without a cost? I doubt you can forge with one hand, can you? So lay down the other and let us finish this." *Preferably before I pass out*, she added silently.

He looked as though he might continue to argue but something in her face stopped his tongue. A strange desperation that mirrored Áine's own came over his face and he placed his other grotesque fist under her waiting palm.

"All right, healer," he rumbled, "make an end of this."

It was at once easier and far more difficult for Áine the second time. She knew what to expect but her strength flagged as she wrestled with the frigid serpent of pain in his left hand. Her heart slowed to match Trahaearn's and her mind felt frozen and raw like meat scraped from a bone in the dead of winter. She wanted to rest, to flee this battle and go toward the warmth she could sense somewhere far away.

It grew harder and harder to recall her purpose here as she shoved and jammed each coil of pain. There was so much pain and she was so very cold. It would be easy, an inner voice whispered to her, so simple to just let go, let the pain have her. She had the power to end it, to let go completely. There was peace there, a void place that lay just beyond her languid heartbeat. The head of the snake reared in her mind and the pain flared worse than before.

NO! She grasped at the last tendrils of icy pain. *No more curses, no more hurting. This, this I can end.*

The stone beneath her palm cracked in half with the ringing cry of a breaking bell. Áine jolted out of her trance, ripping free of Trahaearn's flesh with a strangled cry. The memory of pain hung about her in a strange mist and she forced her eyes to focus on the face of the fairy smith.

He stared at his two beautiful hands as though they belonged to a stranger. Áine smiled to see the joy etched in every line of his strange face. He looked at her with golden eyes and said something. The fog around her swallowed his words and she shook her head. Concern slipped over his features and Áine tried to speak, to tell him that she was all right. Then the table seemed to slip away from her and the torchlight dimmed. *How odd*, she thought, and then she thought no more.

Idrys crawled out from underneath the warm blankets and shivered in the winter chill. His body tingled as the rising sun edged the horizon. The change would be on him soon. He cursed the unusually deep snows that would keep him from ranging out to look for Áine, though deep in his heart he admitted his search had become more habit than true hope.

I can barely recall the sound of her laugh; how much more of her warmth will time steal from us?

Emyr roused from his place at the foot of the bed and whined. Idrys shivered and pulled off the thick woolen shirt he'd worn to sleep. His brother's cold nose pressed into his thigh and Idrys laid a hand on his bony head.

"I wish I could think of something to say, Emyr," he murmured. "There's too much silence between us."

Emyr's liquid brown eyes were far too sad and full of understanding. Idrys looked away and then the change took him.

Emyr dressed quickly for the day and emerged into a sleepy hall. Caron was already awake and building up the hearth fire. She tossed a friendly smile and greeting at Emyr as he walked outside to cut her more wood.

The exertion took his mind off the slumped form of his brother until he returned to the hall to break his fast. Idrys slipped out the door when he opened it and Emyr almost shouted after the hound not to stray too far. He bit back the words. Idrys wasn't an idiot; he knew the dangers of the deep snow and unpredictable winter skies. Shaking his head, Emyr stepped into the dim hall.

"Good morning, Emyr," his mother called to him. She looked healthier than she had, having taken a chill at midwinter. Caron and Melita still babied Hafwyn though her illness only clung on in a lingering cough. She shooed Caron away after accepting a bowl of steaming grains liberally dosed with honey.

"Good morning," Emyr said as he rinsed his hands and then sat across from Hafwyn. Caron placed a bowl in front of him and he blew on it before mixing in the honey.

"Spring is coming," Hafwyn said after a few mouthfuls. "I hear tell that the Chief of Rhufon has a beautiful daughter. An alliance with them would expand our powers of trade through the Cantrefi of Perfeddwl."

Emyr glanced for his brother before remembering Idrys's defection. He tensed and swallowed. "I know the benefit of an alliance, mother. But I am not so old that time makes the need stronger."

Hafwyn sighed and dropped her eyes to her lap. "Not all of us are so young," she said gently, "and it would sit well for the cantref if the chief had an heir."

Someone to rule who is not cursed, you mean. Emyr stabbed his spoon into his breakfast.

Even if it weren't for the dimming hope that Áine would return and agree to wed him, them, there was still the problem of how a wife would handle the curse. Such a thing would be difficult to hide if at every dawn her husband rose and exchanged places with his hound. Better to place a hope on a woman missing for a year and more than to face the unknown, in Emyr's mind. *A pox on you Áine, for giving us hope and ripping it away.*

"Please, mother, don't mention this again until I do. I'll think on it," he said, rising from the table. He barely saw her nod as he turned and, grabbing his cloak, went out to start the day.

Emyr paused as the door shut behind him and reached into his beltpouch. He found Áine's smooth pearl tear with the practice of long habit and rubbed it between his fingers before letting it settle once more.

Áine was warm, blissfully so, and her body rested on a soft surface. She burrowed deeper into the thick quilt covering her and reached a hand out for the twins. Her fingers encountered the edge of her bed instead of warm skin and she jerked awake.

Memory flooded back even as the smell of coal smoke reached her nostrils. She was in a closed-off alcove of the huge hall beneath the mountain, wrapped in a thick if dusty quilt and curled up on a pallet of leather and fur. Through the hide curtain that sectioned off her alcove from the hall, Áine could hear the sound of a hammer beating metal and then the great huff of a bellows.

She got out of bed slowly, her body possessed of a hundred little aches and protests. Áine realized with a start that her dress had been changed. The old one lay in a soiled heap on a rough-hewn wooden chair. She touched the soft blue linen that hugged her body and blushed as she realized that the fairy smith must have changed her clothing.

Beside the bed were two soft leather shoes embroidered with diving swallows. Áine slid her sore feet into them and found they fit quite well once she'd readjusted the laces that pulled them tight to her ankles. She put on her red belt and took a deep breath.

Trahaearn bent over a great pentagonal anvil that Áine hadn't seen before in the room, making a small adjustment to the shining bit of metal gripped by his tongs. Áine looked around her in disbelief.

Gone were the dusty coverings and the chilled touch of neglect. The entire cavern was bright with lamp and torch light and clean but for a fine dusting of coal and bits of metal debris and slag in the area of the forge. A huge fire crackled in the hearth.

"Good morning to you," Trahaern called out to her.

Áine walked the length of the cavern to the forge. She felt blind for not having noticed it before, or at least remarking to herself its apparent absence before.

"Is it morning? I did not sleep long, did I?" Áine halted and blushed, thinking again of how this strange giant had cared for her unconscious body.

"Two days. For a while I thought you'd not rouse at all. Then you started thrashing and screaming and tore your dress," he said and then turned his head away and mumbled. "That's why I had to give you that other one, once you'd calmed."

"I thank you," Áine said. He seemed as embarrassed by the act as she'd been imagining it.

"Dress and shoes were my wife's. I've no need of them now." He glanced at her and then turned back to his work.

Áine saw the tension in his body and her healer's instincts told her there was great pain in that statement. She burned with curiosity but took a deep breath. He'd speak more of it if he wished and she was in no position to pry.

"How do your hands feel?" she asked instead.

His face lifted and his eyes lit up. "Good, wonderful. I've nearly got your clasps done, haven't I? There's a little pain returned today but it's a shadow of what it was. You've given me back to myself, girl."

Áine smiled. She was back to being called "girl" again. She looked about and saw her pack on a newly cleared table near the hearth.

Trahaearn followed her gaze and said, "Go on then, eat some breakfast and I'll be done here quicker for you not distracting me."

Her stomach didn't need telling twice and Áine went to the table to have a breakfast of apple and bread. She ate and stared at the walls of the cavern.

Racks of forged creations hung there. There was a sword as long as she was tall with intricate scrolling work along its blade. There, a collection of spearheads, the leaf shaped blades evoking real leaves in their almost delicate lines and edges. A line of hooks just above the tables against one wall displayed a perfect set of spoons done in copper and silver. Tiny animals graced the bowl of the spoons and Áine rose to take a closer look. She wandered the length of the hall, her heart lifted to see the smith once again taking joy in his craft.

"You like my work?" Trahaearn came to stand near Áine, wiping his hands on a rag.

"It's like nothing I've ever seen. The quality I mean. I'm not even sure what some of these metals are."

"I thank you for your praise. Here in Cymru-that-could-be there are many things not yet possible in Cymru-that-is. Come, your clasps are finished."

Áine went with him to the forge and gasped as he placed two delicate clasps in her outstretched hands. Each was forged of the purest silver into an intricate box.

She set one down and delicately opened the clasp. The sides of the box came apart as she pressed, opening to reveal two boxes now with curving edges. Though the metal seemed thin in her fingers, she could feel the strength in it. She slipped the sides back together and they interlocked so perfectly she could no longer make out the seam. The design was a looping whirl that had no end, though it suggested the shape of something. Áine bent closer to the small clasp, it being no larger than the dip of her palm.

"Oh," she gasped, "it's a hound." She quickly picked up the other to see if it was a match.

"Aye," Trahaearn sounded pleased. "I was able to understand some of what you called out in your sleep. I thought a hound might be fitting."

Áine just nodded and ran her thumb over the design again and again. *Emyr. Idrys. I'm halfway done now, just wait a little longer.* Her tears spilled without thinking and she watched as one touched the floor and bounced away under the table as a tiny pearl.

"There now, girl," Trahaearn said gruffly. He shifted from one huge foot to the other. "I'm sure you'll see your hounds again."

Áine laughed through her sobs. "They're men, not hounds. Well, they are hounds, one by night, one by day. It's the curse I'm trying to break."

"Idrys is one of these men?" Trahaearn smiled through his thick beard at her look. "You called his name."

Áine flushed. "Aye, Idrys and Emyr. They are brothers, twins. I love them," she added as she lifted both clasps and went to gather her damaged dress.

"Both of them?" Trahaearn asked when she returned.

Áine considered this as she tore a large scrap from her already ruined dress. She wrapped the clasps carefully in the fabric and slid them into her pack. *Was it only Idrys's name I cried in my sleep?*

"Yes," she said after another moment. "I love them both. They are different for all it is nearly impossible to tell them apart by looking. One is gentle and calm, the other passionate and stubborn, and..." she hesitated, "broken."

He needed me more than Emyr. If we'd had more time, I would have taken Emyr into by bed as well. I wish...no. We will have time and time enough when I've broken the curse.

Trahaearn nodded as though she'd answered something more for him than just that single question. "They are lucky to have you, girl." He moved away from her, toward one of the tables against the wall. He pulled a bundle of gold cloth free and brought it to the hearth table.

Áine rose and joined him. Trahaearn pulled out the knife he'd shown her before, now in a simple wooden sheath.

He looked Áine in the eye and said in his graveled voice, "There's more than one way to break a curse."

Áine stared at the knife, recognizing the pattern of birds. "The Daughter of the Wind is your wife?" she guessed.

"Aye. As I said, she's quick to anger." He shrugged his huge shoulders. "If she weren't my wife, I'd have broken the curse long ago, but love complicates life, eh?"

Áine shook her head. She could not fathom loving someone to the point of bearing such a curse, nor how someone could love and deliver such a curse. These thoughts raised uncomfortable doubts in her mind and she pushed them away. Instead she stared at the knife and felt a chill creep into her heart.

"How else does one break a curse?" she whispered.

"By killing the one that did the cursing," Trahaearn answered.

Áine's head reeled and her stomach tightened into a lump around her breakfast. "Kill Seren?"

The fairy smith's golden eyes widened and he leaned forward. "Seren? The Lady of the drychpwll cursed your twins?" At Áine's nod, he shook his snowy head. "That's a fine mess you're in, girl. If you kill the Lady, you'll have to take her place."

"Take her place?" Áine shook her own head as the chill at the thought of breaking her healing oaths and committing murder gave way to confusion.

"Seren cannot stray far from the drychpwll, that little lake she makes her home by. She wields great power from there, but her reach in either Cymru is small. If you kill her, you would be bound to the drychpwll in her place, immortal but unable to leave her domain."

"But it would free the twins?"

"Aye. They would be free."

You can free them. Those words which had been such a comfort to her suddenly twisted, turning strange and terrifying in her mind. *At what cost? Am I willing to sacrifice myself for a love I've known only a little while?* Her heart made no answer and Áine felt tears burning at her eyes again.

"There, girl, stop. I did not mean to make you cry again. I'd thought to help, but I can see I've done nothing but upset you. You'll break the curse another way."

Áine rubbed her eyes. "Wait," she said with more force than she'd meant. "Give me the knife. I cannot now say what I'll be willing to do in the future. If I use it or not, I'll see it returned to you before I leave Cymru-that-could-be."

Trahaearn stared at her unblinking for a long moment. Then he wrapped the knife back into its shining cloth and held it out. Her hand brushed his as she took it from her and her healing senses flared, warning her there was great pain there. Áine looked up at him.

"Your hands, they hurt more than a little, don't they?"

"It's nothing like it was." He shrugged and folded his hands into a large pocket on his leather apron.

"Not yet," Áine said. "I can fetch more stones and take the pain again before I go."

Trahaearn laughed, bitter and booming. "I can see what this Idrys shares with you, girl. Stubborn indeed. But the morning wears on and you must go. You've given enough of yourself to me already. Go." He motioned toward the stairs and turned back to his forge.

Áine hesitated, words forming in her mind and disappearing before they could touch her lips. She shivered and rubbed her palm against her forehead.

"Thank you, Trahaearn," she said.

He did not respond nor look back at her.

She climbed the stairs toward the doorway. Sunlight filtered in and the bright leaves of the holly greeted her as she left. The mountain rumbled and the doorway to the fairy smith rose again from the rubble and re-formed behind her one last time.

Áine set out across the moor toward the woods and Seren's home with a heavier pack and troubled heart. She did not look back.

Twenty-two

Warm satisfaction bordering on the smug settled into Áine's heart at Seren's annoyed expression. The Lady was clearly not in the least bit thrilled with Áine's return or her success. Áine kept the smile off her own face, barely.

"These are the clasps you wished, are they not, Lady?" she asked, though the tightness around Seren's mouth and her pinched look of disappointment had already confirmed what the Lady might answer.

"Yes, halfling." Seren's swirling silvered eyes studied her, taking in the new gown, the embroidered slippers.

Áine shifted from one sore foot to the other, the satisfaction fading even as Seren composed her own face.

"Would you care to rest?" Seren said with a cold smile that turned the question into a comment on Áine's appearance.

Áine ran her chafed hands over the soft blue linen and gritted her teeth. Her pack rested against her leg and Áine imagined the slender blade calling to her from within its gilded wrappings. All she had to do to end all of this was take that knife and plunge it deep into this selfish and infuriating creature's breast. No more tasks, no more swallowing pride and anger and begging this woman for crumbs. Emyr and Idrys would be freed.

And I'd be trapped at this pond. I'd have to sleep in her bed, wear her clothes, and become the Lady. Forever.

She realized she'd been staring off into the water over the Seren's shoulder and shifted her green gaze back to the Lady. "No. I'd like my next task," she said and then added as an afterthought, "please."

Seren's eyes narrowed. "Very well. I need strands of hair from the tail of the March Cann."

"A Fairy steed? Where will I find this creature? And how much hair do you need?"

"You ask so many questions." Seren sighed. "To the north lies a lake. In the middle of the lake is an island formed of drowning oak trees. The March Cann can be found there. I need at least two strands, clearly."

Before Áine could ask anything more Seren turned and slipped into her cottage, the heavy door closing behind her. Áine ran a hand through her tangled hair.

"I hate it when she does that," she muttered. A soft laugh echoed across the clearing and Áine snatched her pack from the ground and turned away.

She put the sinking sun on her left and walked toward where this lake might be, shoving away all bloody thoughts about the contents of her pack and Seren's slender throat.

She walked until it grew dark, then called a little ball of light and walked until her legs and feet demanded rest. Áine released her light and wrapped herself in her cloak. She forced herself to eat some bread and then curled against a tree, Idrys's little wooden horse clutched in her hand.

The bright birdsong of early morning woke her and, after a quick breakfast, Áine set out again. She kept herself pointed north, putting one foot in front of the other. In some places the forest grew too dense and she had to pick a careful path through the brush and brambles. She felt as though she made no progress, that she'd be trapped in this wood forever. The trees here were younger and grew so close together that Áine couldn't see the sun, only its light filtering in through the canopy, green and diffused.

Sweat ran in trickles down her back and between her breasts. Her hands stung from tiny cuts. The light grew dimmer and Áine paused to pull another twig from her hair. She wished for her braids, but her hair was still far too short to pull away from her face or the entangling vegetation.

Áine heard the sound of frogs ahead and hope grew in her heart. She had to be close. She shoved her way through another thicket of young poplar and wild cherry saplings clotted around with ferns and abruptly found herself knee deep in cold water.

The forest gave way without warning. Áine gasped at the shock of the water closing over her feet and at the huge expanse of the lake in front of her. Water spread out dark and glassy as far as she could see. The sunlight glinted off its surface in places while other bits of the lake were obscured by wisps of mist the sun couldn't burn away.

Áine twisted around and pulled herself out of the water and back into the thicket. The lake mud sucked at her shoes and threatened to steal them from her but she managed to pull her feet out carefully. Her skirt was soaked up nearly to her thighs and her shoes were a mess. Áine used a handful of leaves to get the worst of the mud off and then tied the shoes to the strap of her pack. She pulled her skirt up and tucked as much as she could into her belt. Then she held on to a slim poplar trunk and looked out over the lake.

Off in the distance, she saw a dark shape. She hoped that was the island but saw no good way to reach it. Áine looked at the forest that stretched to either side and arched around the lake toward the horizon. She wondered if her knife would cut down trees. Perhaps she could make a raft of some sort and pole her way across the lake. She chuckled at the idea and sighed. *Time to get wet, silly girl.*

Adjusting her belt, she bunched skirt to beneath her breasts and stepped barefoot into the water. She held her pack above her head and waded carefully out into the lake. The water stayed at the level of her knees. Little insects dodged away from her along the surface as she walked and the hum of birdsong drifted over the lake. The unseen frogs grew silent around her as she disturbed the lakebed.

Slowly the water deepened until Áine was up to her hips. The cold mud dragged at her feet but the sun shone welcome warmth on her head and back. Her arms ached from holding the pack up and she let it rest on her head as her shoulders slumped. The dark shape in the distance became clearer and clearer as she walked until, after what felt an eternity, Áine made out the shape of a grove of huge spreading oaks rising from the lake.

The sun dropped to the level of the lake and poured a bright spear of light across the surface as though pointing to the grove, Áine reached it and clambered out of the water up onto the huge roots of one of the trees.

The island was made up of five ancient oaks unlike any Áine had seen before. The bark was silver and black and the whispering leaves overhead held all the greens, golds, and russets of spring and autumn mixed. Áine set her pack down in the crook of the nearest tree and let her skirts down.

The roots tangled among each other, creating a platform above the rippling lake. Áine chose the thickest, widest part and sat down to rest and consider her options. The March Cann was clearly not on the little island at the moment.

Áine kicked herself for not asking more questions of Seren. She knew that Seren would disappear as soon as she was able; after all, it seemed to be the Lady's pattern to give Áine as little chance for information as possible. The fairy steed might appear in an hour, or only once a year.

"Or once a century," Áine muttered. She tried to count up how long she'd been in Cymru-that-could-be. A week? No, longer. A fortnight? She decided that down that path lay only madness.

The sunlight died slowly and a breeze drifted over the lake. The frogs resumed their garbled songs. Áine wrung out her damp skirt and pulled her cloak from the pack. She pulled out an apple as well and sent a grateful thought toward Blodeuedd for the gift of the pack and its contents. If she had to wait a year or one hundred, at least she wouldn't starve. "Though I might die of boredom and despair."

Áine sat down with her back to the one of the great oaks and curled into her cloak. She didn't call a ball of light, worried that she might scare off the fairy steed if it came in the night. After a while the sound of the rippling lake and her own exhaustion pulled her down into sleep.

The whirring of wings and a bright glow woke her. The moon rode high in the clear sky and a creature of legend descended to the sunken oaks. Áine's eyes flew open and she forced herself to stay still as the March Cann settled down onto the roots in front of her, its head turned away, looking out over the lake.

It was taller than any horse she'd seen, but its body was whip thin with three sets of wings extending from its withers and spine, more like a dragonfly's wings than a bird's. The fairy steed's body shone with shifting light, orange, yellow, blue, and purple, shining like a rainbow at the edge of where sky meets horizon, bright and diffused all at once.

The March Cann touched down on cloven hooves like those of an ox, its hair feathered at the legs and joints. Áine gasped and the creature turned its head. She held perfectly still, wondering if the two spiraling silvery horns on its forehead were dangerous or only ornamental. She hoped the latter.

Multi-colored eyes stared at her for a moment and then it curved its slender neck back toward the water. Áine shifted slowly and looked out past it to see what the fairy steed might be looking at.

There, out on the water, thousands of iridescent moths danced in and out of the lance of moonlight where it touched the lake. The insects swirled and wove pattern after pattern until she could almost see the story they told. Was that a pack of hunting hounds? There, that pattern, was that a stag? A hunting horn? A sword held by a woman in a flowing robe?

Áine shivered and let her cloak drop slowly. Mentally she shook herself and tore her eyes away from the dance. The March Cann stood still, apparently transfixed by the moths and the story they told.

Áine crept closer, each footstep and scrap of skirt on tree root sounding like the slamming of door or the breaking of a thousand sticks in her mind. The fairy steed did not shift or look her way.

She drew so near she could see its hair waving in the breeze, feel the warmth of its body, see its sides move as it breathed. No, he; this close Áine could tell that the March Cann was clearly a male. His tail was thick and long, the strands multi-colored like his fur. Áine chose two purple ones and achingly slowly stretched out her hand to grip them.

The moment her fingers touched the steed, he jerked, coming alive again and leapt up and away from the island in surprise. Áine gripped the hairs, yanking with all the strength in her arm. She might as well have tried to uproot one of the ancient oaks she stood upon for all the effect it had. For a dizzying moment, the strength of her grip and the fairy steed's tail warred as he lifted her clear of the ground.

Then a rear hoof struck out and slammed into her shoulder. Áine lost her grip and fell back to the roots, her left ankle turning beneath her.

She lay gasping; her sore hand trailed in the water between the roots of the oaks and her other set tight against the burning pain her shoulder. The March Cann flew up into the sky, spiraling higher and higher until Áine lost track of him among the stars.

"Get up," she hissed. "Your shoulder is dislocated. Get up."

The searing pain in her shoulder overshadowed the sharp ache in her ankle as she shifted to kneel, and then stand. Áine limped back to the more solid part of the roots and felt around the shoulder joint of her right arm. It was certainly dislocated. She took a deep breath and immediately regretted it. There'd be quite the bruise on her chest tomorrow.

Áine had reset dislocated shoulders before, but never on herself. She tried rotating her arm with her elbow bent placing her forearm parallel to the ground, but though she could feel things shifting, she couldn't get enough force on her own to pop the joint back into place. She gritted her teeth and looked at the wide trunk of the oak she'd been sleeping under.

She jammed her left fist into her upper arm to help stabilize and then hobbled up to the tree. Closing her eyes, she threw her body forward, jamming her shoulder into the tree. With a horrible grinding sound and pain so harsh it brought instant tears to her eyes and a raw cry to her throat, her arm slipped back into place. The pain faded immediately to just a dull ache and Áine whimpered in relief. She sank down and pulled her cloak around herself.

Though she wanted nothing more than to wrap herself up and wallow in misery at her utter failure to procure hairs from the March Cann's tail, Áine's healer instincts warned her she had to deal with her ankle as well.

She cut the rag from her old dress into three strips and bound the sprain tightly. That done, she put Trahaearn's knife away and lay back against the oak. Out over the lake, the moths still danced in hypnotic patterns, but all the wonder had bled from Áine's mind.

Would the March Cann return? How long must she wait? And how would she get the hairs free? She gingerly set her injured leg out in front of her and sighed.

The knife. Of course. She could use that to cut free hairs from the fairy steed's tail. If he returned. If, if, if. Áine rubbed at her eyes as her tears finally overflowed. A few escaped her hands and touched the wood, turning to pearls that shimmered for a moment before sliding between the roots to sink beneath the lake.

Emyr opened the door to his room and let Idrys out into the hall. He turned back to finish dressing and walked to the window. Unlatching the casement, Emyr leaned out the opening to get a feel for the weather that morning.

Spring mists clung to the buildings in the dawn light, lending a surreal touch to the village. It was still chilly but Emyr guessed the sun would burn away the mist and they might have a more or less clear spring day. He started to pull the wooden shutters back closed but stopped as something caught his eye. A weak ray of sunlight sparkled on two tiny white droplets resting on the window's ledge.

Emyr's heart leapt into his throat as he realized what they were. Pearls. Two perfect teardrop pearls that he guessed would be a match to the one even now resting in his beltpouch. He snatched them up and threw wide the casement, dark eyes searching the passages between the buildings.

Nothing stirred and he managed to stop himself from yelling her name. "Áine," he whispered. "Áine."

Two pearls. Two years. Does it mean something? Emyr clenched his teeth and abruptly threw the pearls away, out into the muddy ground beyond. *Does it mean wait? Two more years? Why? What's the point of waiting for a woman who walks away the moment a terrible secret is shared? Can you see us, Áine? Do you see our hollow hearts, our hungry eyes?*

He slammed the shutters closed and wrapped his arms around his chest. He could feel more ribs than usual, even after as hard a winter as the last had been. Idrys had grown thin as well; both of them were locked into a war between hope and despair, trapped in the monotony of their own lies, of the curse.

"We're lost, more lost than if you had never come into our lives," he murmured. "Without you, there is only hope, and we're running thin on that, aren't we?"

Before her, there was no hope at all, a traitorous voice in his mind whispered.

With a soft cry, Emyr turned back to the window and opened it again. He climbed through the opening, barefoot in only his pants, and bent to search the freezing mud. He found the pearls, one a mere arm's length from the other.

He clambered back through his window and rinsed his muddy hands and feet off in the basin near the hearth. Then Emyr added the two pearl tears to the third in his belt pouch.

Three pearls. Mother is silently pressing us to move on, to attend to our duty as Llynwg's Chief. One more winter, Áine. I can give that much, just come home to us; I promise we'll forgive the absence. Please come home.

Áine slept fitfully throughout the remainder of the night and into the day. The sun was high overhead before her stomach reminded her that she still needed to eat. She rose reluctantly and pulled bread free from her pack. Her ankle felt tight and ached but looked well enough. Her shoulder was a different story. She pulled aside the neck of her gown and winced at the deep purple and red bruising that traced the hoof of the March Cann.

Mechanically, Áine chewed her bread and drank from the waterskin as she considered the coming night. She couldn't try the same thing again. Assuming the steed showed again and landed in the same place, she'd likely face the same outcome without a better plan.

She recalled the speed at which the creature had reacted to her touch. There was no way she'd get a good grip on its tail and have time to bring up the blade with her other hand before it pulled her off the ground again, especially since her right arm was already injured and therefore slowed.

Shaking the crumbs out of her skirt, Áine watched absently as they filtered between the roots and into the lake. She jerked and looked over to where the fairy steed had landed the night before.

The roots there were thinner, more spread out as they arched gently above the water. There was room enough between some for her to squeeze herself down and the lake here was only waist deep. She could hide there to the side, and out of range of the steed's powerful kicks. She'd be pulled into the air; she knew there was likely no way to avoid it. But she hoped she'd cut the hairs before they flew too high, and the lake would cushion her fall if she landed in the water.

Her plan firmly in mind, Áine sat back against the broad oak to wait for dark. She wasn't thrilled at her chances and held Idrys's little wooden horse in her palm, rubbing a thumb over it.

Emyr had been teaching her to ride. She wished he'd taught her more, that she'd had more time, more skill. A true heroine, like one from the tales Tesn had told her as a little girl, would leap fearlessly to the fairy steed's back and ride it into the sky until the creature grew tired and had to land. Then she would climb down and triumphantly cut free two perfect strands of hair from its tail and stride back to the evil fey Lady and demand the curse be broken.

Áine snorted and tucked the little horse away in her pack again. *Too bad I'm all they've got, isn't it?*

The day passed with the sluggishness only boredom can lend. Áine ran through every recipe and cure for every common ailment she could think of before abandoning that to make little oakleaf boats that she sent out on the lake. The pain in her shoulder died down to the ache of a bad bruise and her ankle let her put a little weight on it by the time the sun slipped down behind the forest.

Áine put her pack up in the tree after tucking her dress, belt, and cloak safely inside. She kept only the knife, removed from its sheath and gold wrappings. Her right hand's grip still felt weak to her, so she put the knife in that hand and decided she'd use her left to catch the tail when the time came. If the time came.

The lake water was cold and her feet sank into the mud up to her ankles. She could feel submerged edges of smaller roots beneath her feet and against her thighs as she slid down into her hiding place. *Gods, let this work, please.*

The stars emerged and the moon peeked over the lake to the east. Crouching there in the dark, Áine fought the cold and her own doubts. *Emyr, Idrys, I'm a world away from you. Did I only imagine your love? If I fail, if I die, you'll never know what I tried to do for you, for us.*

For myself.

Her teeth chattered and her skin felt as though it might crawl free of her bones in protest before the moon rose far enough to send its light out over the water like the broad blade of a spear pointing straight at the island. Áine nearly cried out with joy as she heard the whirring of wings and felt a strange wind lift her blood-red hair from her damp cheeks.

The moths returned, appearing as if by magic over the lake, swirling in their tapestry patterns as they'd done the night before. And above her, like a gift descending from the gods themselves, came the March Cann. He settled in the same place he'd been the night before, snorting and pawing at the roots and looking around the island before turning his attention to the moonlit dance over the lake.

His tail was a hand's breadth from Áine's face, its ends resting on the root in front of her. Hardly daring to breathe, she turned her body toward the steed and slowly raised her hands. She'd positioned herself perfectly off to his side where she hoped his kick wouldn't touch her. She inched her hands forward and with a last prayer grabbed a thick handful of tail and pulled it toward herself.

Again with preternatural speed, the March Cann sprang into the air. Áine held fast even as she was ripped free of the gap in the roots and dragged upward. Her body swung hard to the other side of the steed and his kick went past without connecting. For one terrifying moment Áine saw how far over the island they were, the lake with its moonlit spear looked as tiny as a lady's polished hand-mirror. Then she swept the blade up and cut into the tail as high above her fist as she could reach.

The hairs parted. With an iridescent fistful of hair and a triumphant yell, she fell out of the sky.

Twenty-three

As though emerging from the very darkness of the night itself, hundreds of ravens appeared beneath her as Áine plummeted toward the lake. A cacophony of cries echoed through the air as body after body buffeted her, slowing her descent. She rested on the back of each raven only a moment before it would drop away and another would sweep in to take its place.

Áine dared to look when she realized she should have touched the water already and saw that with their strange method the ravens were carrying her out over the forest.

It felt like no time at all to her racing heart before she was allowed to fall to the soft ground at the base of a hill. All around her ravens landed, some shifting into dark-skinned people. Áine shivered, naked except for her fistful of fairy hair and her knife. Her head spun and she took deep breaths before rising.

"Thank you," she called out to the raven people.

An odd clicking laughter rippled through the gathering crowd. She stood carefully, keeping the weight off her injured leg, and noticed that they parted before her in a clear path toward the crown of the hill. Taking the hint, Áine limped between the laughing people.

Her eyes widened as she reached the top. The top of the hill was a huge marble slab of purest white that glowed in the moonlight. And on it stood a handsome youth with glossy black eyes and a brilliant white smile in his blue-black face. He was clad only in a cloak of raven's feathers that fell from shoulder to ankle in thick gathers and a simple silver circlet that bound his curly black hair.

"I greet you, Áine," he said.

"I greet you," she answered, "but I do not know you."

He laughed and a flash of recognition came to her at its harsh sound. "You do not recognize me, yes, but you do know me."

"Bran?" Áine guessed.

"Aye." His grin grew wider. "I told you I was the king of the ravens, but you seemed only to humor the child. I thought you might better believe the man."

"Forgive me, my lord." Áine flushed and stared down at her toes.

"No offense was meant, and so none has been taken." He reached behind him and brought out her pack. "I believe this is yours?"

Áine nodded and came forward to take it from him. His smile deepened as she blushed even further. This close she could feel the heat from his nearly naked body and was very aware of her own bare and chilled skin.

Focus, you goose. She bent and put her handful of hair into the bag, then pulled out the knife sheath and her dress. Bran stood over her and watched with that insufferable grin on his face. *No wonder they call it an "unkindness" of ravens; I think he's doing that on purpose because it makes me blush.*

She stood, clothed now, and tied her belt around her waist. Bran was only an arm's length away and Áine took a step back and another deep breath.

"I thank you and your people for saving me," she said.

"I told you, I owed you a favor. It was an honor to save you, Áine."

She narrowed her eyes. "When you were trapped in the thorn bush, why didn't you just shift into a man and untangle yourself?"

He threw back his beautiful head and laughed.

Áine crossed her arms and started to turn away. The ravens might have saved her, but she was cold and exhausted and had a long walk to Seren's if her ankle would hold and she could find the way from this strange hill.

"Áine, please. Take no offense." He stepped forward and caught her arm with one long-fingered hand. "I did trick you before, but why save myself when a beautiful woman is nearby? Come, rest this night with us and feast. In the morning I promise to show you the way to the drychpwll."

Raven people came up the hillside, laying out a thick woolen blanket and many cushions. Áine allowed Bran to lead her to the blanket and she sank down with a sigh, though she tucked her pack carefully against her side before relaxing.

A feast was laid out before them: piles of ripe berries, a platter of cooked grey partridge basted in drippings and stuffed with herbs and roots, warm rolls, soft white cheese, stewed pears, nuts mixed with sea salt, and a clay pitcher of sweet mead.

At Bran's gesture, Áine filled the wooden platter in front of her. She'd eaten nothing for weeks but apples and bread and while they sustained her, she realized now how much she missed the textures and flavors of other foods, especially the cooked meat.

Finally her body warned her not to eat another bite and Áine leaned back on the cushions, sipping the mead. Bran sat across from her, his feather cloak wrapped around his body, watching her. As though something in her posture invited him, he rose and moved to her. Áine stiffened as he sank down beside her and reached to pull her against him.

"No, please," she said, though the warm touch of another nearly made her cry out. *To think, I've almost become accustomed to loneliness.*

"Shh, Áine," Bran murmured as he wrapped his feathered cloak around her. "I know your heart is given. Rest now, halfling. I'll watch over you."

Halfling. That was what Seren called her as well, but on the raven king's lips it was more endearment than insult. The bone-weariness that these days seemed to eternally hover over her seeped into her warm body and she let her head fall against Bran's chest. It felt good to be held thus and tears welled in her tired eyes.

"I come to Cymru-that-could-be," she whispered. "And it seems I spend half the time weeping."

"If it's only half, this land hasn't yet broken you, has it? Sleep."

A question flitted through Áine's mind but it slipped away before she could grasp it. With a deep sigh she drifted off to sleep.

Emyr and Idrys stood behind a curtain of falling water, perfect mirrors of each other. Áine rose from the ground, glancing around at the towering stone walls that bound her.

"Áine," Idrys cried out to her and stepped forward. Emyr grabbed his hand and pulled him back.

"Cruel to leave us so, aren't you?" Emyr's eyes were dark and angry.

Áine opened her mouth but found she could not speak.

"Áine, Áine, my love," Idrys said, "Come home to us."

"Come to us," Emyr echoed, his expression softening. "Return here, return now."

Áine shook her head, holding out her hands. She stepped toward them, reaching through the cascade of water. The water was warm and thick and she looked down, recoiling in horror.

Her hands and arms were soaked with blood. She found her voice in a long raw scream.

The twins turned away and faded into the darkness beyond, hand in hand.

Áine woke, still calling to the twins. She jerked away from Bran's comforting arms and blinked down at her hands in the weak sunlight. As far as she could tell, it was just past dawn. Slowly she brought her breathing under control as she stared at her clean, pale hands.

"All right, are you?" Bran asked. His glassy eyes watched her closely.

"There was so much blood," Áine whispered, "but it was just a dream. Only a dream."

"Not all dreams are dreams."

"Comforting me, are you? You've a funny way about it." She glared up at him before flushing and looking down. She smoothed her skirt over her bruised legs and sighed.

"You've taken on a difficult journey, Áine. Accept the warnings and the help as they come." His feather cloak swirled around his dark body as he rose to his feet.

"Forgive me," she said and stood as well. "Sometimes I think I've forgotten what help is, or what it felt like to be rested and content."

"Would you break your fast before we leave?" he asked.

Áine thought of the dream and all the blood on her hands. She shook her head as her stomach turned.

"What is this place?" she said instead.

In the sunlight the white marble glimmered with thin veins of gold and she could see the crown of the forest stretching all around the hill. It was higher up then she'd realized in the dark.

"White Hill," Bran said, "my llys, the center of my kingdom." His lips twitched in an ever-ready smile. "Ravens are not exactly the most clever of creatures when it comes to naming, are we?"

"I love a man who calls his hound Cy," she said and smiled back at him. *Calls his brother Cy.* She wondered which twin had come up with that name and couldn't decide.

"Are you ready then?" Bran motioned to her pack and she wondered at the sadness in his face. "I'll take you to Seren, since I doubt that ankle will carry you far."

Áine hobbled to her pack and slipped the strap over her shoulder. She rubbed the sleep from her eyes with one hand and ran the other through her short hair. Her body felt bruised and sore from the buffeting of wings and her cold wait the night before and she felt as though she'd hardly slept at all. Her ankle throbbed and didn't want to bear her weight.

Áine worked her ankle around in a circle each way and then sighed. "All right," she said, "take me to Seren."

Bran held out his hand and Áine stepped forward with a quizzical look and took it. He clasped her wrist higher up and with a harsh laugh pulled her into the sky.

"Don't let go, eh?" Bran laughed as Áine clung to his arm with both hands, clutching her bag tight between her arm and her body as they flew out over the trees.

As if I'd even consider it, you oaf. She pushed away the uncharitable thought and stared down at the trees as they flew past. Her stomach churned and she focused on the horizon instead. Bran's cloak swept back from them, snapping as it billowed in the wind.

Too soon and yet not soon enough Bran brought them down in a spiral to land in a clearing that Áine thought looked familiar. Her legs went out from under her and she sat hard onto the ground as her heart slowly found a calmer rhythm and her eyes stopped watering from the flight. Bran stood silently beside her, his cloak wrapped around his body, his black eyes watching her.

Áine struggled to her feet and lifted her pack once more to her shoulder. "Thank you, King Bran."

"It was my pleasure," he said with a wide smile. "Seren's home is the next clearing to the west. You should be able to get that far on foot. I will wait for you here."

"Wait for me? Why?"

"You have more tasks, do you not? You do not seem like a woman triumphant."

"Yes, I think one more, provided Seren did not trick me in some way. But she said four when this began and she cannot lie about such things." Áine sighed. One more task. "But why would you wait? You've already given me more help than I know how to repay." She looked into his beautiful face and hated that she mistrusted his motives so, but this place was teaching her quickly that nothing came without some price.

Bran shrugged, his cloak rippling with the motion. "I have my reasons, not the least of which is that if you succeed, you'll be making no friend in Seren, and the Lady is no friend to my people. And I like you. Another might have long since given up. Your heart is a tiny sun within you."

Áine flushed, knowing how close she'd come to giving up more than once on this journey. *I almost gave up right as it began.* She nodded.

"All right. Thank you, Bran." She touched his feathers and turned away. What with the strands of the March Cann's tail, she was nearly done. She smiled to herself in satisfaction. Seren would be quite disappointed to see her, wouldn't she?

Áine's satisfaction was short-lived. The Lady greeted her with a smile that raised goose flesh along her arms and made Áine's scalp crawl.

"You return with the tail hair?" Seren asked and her perfect white teeth looked almost sharp as she parted her full lips and leaned slightly forward.

Áine reached into her pack and felt the cold metal hilt of the knife. She was little more than an arm's length from the Lady. It would be easy: draw the blade, one thrust into the perfect white of her breasts that swelled over the low line of her gown.

One little cut into Seren's heart and the curse would be over, that condescending smile and all the pain she'd caused wiped away in a single motion.

Áine swallowed hard and grasped at the curled hairs beside the knife. She drew out the shimmering handful; translucent blues and purples cascading over her fist.

"There, tail hair from the March Cann. More than you asked for as I thought you'd like your pick." Áine bit her lip and raised her chin.

Seren gracefully plucked two purple strands from Áine's hand as she opened her fist. The other hairs slid to the ground where they evaporated upon touching it.

Áine stared down at them in surprise, wondering how close she might have come to dropping the precious tresses. She narrowed her eyes and looked back up at Seren who merely raised a single pale blood-red brow and widened her predatory, knowing smile.

"My final task here in Cymru-that-could-be?" Áine prompted. Bran was waiting for her, and even his strange oscillations between gentle teasing and tense scrutiny were preferable to Seren's sudden smugness.

"It is simple," Seren said and she motioned with one hand. The hairs of the March Cann disappeared and a small horn bowl appeared in their place in her palm. "Go to the Yfwr and collect her tears. Bring them to me and I will complete the charms that will break the curse."

"Collect them in that bowl? How do I do this? Who is the Yfwr and where does she live?"

Seren laughed, a sound like bells on a cold morning. "Ah, halfling, you ask so many questions. Yes, collect them in the bowl. Make her cry and it will be an easy enough task. You will find the Yfwr by the fairy ring beyond the lake."

"How do I make her cry?" Áine clutched at the bowl that Seren extended to her. *Why are you answering my questions now? Why are you acting so helpful?* Áine tried to think what might have changed but her mind swam in tired circles.

"You've proven a very resourceful one, haven't you?" Seren shrugged and vanished.

"I do hate it when you do that," Áine muttered to the empty clearing and shivered. She turned and tucked the bowl into her bag. *I could have ended it all. Selfish of me, wasn't that? I'm a coward. No, I'm a healer. Do no harm. I will end this my way.*

She hobbled slowly back toward Bran, wondering what the price hid in this new task.

"Emyr, please. See reason on this." Hafwyn touched his shoulder as he threw wide the hall door and set one foot out into the crisp spring evening.

Melita rose and left the hearth with a murmured excuse. Alone now, Idrys turned back to his mother and glared down at her. There were tears in her warm brown eyes and his heart softened.

"You'd have me marry, would you?" He glanced around and added. "Have us marry? Do you know what that might mean?"

"I know, Idrys, I know." She dropped her gaze. "But life goes on, with or without curses, with or without love."

"Not Idrys," he said bitterly. "Emyr. This would kill Idrys forever."

With a harsh moan, Hafwyn reached out to him again, her shoulders slumping. Behind her Emyr gave a soft whine and dropped low to the rushes, resting his bony head on his paws.

Idrys wrapped his arms around his mother, noting the white that dusted her dark hair; it seemed more than the previous spring. He took a deep breath and stepped away from her, pulling them both into the hall and closing the door behind him. He stared beyond his mother to the hound sitting by the hearth.

His brother watched him with sad, liquid eyes, a dark shadow against the stones. Idrys shivered. *It wasn't loving the same woman that pulled us so far apart. It was losing her.*

Idrys looked down at Hafwyn. "Comely, is she? Well. All right, mother," he said, "it cannot hurt to at least meet this chief's daughter."

Twenty-four

His glassy black eyes narrowed in an otherwise impassive face, Bran stared at her in silence for a long moment before his shoulders rose and fell in a very bird-like gesture that Áine wasn't sure how to read.

"The Yfwr was the first creature of the water. There is a legend among my people that she saw Amathaon, son of the goddess Don, tilling a field by her lake and fell in love. She shifted into a maiden and seduced him. After he lay with her she turned back into a creature and when Amathaon realized the deception, he left her. It broke her heart. She bore him three children, then turned into a weeping willow, which is how you'll find her now."

Áine mulled this information over. "How do I make a tree cry? Seren said this task would be simple, but I cannot see how that was not a lie."

Bran's jaw tightened and he pulled his cloak around him, turning half away from her. "It is simple, she did not lie. To make the Yfwr cry, you need only wound her."

Áine clutched her pack to her chest and sighed. "I do not like this. But I have a knife of cold iron, and if it must be so, I will do what is needed."

Bran turned back to her with a melancholy smile. "Yes, you likely will. Shall we go?"

"More flying?" Áine took his blue-black hand in her own milk-pale one.

"Rather walk, would you?" Bran's smiled warmed slightly.

"More like hobble. And no, thank you." She hesitated, looking up at him. "Thank you, Bran."

He chuckled without mirth and shook his head. "Don't thank me yet," he murmured, but before she could respond, he lifted them into the air and they flew out over the forest, back toward the lake.

Bran brought them down in a slow spiral beyond the lake, along the banks of a little stream. Áine knelt in the thick, soft grass as the world to stopped spinning and her stomach unclenched. When she finally felt somewhat close to normal again she looked up and gasped.

Across the stream was a huge weeping willow. Its bark was the grey-blue of the sea just before a storm and the leaves shimmered silver and gold, trailing down into the water. Áine had to crane her neck to see the crown of the tree and she thought that it would take five or six grown men to span the trunk that leaned out over the stream with their arms. Beyond the willow was a circle of white stones, a fairy ring within the shade of her giant canopy.

Áine took a deep breath. She did not like the idea of harming anything, but this was only a tree, albeit a magical one. *I eat the flesh of animals, I sit on wooden chairs in front of warm fires; cutting into a tree is no different from these things. And I'll make the cut small as I can.*

She reached into her pack and drew out the knife. She unsheathed it and picked up the horn bowl.

The stream was shallow and Áine forded it by stepping on the half-submerged stones. She went to the base of the Yfwr's trunk and chose an exposed root. With a silent prayer and apology, Áine drew the knife blade quickly across the root.

It did not cut. The knife failed to even score the wood. Áine did it again, this time putting all her weight behind the blade. Nothing, not a mark, though the blade sparked against the surface.

Áine touched the root and found it hard and cold like metal. She raised her hand to brush against a clump of leaves and found they too were cold and hard as though formed of actual silver and gold.

She turned and looked back at Bran who stood just across the stream watching her, his expression unreadable.

"I don't understand," she called out. "I can't wound it, the blade does nothing."

"Áine," Bran said. "Come to me and I will try to explain."

Áine limped back across the stream and sank down in the grass to take the weight off her sore leg. Bran settled across from her.

"The Yfwr changed into what you encounter now to prevent herself from ever feeling pain again. The tree cannot be harmed."

"But I have to wound her to get her tears," Áine said. "This doesn't make sense, does it?"

"Think, Áine!" Bran hissed. "There is more than one way to wound."

Áine stared at him with wide, confused eyes. *I don't know what he means. Well, that's untrue. I know what he means, but how would one hurt the heart of a tree? I do not understand.*

"Her children," Bran said finally, "her three children are her last weakness. If they come to harm, she will wake and weep."

Áine wrapped her arms around her chest. "You want me to wound children?"

"No, you cannot merely wound them. They have powerful gifts of healing; momentary pain would not wake their mother." Bran pulled his feather cloak tight to his body. "To make the Yfwr weep, you must kill them."

"Kill them? But..." Áine rose to her feet and winced. "No. No, I won't do that. I cannot do that."

Bran stood with strange, intense expression on his face. "You want to free these men you love, do you not?"

"Aye. And I will. But there has to be another way."

"There is," he said simply and Áine remembered what Trahaearn had told her when he made a gift of the knife she now held in one hand.

"Kill Seren," she said.

"Kill Seren," he echoed and took a step toward her, his eyes bright.

"Why do you want her dead? That's it, isn't it? You've stayed with me, helping me all this time in hope that I'll make that choice. You knew before we flew here what I would have to do, how to make the Yfwr weep. You could have said something back there, couldn't you? But you wanted me face her, to see the impossibility of all this so that the other choice would look more attractive, didn't you?"

She pulled out of reach of his arms as he moved toward her and threw the knife down at his feet. "No! Don't touch me. If you want her dead so much, kill her yourself."

"Áine," Bran said sharply, then more softly, "Áine. Aye, I want her dead. The Lady took offense to my father paying her court a long time ago. For his apparent insult she drowned him in the drychpwll and to this day hunts down my people for sport with her hounds. Do you not think I desire nothing more than to take that knife and thrust it into her cold, vain heart? But I cannot set foot in her clearing, and if I could she'd still never let me near enough to do harm."

Áine took a deep breath and willed her shaking hands to still. "I'm sorry Bran. I know that my coming here must look like salvation for you, but it isn't. If I kill her, I break the curse and yes, free your people from her ire. But I would become the new Lady, trapped forever in the boundaries of her domain. Emyr and Idrys would be free of the curse and lost to me. There must be some other way, some path that doesn't involve killing anyone."

Bran laughed and it was not a pretty sound. "Cowardly Áine, driven from her quest by a little blood. If your love falters so easily, you hardly deserve it."

He swirled his cloak around himself and turned into a raven. Heedless to her calling his name, Bran leapt into the air and flew off over the lake.

Áine sank to the ground and wrapped her arms around her knees.

You can free them.

Follow your heart.

The words whispered in her mind, once a comfort but now their own kind of curse. "Tesn," she said to the empty field. "You taught me never to cause harm. I've come so far."

She pulled her pack to her and groped around inside it for the tiny wooden horse. She sat for a long time as the sun slowly sank toward the water, stroking her fingers over the horse's body, memorizing each nick and cut.

"Idrys," she murmured. "Do I only imagine that you made this thinking of me? What would you do?"

But her mind pulled away from that answer. *You'd kill Seren, wouldn't you? He'd do anything to free his brother of this curse if he knew the way.* Tears stung her eyes. *But he isn't here, is he? He wasn't the one chosen, the one given this chance.*

She curled into the grass and fell asleep as the sun set, her hand clutching the little horse.

It was the same dream as before. Emyr and Idrys stood, hand in hand, parted from Áine by a sheet of falling water. This time it was Áine who backed away.

"I'm sorry," she whispered, "forgive me. I just want to be with you. To have a home. But not like this."

The twins came toward her, moving as one. As they touched the waterfall it turned to blood, soaking them both and turning their visages into something alien and terrible, something Other.

"Áine, my love. Why do you abandon us? Don't leave us."

Áine felt movement in one hand and something horribly cold and still in the other. She looked down. In one palm the little horse came to life and squirmed, soft and warm between her fingers. In the other, she held Trahaearn's blade.

Áine woke, her throat raw and her face hot from crying. She still clutched the wooden horse, but in her other hand she grasped the knife. With a cry she sat up.

Three slender sprites surrounded her, peering down at her with curiosity in their wide silvery eyes. They each stood about the height of her waist, with perfectly hairless bodies and long limbs. In the moonlight they looked like tiny tree sylphs with branch-like noses, sharp chins, and smiling pink children's lips. Their eyes, too big to be human, were without pupils or irises.

One slender hand brushed her cheek; another child stepped in and stroked her hair. Áine stared up at them, realizing they must be the Yfwr's offspring. The knife was a cold, hard weight in her hand and she pulled away from their touch.

"I'm Áine," she said. "I greet you."

A sound like a muffled harp issued forth from one child's mouth and the other two joined in, speaking a musical language Áine could not comprehend. She shook her head. They pointed to the fairy ring and Áine saw that it was lit up by the moonlight. One slender child danced away from the others, moving in hypnotic spirals over the ground toward the ring of glowing stones.

"I cannot dance with you," Áine said, guessing at their intentions. "My ankle, it's injured." She motioned to her wrapped ankle.

The child who had touched her cheek bent over her leg and laid a warm hand on her skin. Heat suffused her leg, spreading down into her ankle and foot. It lasted only a moment, followed by a sudden cessation of pain. The sprite rose and smiled at Áine.

Áine worked her ankle around slowly and then stood carefully and put weight on it. There was no pain. Áine smiled down at the children as they waved to her again and danced away toward the fairy ring, their singsong voices drawing her along with them.

She looked down at the knife in her hand and a sickening thread of fear twisted within. Pushing that fear away, Áine tucked the knife into her belt and followed the children across the stream, letting the little wooden horse fall from her hand.

She hesitated and then stepped within the fairy ring. Music greeted her as she crossed the threshold, unlike any she'd ever heard before. It sounded as though a hundred harps and wooden flutes played in glorious harmony, the music nearly alive around her, a tangible thing that pulled at her skirt and hair, begging her body to move with its power. The children brought her into their spiraling dance, grasping her hands and turning her this way and that with their little faces turned upward to the stars that winked between their mother's leaves.

The sprites spun and spun, the music growing louder, faster, wilder. Áine danced with them, her mind emptying of its cares, her heart light with joy. Every ache and pain, every ounce of exhaustion in her weary body fled in the whirl of the dance until only the rhythm mattered and all she felt was the beat of her own heart and the warmth connecting her to these strange children. Her mind sank into the bodies connected to her and she found only joy and a weightless power. There was nothing to be healed here, no sickness or wound, just the delight of sharing in connection with another.

They danced until the moon set and the sky turned grey with false dawn. The children slowed their steps and moved in close to Áine. As if it were a natural end to the mad dance, she sank to the ground, her skirt spread out around her, and the children curled with their heads in her lap. She watched sleepy eyes close and their thin bodies settle into slumber.

The carved bird on the hilt of the knife dug into her ribs, a harsh reminder of her purpose here. *Not my purpose. I cannot do this. They are so little, so trusting.*

Does not Idrys trust you? Is not Emyr waiting for your return? Did you not tell him as you slipped away that you would come home?

Her mind warred with itself and Áine felt torn apart from within.

She counted the days slowly. Not even a fortnight. It felt like so much longer since she'd lain in Idrys's warm arms, teased Emyr, and seen the responding love in their eyes. *Two weeks. They are waiting for me. I could just go home.*

Go home? What home? A chief is not free to marry without thought for the future. Look at you, silly girl. They call you halfling, they call you Other.

"No," she said aloud. One of the Yfwr's children shifted and Áine jammed her fist in her mouth. *Emyr and Idrys don't care about that. They love me. I love them.*

Is love enough? If they learn that you could have freed them but walked away? Or will the guilt of the curse and your failure here pull you all apart?

You can free them.

Follow your heart.

"Which heart?" Áine murmured.

A memory came to her then, an image as clear as if it played out again right in front of her. She stood in the snow, her body half-turned away from the forest. An owl alighted on a branch, catching her attention. Áine remembered she'd almost given up before the journey even started.

She remembered her vow not to do so again.

What price, love?

Her body shaking, her hands cold, Áine slid the knife out of her belt. She laid one hand on the forehead of the first child. Tiny green veins threaded through the sleeping child's lids and Áine choked back a sob as she bent forward and brought up the knife.

"Forgive me," she whispered, "I must follow my heart."

She drew the knife across the child's throat.

Blood bloomed around the blade in a scarlet flood. The dying sprite made no sound, just opened its silvery eyes and watched her with an ancient sadness at odds with its youthful appearance. Áine stared down at it in horror and then twisted away, stabbing the second child through the neck and then the third, her eyes pressed shut, her lips bleeding as she bit them. Blood soaked her skirt, climbing up the bodice of her dress and turning the sky-blue linen dark crimson.

With a cry she rose, flinging the knife far from herself. The dead children's heads dropped from her skirt and they lay in a strange parody of their own sleeping forms; bodies curled and eyes half-shut.

She stumbled away from them to the stream and fell into it, dry heaving. Her stomach, empty for lack of food the day before, had little to bring up but acidic bile. She scrubbed at her bloody hands and then her skirt. The blood washed from her hands, but the scrubbing only seemed to spread it on her dress.

Behind her, the willow began to shake and scream.

Áine looked back and saw the tree sweeping its arms through the air as it cried out in pain, the sound like the smashing of a thousand harps, the wail of a thousand suffering throats. She crawled from the stream to where she'd left the horn bowl and snatched it up.

Rising, she walked back across the water to the tree. Its leaves were hard and sharp and cut into her body as she pushed through its raging branches. Her dress was cut to rags and her flesh marked with hundreds of shallow wounds. Áine blinked through the blood that seeped into her eyes and pressed the horn bowl into the Yfwr's bark.

Thick, glistening tears flowed from deep cracks in the skin of the tree and ran down, caught in Áine's bowl. She stood there, sick with grief and guilt, barely feeling the leaves that lashed her skin, the cuts on her face, back, and arms. When the bowl brimmed with the sap-like tears, Áine turned and walked toward the lake.

At the shore she paused and looked back. The tree still thrashed and wailed, and the rising sun shone down on the crumpled bodies of the children. Stuck upright into the earth beside one of the standing stones, the Trahaearn's knife sparkled in the light and Áine recalled her promise to return it to him.

She moved toward it and another spear of nausea and horror stabbed through her. She set down the bowl of tears carefully on one of the standing stones and walked to the bodies of the children. Bending, she laid the children out straight and closed their filmy, staring eyes.

Her hands were slick with her own blood, but she managed to unknot her belt. The red leather slipped off her hips and fell into the grass beside their bodies, a crimson gash on the stained ground.

Áine left the knife where it lay and picked up her bowl of tears. She walked to the lake and stepped into the water. Her foot did not sink; instead it rested on the surface, the lake giving like soft moss under her weight. She hesitated and then stepped forward. Her heart was a stone in her chest, her mouth a determined line. Áine stared straight ahead, placing one leaden foot after the other.

Empty and aching with grief, she walked out over the lake, away from one heart and toward another. Far above her drifted the shadow of a raven.

Twenty-five

The trees pulled back their branches, the ferns curled away from her ragged skirt. The forest itself recoiled from Áine, laying a clear path to where Seren waited. The grieving woman hardly noticed. Her green eyes were hot and damp with tears but focused as though seeing something always just ahead. She held the horn bowl steady in both hands in front of her body as one might carry an offering or a shield.

The sun slid over the sky and sank again. Áine did not waver in her step but called on the glowing fairy light. It ringed her, casting terrible shadows in the trees. The myriad tiny cuts on her arms, back, legs, and face ceased to sting and the blood covering her body dried, making her dress stiff and coarse against her raw skin.

She reached the drychpwll and Seren's cottage in the middle of the night. The cottage window was dark and no light shone from beneath the heavy door. Áine kicked the door hard with one foot, holding the horn bowl high above her head to keep it steady.

"Seren! I have completed your tasks here," she yelled in the still clearing. "Arise, Lady, and finish this that I might go complete the final task and free them."

Soft white light bathed the clearing suddenly, limning the branches of the trees and reflecting off the pond. Áine blinked and Seren appeared. The Lady's hair hung loose down her back and she wore only a thin undergown of the lightest green. No rings or combs adorned her this night, but the eerie light shifted her features as far from human as Áine had ever seen.

Her silvered eyes glinted and her skin glowed as though it had taken the moon into itself. Her hair was a ruby cascade over her shoulders and when she smiled there was something predatory and sharp hiding within.

"You look like quite the Bean Sidhe," Seren said. "Shall I finish this?"

She waved a slender hand in the air. The two crystalline stones, the strands of hair from March Cann, and the clasps Trahaearn had forged for Áine all manifested in the air, floating as if they balanced upon some invisible surface. "You have the tears?"

When Áine blinked at her and held out the bowl with a snarl, Seren took a half-step back. She shook her head, sending her hair rippling, and glared at the bloody woman. Áine didn't care and glared back. She was exhausted, too tired for Seren's games.

"Take it," she said. "Give me what I need to break the curse. I just wish to go home."

Seren took the bowl from her, avoiding touching her hands as she did so. Into the gleaming liquid went the stones, the clasps, and the fairy steed's hairs. The contents of the bowl seemed to boil over as thick gold foam poured over the sides. As the foaming slowed and finally stopped, Seren reached within and drew forth two necklaces, each as alike as the other. The tail hairs of the March Cann had turned into a delicate cord of deepest purple; the two gems shone white and faceted; the claps closed each off with their delicate filigreed closures.

"This is your final task. You must place these over the heads of the twins, one for each. This must be done at sunset when they change." She held them out.

Áine took the necklaces and nodded, then paused. "Any sunset?" she asked, having learnt to be suspicious and not so tired as to have forgotten that lesson easily.

"Sunset on the longest day, at midsummer." Seren's mouth tightened and then relaxed into a smile. "One more thing, Áine."

Seren reached out and touched Áine's shoulder. Áine had just long enough to wonder if this were the first time Seren had touched her or used her given name before she felt a strange tingle in her spine and then sharp pain.

She jerked away, clutching the necklaces. Her body twisted and bent and her clothing changed, becoming heavy and dull, like a beggars robe and rags.

"What have you done to me?" Áine cried out, or would have. Nary a sound came from her lips.

She touched her throat and then felt inside her mouth. She had nary a tooth and at her neck she felt the thin skin and thick wattles of an old woman. She hobbled to the pool, staring down into the calm waters.

A wrinkled old face peered back at her, distorted by the water but clear enough that her own familiar features had been wiped away. She turned back to Seren, aged eyes hurling accusation and hatred.

"Ah, halfling. You'll not stay this way forever, well, not if your princes love you as you seem convinced. If they recognize you before you break the curse, your own body will be returned. A simple enough task for true love, is it not?" Seren laughed. "Come now, you'd not deny me all my sport."

Áine slipped the necklaces over her head and advanced on Seren, her wrinkled, bony hands extended and violence in her mind. With another laugh, Seren disappeared but her words rang out across the clearing.

"Sunset, Áine. You'd best go; the journey will be longer on those legs."

Silently screaming in rage and despair, Áine turned and hobbled from the clearing, Seren's cold laughter echoing behind her.

She stumbled in the dark, her memory guiding her back toward the Ilswyn and Blodeuedd. Her newly old body wouldn't hold her up anymore, exhausted as she'd already been, and finally Áine collapsed onto the ground and slept where she was.

Dawn's light woke her, but no birds sang. It was as though Cymru-that-could-be held its collective breath. The eerie silence suited Áine's black mood. She found a fallen branch that would serve as a walking stick and pressed onward. Her stomach complained about the lack of nourishment but Áine shoved the feelings aside. She didn't want to think, to feel. She fixed the image of Idrys and Emyr's faces in her mind and stumbled ahead, one foot after another.

As she walked she tried to look at the better side of the situation. She had the means to free her lovers now. It had been midwinter when she'd left, so that would leave at least a season between her return and midsummer. She'd found a way to free them, traveled to this strange land and done all that Seren had asked; she could find the means to make the twins recognize her. It was just another task, she told herself.

One more task.

You can free them.

You can have a home.

She entertained herself through the day by trying to guess their reactions and imagining their warm embrace. Idrys would lift her up and call out to the sky in his joy. It was his face she held the most dear in her heart, the guilt that lined his features, that unspoken burden of his secrets. It was Idrys she would confide the truth in, the terrible deed and choice she'd made. It was Idrys who would understand and take her in his arms and whisper his forgiveness. It was Idrys who, she was convinced, would have done the same and worse to set his brother free.

Emyr would smile; kiss her face, her lips. His joy would be contained, reserved. He would think of a good tale to tell about his brother's miraculous return. And Áine would never tell him the truth of what she'd done. Not the whole of it. Emyr would be the one to look upon her with clear and loving eyes, no shadows or secrets clouding their love. After all this, she and Idrys would need his sweetness, his steadying presence.

I need each of them, each for his own ways and own gifts. I've missed them both so very much. They will know me. They must know me.

The trees gave way to meadow and Áine found it easier going. No swallows danced around her, and she saw no insects resting in the bent grasses. The sun was pleasantly warm on her back and with the use of her makeshift cane, she trudged over the silent wold.

It seemed a lifetime ago that she'd searched for the Ilswyn and emerged into Cymru-that-could-be. She recalled the pure white marble, the strange mists, and that Blodeuedd had told her the Ilswyn was only open when the veils between worlds grew thin. Áine hoped that only applied to passage from the world that is to the world that could be.

Despair rode her heart like a threatening storm cloud, hovering on her worst thoughts. What if the gate weren't open until midsummer? How many months would she have to wait? How would she find the gate at all? Seren had said the curse must be broken on the longest day. Which longest day? The next? She'd certainly implied as much. Áine ran a dry tongue over her soft, bare gums and shuddered.

A soundless cry of relief broke from Áine's lips as an opaque doorway appeared just in front of her as she crested a hill. Her heart beat painfully strong and forced her to stop and catch her breath, one hand pressed against her breastbone. She felt the hard stones of the cursebreaking pendants.

Grinding the end of her cane into the thick grass, Áine strode forward through the gate, leaving Cymru-that-could-be far behind.

This time things in the mists bumped against her and she heard voices crying out in a language she could almost understand. At one point, she nearly fell, stumbling over something in her path.

For a moment the terrifying visage of a dead child leered up at her, its neck a gaping wound from which colorless blood poured like a fountain. Áine recoiled and it was gone in the blink of an eye and she was alone again with the swirling mists.

A bright line pierced the gloom in front of her and Áine pushed her aching body toward it. The line thickened and formed into a doorway. Áine stepped through and fell to her creaking knees in relief. The valley of the Ilswyn spread out before her, the trees in their strange state of fruit and flower all at once. What had been strange before was comforting now and Áine choked down a sob.

"Áine, Áine, what has been done to you?" Blodeuedd's voice sounded from beside her.

Áine turned her head and saw the fairy woman standing beside the huge marble slab where the gate had been. Her blue-violet eyes were dark with pity and pain. Áine raised one hand to her mouth and shook her head.

"You cannot speak? Did you find what you sought?"

Áine nodded and pulled the pendants from underneath her ragged robe.

Blodeuedd smiled, some of the worry leaving her features. "Good. We must get you to the village. I fear that things are not as you left them."

Áine raised her eyebrows and tried to communicate her need for information. She pointed to the sun, which rode low in the eastern sky and then pointed to the west and down.

Blodeuedd pursed her lips and thought for a moment. "Do you mean you need to be there by sunset? Or do you wish to know the time that has passed? It's been a few years in Cymru-that-is, Áine."

A few years? Áine jerked back and carefully rose to her feet, leaning hard on her makeshift cane. She pointed at the trees and willed her question be understood.

Blodeuedd read the question clearly enough. "It's summer here, not just in the Ilswyn. Tonight is midsummer's eve."

No. No. I've arrived too late. I barely made the walk here in a full day on young and healthy legs. I have lost before I could even begin.

The vision of having months to convince the twins of her identity slipped away with this new knowledge. Blodeuedd said it had been a few years; did the twins even still love her? Or remember her? Despair swamped her and Áine would have crumpled to the ground again had not Blodeuedd's strong arms caught her up. Áine wept into the fairy woman's warm shoulder.

She had failed and her heart felt as though it would never stop dying. She couldn't breathe, her throat choking closed on grief.

"Áine, no, do not give up hope. I can get you to the village if you'll trust me? There is still time, Áine, still time."

Áine raised her eyes, which were no longer the green of new leaves but a faded grey-green of old moss, and nodded.

If Blodeuedd could get her there before sunset, Áine would find a way to tell the twins what she needed. She'd communicated easily enough with Blodeuedd, and the fairy woman had recognized her, hadn't she? There must still be a way.

Stop it, silly girl. Don't give in so easily. You've come far too far for this weeping and wailing at the smallest hitch.

She dried her face on her sleeves and gave Blodeuedd a wan smile. The beautiful fairy woman stepped away from her and raised her arms to the sky. She shifted, her body sparkling like waves in sunlight and turned into a huge white owl. Before Áine could fully take in the change, the owl beat her wings and rose into the air. Áine put an arm up to block the dust from her eyes and soundlessly cried out as the owl snatched her up in her claws.

When she'd flown with Bran, Áine had been nauseated and disoriented. She'd have never thought she would wish for that kind of flying again. It was much worse clutched in the claws of the owl. Her bones screamed in protest at the heavy weight of the talons gripping her tightly and feathers tickled her face, which was crammed in close to the owl's underbelly. Áine squeezed her eyes shut and tried to breathe shallow breaths.

It felt like an eternity before the owl dropped her as gently as it could to the soft grass beside a road. Blodeuedd appeared again, her body strangely transparent.

"I cannot stay here long, but down this road lies Clun Cadair. I wish you all luck and happiness, Áine. May your love bring to you more joy than mine brought me," Blodeuedd said. "But if it does not bring the happy ending you might wish, return to me. I would gladly share the Ilswyn." Then she shimmered back into a smaller owl and winged away toward the forest.

Áine dragged herself to her feet. Her body wanted to rest, to lie on the somewhat soft ground and settle, but there was not time for that. She still had a long way to walk and a lot of thinking to do about how she would tell Emyr what must be done. He'd likely be in the middle of a feast on this day, but at least in summer the llys would be more or less empty of people and Áine doubted she'd have trouble getting an audience with the chief.

Just have to decide how I'm going to tell him who I am and what I can do. I just have to hope he somehow knows me or find some familiar gesture or thing to show him.

She hobbled down the road, leaning heavily on her cane. The sun rose higher, beating down on her with the full force of its summer heat. Her robes grew damp with sweat and grit itched at her legs and wormed its way into her shoes. She thought she heard voices and wondered if she were hallucinating again in her exhaustion and worry.

She wasn't going mad, for soon behind her came a little cart pulled by a dun mare with a man of middle years singing happily on the seat. He waved to her as she stepped to the edge of the road to let him pass. Áine waved back and the man pulled the cart to a halt.

"I greet you, old mother, do you make your way to Clun Cadair?" he asked.

Áine nodded, motioning to her mouth to show she could not speak.

"The day is hot, the road dusty. Please, hop into my cart and I'll take you with me, for I too travel there and on this fine day I'd hate to have it said Aled Ap Aled let one of his elders walk in the heat."

Áine smiled up at him, careful to keep her lips shut tight over her empty gums. She accepted his arm and sat herself in the back of the cart, her legs dangling off the end. The cart was loaded with three large casks and Áine motioned to them with a clear question on her face.

"Aye, that is my family's specialty. We're brewers, you see, and I'm bringing our finest for the Chief's wedding feast tonight."

Twenty-six

Emyr pulled his tunic to lay straight over the soft linen shirt beneath and sighed. He'd gone over and over the marriage contract with the lawgiver. He was clean and dressed in his finest clothing, despite the warmth of the summer day. Idrys stared up at him from his place on a sheepskin by the hearth in their room.

"You think you're a sneaky one, don't you? Scheduling the wedding for the daylight." Emyr shook his head and glared at his brother. The hound's dark eyes met his without expression. "Deal with none of the ceremony and reap all the rewards of the lovely bride." He tried to keep his tone light and teasing.

Emyr knew Idrys was not looking forward to his wedding night. It had been a terrible battle of wills among Emyr, Idrys, and Hafwyn to get Idrys to agree to marry at all. But reason had won out in the end. The twins needed to produce an heir. Being cursed did not free them of this duty.

Idrys rose and paced to the door, whining in his throat.

"All right. You're right; I can't avoid the hall forever." Emyr adjusted the beaten silver torque at his throat and opened the door, following his brother into the great hall.

The door to the courtyard was thrown wide, allowing sunlight and air to penetrate into the busy room. A fire burned in the great hearth despite the weather and women of both cantrefi worked around it. The tables were arranged both inside and out so that all might share in the feast. Much of Clun Cadair's population was missing due to the season, however, with the addition of the people from Rhufon, the llys felt as full as it ever did in winter.

Emyr's bride stood near one laden table, helping to arrange a last minute garland of flowers down the center. He paused and watched her, his heart lifting as she turned a gentle smile toward him. Eirian's mother had been a Mercian. She was small like the people of Cymru, but fairer of skin, with golden-brown hair like good honey and eyes the color of a winter sky. Her blue wedding gown hugged her slender frame and pert breasts, the embroidery at the neck and cuffs done in gold and red thread, cleverly depicting little birds and flowers intertwined. Her hair was loose and long down her back, contained only by an etched silver circlet and a few summer blooms woven into her curls with silver wire.

Eirian was soft-spoken and loved hounds. It had not been so difficult to make her understand that her husband's favorite hound would sleep in the room with them, nor had she said one word about Emyr and the hound disappearing at sunset thus far.

Who knows what she'll think of me rising before dawn, but by then we'll be wed and she'll adjust. All husbands have oddities, I hope.

Emyr smiled back at her. This marriage was a good thing, he knew. Good for the cantref, good for the twins' spirits. Idrys would not be unkind to Eirian, and Emyr hoped that in time her gentle ways would wear down his brother's stubborn sorrow. *The gods know I haven't had the greatest luck.*

A commotion in the courtyard drew many looks toward the door and Emyr followed his brother's dark form outside into the bright sunlight. It was only an hour or so before the ceremony; Emyr hoped nothing had gone too horribly awry outside. He guessed that Llew or someone had dropped some of the meat roasting for the feast or somewhat like that.

He had not expected the cause to be a bent bundle of rags and dirty grey hair waving what looked very much like a fallen branch. The old woman poked her makeshift cane at Urien again as he tried to block her path into the great hall. The big man leapt back to a gale of laughter from the bystanders.

"Come now, Urien," Llew called from by the pits of roasting meat, "one poor old woman isn't going to topple you, is she?"

"She certainly seems determined," Urien said and waved his hands at her. "Old mother, old mother, calm down. There's a wedding today, you can't disrupt the preparations so."

"Easy, Urien," Emyr came up behind him and laid a hand on his shoulder. "I'll see to her." He stepped forward and saw the muddy green eyes of the old woman light up. "I am Emyr ap Brychan, Chief of Llynwg, perhaps I can help you?"

The woman came right up to him and Emyr lifted his face away from her smell. She was filthy with road grit and her hair hung in thin greasy locks around a deeply wrinkled face. He had never seen a woman so old and wondered that she'd even made the journey here. She stared up at him with an intense familiarity, but he was sure he'd never met her before as he would have recalled such an ancient crone.

"Please, what is your name? Do I know you somehow?" he asked, catching her thin wrist in his fingers as she reached to touch his face.

Her eyes lit up and she nodded vigorously and then pointed to her throat as she opened a mouth long deprived of teeth. Emyr realized then that of course the poor woman could not speak.

"Did I meet you when you were younger?" he guessed, for he could not place her.

Again she nodded.

"An old friend of my mother's, are you?"

She thought for a moment and then shook her head.

Curious. Emyr looked up and motioned to Urien. "Who brought her here? I can't believe she walked, eh."

"She rode in on Aled ap Aled's cart," Urien answered. "I'll fetch him."

Emyr released the crone's wrist and smiled at her in what he hoped was a reassuring manner even as he took a step back. He turned his head back toward the open door of the hall and called for Hafwyn to come out.

Hafwyn emerged into the summer sun, dusting her hands off on her skirts. Emyr motioned to the strange old woman.

"Do you know her, mother? She says she knows me, or at least implies. She cannot speak, poor thing."

Hafwyn looked at the crone who immediately turned beseeching eyes toward her. She studied the old woman a long moment and then slowly shook her head.

"I'm sorry, I don't recognize her. If she's a friend from my youth perhaps Melita might recall her, but I think it unlikely she'd know her when I do not."

The crone stamped one foot into the ground and wobbled precariously for a moment, clearly frustrated. She pointed vigorously between Emyr and herself, and then, to everyone's surprise, to Emyr and his dog.

Does she know somehow? Has she been sent here to disrupt the wedding? To reveal our curse? Is she some manifestation of the Fair Folk? Emyr turned a worried gaze on his mother and found his fears reflected in her eyes.

Urien returned at the moment with the brewer in tow. Emyr motioned the man forward and asked him to tell what he knew of the old woman.

"From where and why did you bring her here?" he asked gently, pressing down on his fear.

Aled looked between the chief and the crone with wide eyes. "I did not mean any harm, I didn't. She was walking on the road down from the woods and seemed to be heading to the feast. It seemed a terrible long way for such as she to walk, so I offered a ride in my cart. She gave me little trouble; does she bother you now?"

"She seems to think she knows me."

Aled swallowed hard. "Well, there was one odd thing." He paused and glanced at the crone again. She stared back at him, that same intense determination on her face as before. "Well," he continued "When I mentioned that I was on my way to your wedding feast, the poor woman fainted dead away. And when she came to she seemed doubly determined to reach the llys. But she can't speak, so I'm not sure the meaning of any of it. Sorry, my lord."

Emyr sighed. This news only raised more questions and did nothing to quell his fears. "There is nothing to forgive, Aled. Go about your business now, and thank you for your kindness. It surely would have been too far for her legs to take her." *Though I ungenerously wish you'd been a harder man and left her behind.*

Aled nodded, glanced between Emyr and the crone one last time, and then fled the courtyard.

Emyr looked down at the crone. He didn't want to be rude or give offense in case she was one of the Fey, but he could hardly let such a shadow hang over his nuptials.

"Forgive me, old one, but I must ask it. Are you one of the Fair Folk?" he said and then held his breath.

She hesitated, a strange look on her face. When she did finally answer, she shook her head slowly. Her hesitation and tense face were answer enough for Emyr. He let out his breath and ran a nervous hand over his tunic.

"Today is my wedding day. I mean no offense, but I cannot allow you into the hall until I have the time to sort out where you are from and why. Please, go and seat yourself there by the forge. I'll have someone bring you soft food, and you may enjoy the merriment from there."

She looked at him with what he would have sworn was terrible despair and shook her head. She pointed to him again, and then to Idrys, who sat up and cocked his black head to one side, watching her as intently as she watched him. Then the crone pointed to herself and repeated the triangle.

Hafwyn touched his arm. "Come, my son, we'll have time and time to sort this out tomorrow. The lawgiver stands ready and the feast nearly set. We should make sure to finish this before the hour grows late." She gave him a meaningful look.

Emyr nodded, pushing all thoughts of the strange old woman aside. "Urien, seat her over there and see that someone brings her something soft enough for her to swallow." He left the 'and see she doesn't enter this hall' portion of his orders unspoken for the sake of courtesy.

The crone gave a silent, open-mouthed cry and threw herself at him, waving her branch. Urien stepped in just in time to prevent her from actually leaping upon him and hauled the crone away. Emyr winced and hoped his friend was being gentler than he looked to be since the poor old woman appeared fragile enough that a summer breeze might break her. At Hafwyn's second tug on his sleeve he turned and followed her back into the hall.

Idrys turned to follow his brother, then paused. Something about that old woman was terribly familiar. He slipped around the edge of the courtyard and waited until a very firm Urien got her seated on a bench and took away her branch. Idrys came up alongside the crone. She smiled shyly at him and stretched out a thin, veined hand.

Idrys sniffed at her fingers. She smelled of dirt and sweat and more faintly of horse and owl. He wondered at the owl part and his furry body shivered as he recalled the owl who shadowed him often as he sat out staring into the distance each night. There was something else under these smells, something familiar and yet strange.

Idrys jammed his bony head into her thin thigh, snuffling at her skin through the rags of her robe. There was a smell there of herbs and beneath that a scent of both spice and fruit. He knew that scent, knew it in every part of himself.

Áine.

With a surprised yip, Idrys sat back on his haunches and looked up at Áine. She looked down at him with an unfamiliar face and eyes no longer the fresh green of new leaves but the tired color of dead moss. They stared into each other's eyes for a very long moment and then Idrys jumped up into her lap and licked her face. He had to let her know that he knew. And as soon as darkness fell, Emyr would know as well from her scent if not from Idrys telling him.

Idrys dropped back to the ground as Urien stepped over and pushed him away.

"He's not usually so friendly, I'm sorry. Go on, Cy, leave the woman in peace, eh?" Urien gave Áine a halfhearted smile of apology and shoved at Idrys.

Idrys barked. He did not want to be parted from Áine. He had no idea how she'd come to be this way, though he had a few guesses, and he had no intention of letting her out of his sight again, at least until after the wedding when he could be a man again and let everyone know who she was. And find a way to put her back to what she'd been.

The wedding! The wedding cannot happen.

The thought struck him hard and he redoubled his barking. Emyr would come, would know something was horribly wrong. Idrys rarely barked or howled, only ever when there was terrible danger or when he felt deep sorrow. *Áine is returned to us; we cannot marry that other woman, not until we know how and what has happened.* And, following on the trail of that thought, *I pray that I did not somehow cause this for her. Let it not be because I loved her. Hasn't Seren punished us enough?*

He growled and snapped at Urien, placing himself in a guard position in front of Áine who was making frantic motions behind him. Urien backed away in shock and yelled for Emyr.

Emyr came into the courtyard at a run, ducking out of the hall and looking around for the danger. He strode over to Idrys and looked between the hound and Urien.

"What is happening here? Is everyone all right?" he asked, still casting about as though wondering who was bleeding to death and where.

"That damn hound. I don't know. He's never acted this way before." Urien looked bewildered. "He jumped up on the old woman, and then when I pushed him away, he started snapping and howling."

"Cy, Cy, easy there old friend." Emyr approached Idrys with fear in his eyes.

Idrys quit barking and looked between Emyr and Áine in what he hoped was a meaningful way. He understood Áine's frustration at being unable to speak; it was how he spent half his days.

"Did she do something to you?" Emyr asked him as he stroked his ears in a soothing gesture.

Idrys shook his head in a very undoglike way that raised the eyebrows of the little crowd gathering.

"I swear that hound just shook his head in answer," said Gwideon ap Rhys, who was the Chief of Rhufon and father to Eirian.

Emyr stiffened and looked at his soon-to-be father-in-law. "Aye, we've a rapport, Cy and I, he half-fancies himself human sometimes. But clearly something has disturbed him. I'll just bring him inside and we'll get the ceremony started. Go on in, please."

The small, wiry man, who was about the same age as Hafwyn, nodded. "The lawgiver is ready, and so be my daughter. I'd hate to have a hound hold up the wedding." He smiled but it didn't push the worry out of his eyes.

Idrys understood everyone's reservations. A black hound howling was an omen of death, and the strange old crone didn't set any nerves to rest either with her presence. He hoped to use that to his advantage, for this wedding must not occur. He rose to his feet again and started howling.

"Cy, cut that out, will you? Come on, boy. Inside the hall, now." Anger flashed in Emyr's eyes, mixed with confusion and worry.

Idrys refused to budge, howling more loudly. He turned his head and looked up at Áine. She leaned on the bench with a wild smile on her face. She understood what he was trying to do and clearly approved. Given heart, Idrys started running in tight circles around Emyr, keeping him penned in the courtyard.

"Enough!" Emyr yelled. "Whatever game you've got in your head, now is not the time for playing. If you don't calm down, I'll have to lock you in the barn." He looked surprised that the threat had even left his mouth, but Urien and Llew, who'd come over to see if he could help, both nodded.

"Might be best, Emyr. At least until after the wedding and feast, eh?" Llew clapped a hand on Emyr's shoulder, stepping nimbly through the circle howling Idrys wove.

Idrys stopped and snarled before resuming his mad circling.

"Mayhap he's ill," Urien muttered.

Emyr started to run a hand through his hair before he recalled it was pulled back for the occasion. "Urien, get a rope," he growled.

Idrys barked and snarled and darted about the courtyard, upsetting a table before the determined men cornered him and pulled him into the barn. Emyr tied him up with an apologetic look and whispered "We'll sort this out tonight, I promise."

He jerked and pulled and bit at his makeshift collar but it was tied well. The rope was thick and coarse, but Idrys set to work, determinedly gnawing away at the strands.

Keep faith, Áine. I know you, I won't let this happen. Somehow I'll stop it all and set it all to right. I've failed everyone for so long, I cannot lie down and let this, too, pass. Áine. Áine.

Áine watched in horror as the three men wrestled with Idrys and then dragged him into the barn. She rose unsteadily to her feet and lurched toward them as they emerged and barred the barn door behind themselves.

Urien rolled his eyes and moved toward her as though she were an unruly child unable to follow direction. Áine glared at him and tried to push past, hesitating between going to Emyr and going to the barn to free Idrys.

Emyr advanced on her also, his face red and his lips pulled back from his teeth in a tight grimace. "You!" he cried, "I don't know who or mayhap what you are, but you've caused enough trouble for an afternoon. Sit there and if you make another motion toward myself or my damn hound, I'll see that you're set out of the village, courtesy or no. If you've worked a spell on my old friend there, I'll have you strung up for witchcraft. No, I'll do the stringing myself."

Áine recoiled from his anger and stumbled. Urien reluctantly caught her with one arm and helped her back to her bench at the edge of the courtyard. A goodly crowd had gathered and even the faces Áine knew gazed at her with curiosity and fear, and entirely without recognition.

Idrys knew me, why doesn't Emyr? He marries another; has his love for me flown? She shivered and gazed at Emyr as he took several deep breaths to regain control of his temper. *Idrys is a hound, he has a hound's senses. At nightfall, Emyr will know me as well.*

At nightfall, it will be too late.

Emyr turned away from her and motioned to the gathered people. "Come now, the others stand ready. The sooner we bind the contract, the sooner we feast." He put on a brave smile and strode back into the hall.

Áine felt as ancient as her bones. Her spirit cracked and her heart slowed to a deep, painful rhythm. She felt as though her hope were a tangible thing draining out with every tired breath. A harsh sob wracked her frail body and she doubled over, clutching at herself with weak, unfamiliar arms. It would all end here, this night. She would remain an old woman forever and her lovers would be bound to another.

From inside the barn came a mournful howl. *Idrys. You are as helpless as I to stop this wedding, to communicate the truth. I have failed us both.*

At dusk, they would change and she would not be near. Emyr had threatened to throw her out of the village if she approached him again, and Áine knew that, once in the wild, she'd likely give up and die alone of a broken heart or old age, whichever proved a swifter end.

Dusk. The change. He has to return to Idrys to switch places. I'll have a chance to free them at least. If I can somehow follow him into the barn, for I doubt that Idrys will go quietly into the hall.

There was still hope. Áine raised her worn and reddened eyes. She would have one final chance. She touched the curse-breaking necklaces where they rested under her ragged robe. She'd not brought them out to show Emyr for fear that he'd take them from her, since he seemed determined to misinterpret all her actions for the ill.

She took a steadying breath and rubbed her arms. A young girl approached her cautiously with a bowl, glancing up at Urien who nodded. Áine took the bowl, thinking the girl looked more than passing familiar. With a start she realized it was Maderun's elder daughter, Geneth. She stopped herself from touching the girl's face, reading the fear in her eyes. She'd cared for the girl when she was sick, and now there was no recognition at all.

She sighed and sipped at the warm goose broth. She could not prevent the wedding. Even now she could hear the crowd inside the hall responding with the traditional words of promise and witness. But she would be trapped in this hideous form, so perhaps the wedding going forward was the best thing for Emyr, and Idrys.

Idrys. You love me still; will you care for me in my strange old age? Or will this become another thing with which you torment yourself? She touched the cheek he'd licked so enthusiastically and felt a little warmth creep into her heart.

It was too late to prevent the wedding, yes. But only Emyr was in there saying those vows, agreeing to the contract between cantrefi. Idrys would be free, he'd be hers.

You can free them. Yes. And I will.

Twenty-seven

Emyr hardly tasted the food he ate from his plate more by habit than desire. All around him swirled happy conversation and he felt Eirian's thigh pressing into his as they sat side by side on the bench. Beneath the voices he imagined he could still hear the desperate howling of his brother and the muddy green eyes of the crone burned into his mind. He did not know her, but clearly there was something Other about her.

Idrys had been trying to tell him something, he was sure of that. But had it been a warning or some different message entirely?

He picked at a dormouse baked and stuffed with sweetmeats and then took a deep drink of ale. The shadows outside in the courtyard were growing longer and he felt the familiar tingle in his blood. It was nearly time for him to leave, but he would need to think of a good excuse to rise and leave his own wedding feast for time. Emyr turned his head and watched his bride. Her pretty face turned up to his and she smiled shyly.

Emyr was about to ask her forgiveness for his rude leave-taking and beg the need for the latrine or some such when Urien darkened the doorway and looked about the hall, meeting Emyr's eyes with a worried face. Emyr motioned to his friend and Urien glanced behind and then crossed the hall to the chief's table.

"Forgive me, Emyr, but it's Cy. I think he's chewed himself free of the rope and is now throwing his body against the stable doors. I'm not sure they'll hold." Urien glanced back toward the courtyard again.

Now that the hall had quieted on his entrance, the banging of a body hitting wood rang clearly in the late afternoon air.

"Thank you, Urien. I'll see to him." Emyr rose.

"Why not let your man take care of it? A man should not leave his own wedding feast." Gwideon ap Rhys looked between the two men. His eyes were full of suspicions and Emyr knew that the events earlier with the dog and the old woman had raised some doubt in the Chief of Rhufon's mind. A black dog and a crone were ill omens.

Emyr sighed. The tingling in his blood grew stronger and he knew he'd need to leave soon anyway. Idrys's strange actions had at least given him a good excuse.

"Cy is acting strangely, Gwideon, and while I have no fear my hound will bite me, I'm not so certain of the safety of others right now. I'll not send a friend into danger." He turned and looked down at Eirian. "Forgive me, my lady. I will return shortly." *Well, I won't, but I hope whatever is infecting my brother doesn't carry over to his human form.*

Gwideon looked as though he would protest further but Eirian rose as well.

"Hush, father. Emyr's hound has been his companion since boyhood. It is only right that he show such care for the poor beast." She turned her radiant smile on Emyr and he felt his heart leap. "Here," she said and wrapped up a lamb shank in her napkin. "Take this to Cy."

Her kindness hurt, since Emyr knew by the feeling in his blood that it would be he who gnawed the remaining meat from that bone. He took it from her with a pained smile and left the hall with Urien following close behind.

"Watch the old woman," he said to Urien.

The crone looked up from her bowl of broth as the two men emerged from the hall into the courtyard. Her face lit up with the same mix of determination and recognition that he'd noticed before and Emyr glared at her. He didn't have time for any more of her strange antics. The tingling in his blood had become a clarion call to shift and the sun rode very low, dropping behind the houses.

Another huge crash sounded from the stable and Emyr saw the barred door splinter and buckle outward.

"Cy, I'm coming, stop," Emyr cried out to his brother as he walked across the courtyard.

He wanted to run, but there were people from both cantrefi seated around, watching the chief with curious faces. He gritted his teeth and forced himself to stride calmly as though he were only seeing to his dog, gripping the lamb bone like a weapon in his fist.

"Woman, no!" Urien's cry stopped Emyr.

He turned and saw the crone had risen from her seat and was trying to get to him, her hands at her neck. Urien grabbed her around her waist and she kicked at him viciously, with more strength than Emyr would have given her credit for. Tears streamed down the old woman's face and her eyes were full of so much pain and despair that Emyr froze, watching her in wonderment.

Áine winced with each crash as Idrys threw himself against the stable doors and she looked pointedly at Urien where the bluff man leaned against the eave support of the smithy. He sighed and, with a clear warning glare to behave herself, took off for the hall. Áine watched and debated going to open to the stable doors, but there was still a score of people talking and eating in the courtyard and the stable was just far enough off that she worried she might fall before she reached it without her branch for support.

With a sigh she sat back and waited. The sun had dropped precariously low in the sky. Emyr would come, would go to Idrys and Áine would need to be ready.

Emyr emerged from the hall a few moments later with Urien in tow.

"Watch the old woman," he said to Urien and Áine grimaced.

It would be harder to get to them in time with that great oaf breathing down her neck. She carefully gathered her feet underneath herself, knowing she'd need to find a way to move more quickly than her old body would want. She had to be ready, had to get to the stable before the sun set, Urien be damned.

Tears burned her eyes and she took a deep breath. *Tears.* Áine suddenly wondered if her tears would turn to pearls while she was in this form. Could she manage to make Emyr see? Would he remember? She shuddered but let the tears well in her eyes. *I must take any chance.*

Idrys threw himself into the door again and this time it splintered, buckling outward. Áine started to her feet and angled toward the stable, reaching for the necklaces with both hands.

"Cy, I'm coming, stop!" Emyr cried.

Áine tried to duck Urien's arms as he reached her, throwing her body forward toward Emyr.

"Woman, no!" Urien's strong arms closed around her waist and she silently screamed in frustration.

He was going to ruin everything. With strength born of desperation, Áine kicked at the man and his grip loosened. *I cannot be so close and fail, release me, Urien, damnit let go.*

Tears of rage and despair flowed from her eyes and ran off her chin. A few hit the ground, turning to pearls and bouncing. Áine wanted to shout with triumph, praying that Emyr would notice. She had nothing to lose any more, not if she couldn't get to the twins before the sun dropped completely out of the sky.

Emyr froze, staring at her with a haunted and pained look. He opened his mouth as though to speak but with another huge crash, Idrys broke through the stable door and rolled into the courtyard with a mournful howl.

Did he see? Áine could not tell and tore her gaze from Emyr to Idrys's dark hound body lying in the ruins of the stable doors.

Idrys knew he would be too late to stop the wedding but still he chewed on the rope that bound him. He had to get out, to try. He could at least perhaps protect Áine, though from what he wasn't certain. A terrible foreboding rode his heart and so he gnawed and gnawed at the coarse rope until his teeth hurt and his gums bled freely.

After what felt far too long, the rope snapped and he was loose in the stable. The few horses not out on summer pasture whickered nervously and danced in their stalls as Idrys leapt free of his own enclosure and made for the stable door. It was barred from the outside and he howled his frustration to the dark stable. The tingling in his blood warned him that it was nearly sunset and a more rational part of him told him that Emyr would come for him before dark.

Áine was out there and Idrys wasn't about to listen to any rational side. He'd waited years for her and now he was supposed to be married to another. Every thought of future happiness lay in the memory of the strange wisewoman he'd fallen in love with. Áine had returned, as she'd promised. He would find a way to keep himself true for her.

He threw his body into the door and felt it give a little. Idrys backed up down the stable's aisle and raced at the door, leaping high at the last second to slam his full body into the thick wood. It buckled. With a growl, he raced back down the aisle to try again.

And again. And again. Splinters dug into his fur and his shoulders protested with a deep ache. The fire in his blood grew, the need to shift becoming stronger and stronger with each passing moment.

Emyr? Where are you? Idrys thrust his body against the door again and this time felt it give more than a little.

"Cy, I'm coming, stop!" Emyr's voice pierced the door and Idrys paused.

Then he heard Urien yell something and the sounds of a struggle in the courtyard. With a final leap, Idrys broke through the door and fell out into the courtyard, rolling hard with the impact. He scrabbled to his feet, dazed.

The prickling of his blood became a fiery roar. The change was nearly on them. Idrys twisted his head and saw Áine battling with Urien. Halfway between the hall and the stable stood Emyr, who was staring at Áine with a strange look on his face. Idrys started toward them, caught between going to this brother or going to help his love.

Áine saw Idrys's dark body roll into the courtyard and she feared he might be seriously hurt. She kicked at Urien again but the man had gotten his grip back.

No, no, you stupid man, let me free. She screamed silently, her mouth open as she struggled.

Idrys rose and shook himself, then started toward his brother, paused, and turned toward her. The shadows had grown very long and Áine knew that time was nearly run out. She dragged the necklaces over her head, managing to keep her arms free from Urien's grip.

Idrys hesitated. Áine had pulled something out of her ragged robe, something iridescent that reeked of otherworldly power to his keen senses. Hope and fear burned through him. Had she found a way to break the curse? He looked between her and his brother.

Emyr jerked as Idrys broke through the stable door and he too worried for a moment that his twin was seriously injured. The crowd was forgotten as he turned toward Idrys, but his brother rose and shook himself off, then started for him before hesitating and turning to the crone.

Emyr, too, turned back toward the crone as a glint caught his eye. Her tears poured down her face, some dripping to the ground. She hauled a pendant, no, two pendants from underneath her rags and they glimmered in the dying light, iridescent and strange. But there was something else, something Other and odd about the scene that Emyr could not place for a moment. The feeling of the change in his blood distracted him and he shook his head to clear it, dropping his gaze.

Áine drew a desperate breath and with a final prayer, threw the curse-breaking pendants as the sun sank below the horizon. She threw the one in her right hand at Emyr and the one in her left toward the advancing hound. They arced through the air in a moment that seemed to last for eternity.

"Áine?" Emyr said and lifted his head just as the necklace descended.

Twenty-eight

Emyr watched a tear fall to the ground as though the whole world had slowed. The tear touched the packed earth and stone of the courtyard and bounced away in a shining spin as a perfect pearl. A pearl just like the ones he kept hidden away in his belt.

Everything came together then in his mind. The crone's gestures, Idrys's strange behavior. His heart beat hollowly and he looked up at the old woman as she tossed the shining pendants into the air.

"Áine?" he said.

Oh Áine, what have I done?

The necklace slipped over his head and a terrible shivering wave washed over him, clearing his blood of the burning rush of the change. The sun dropped below the horizon and for the first time in ten years, Emyr did not turn into a hound.

Idrys saw the necklace arc toward him and realized it wouldn't make it. He jumped, snapping his jaws to catch at the gossamer pendant. He heard Emyr cry Áine's name just as the necklace slipped between his teeth.

The strand broke and its pieces fell to the ground, dissolving into an iridescent mist even as the sun set and the change took him. Fur and bone flowed upward to form his human shape and blood rushed in his ears even as horrible despair took hold in his heart. The curse was unbroken; he'd failed to get the necklace.

Áine watched the pendant slip over Emyr's head and saw the full-body shiver that took him in that moment. She had a moment to feel triumph before she heard the snap of jaws as Idrys tried to catch his own pendant.

Turning her head, she watched in horror as the necklace snapped and fell to the ground, disintegrating into mist as it touched the earth. The hound's dark eyes met her own and then he shifted, pouring upward into the shape of a man. Her own body spasmed and she cried out, surprised when sound issued from her lips.

Urien released her, falling backward onto the ground. A deep, twisting pain wrenched at Áine's limbs as her ancient body straightened and her rags were transformed back to the shredded and bloody dress she'd been wearing in Seren's clearing. Her limbs turned milk-pale and strong again and blood-red hair fell over her eyes. She brought familiar hands up to her face, feeling the tiny ridges of healing wounds across her own features.

Her twins had both known her before it was too late. Her body was restored and she was free.

Silence owned the courtyard as everyone stared in shock. Idrys looked down at his own naked body and then to his brother who stood as a man before him, still clothed in his wedding finery. With aching steps he walked to Emyr and the two men clasped arms, each staring into the other's face.

"Emyr," Idrys said softly.

"Idrys," Emyr responded.

Too many years of pain and silence between them. They stared at one another, unable to find the words for all that each wanted to say. After a long moment, they turned as one and looked at the woman who had freed them.

"Áine."

She stumbled toward them and they took her in their arms. Her hair was still short around her cheeks but she looked very much changed. Her torn, light blue dress was soaked with dried blood and every bit of exposed skin was covered in pink healing gashes that looked as though they'd scar. Her leaf-green eyes held shadows behind their joy and the twins wondered what this miracle had cost her.

"Idrys, Emyr. My loves. I've freed you and you freed me." She smiled at them, tears streaming down her cheeks. "How did you know me, Emyr?"

"Your tears," he answered with a laugh. "I've kept your pearl tears with me all this time, secret and safe. I saw you crying there in Urien's arms and one of your tears fell and bounced and I knew it must be you, for only my dearest love had tears so strange."

"You call me your dearest love," Áine said softly. "But you married another."

Before Emyr could respond, as if on cue, the wedding party emerged from the hall and the crowd around them lost their reluctance to speak. People surrounded the three, calling out questions and exclaiming.

Many of Clun Cadair's fold recognized Idrys, and others had heard his brother call his name. Nearly everyone, both of Llynwg and of Rhufon, knew the story of the tragic rockfall and Emyr's twin's horrible death ten years before.

"What is this? Who is here?" Gwideon cried, his voice cutting through the babble of the amazed crowd.

Instinctively, Urien and Llew pushed through to their friend's side, and though they too threw troubled glances at the twins, their posture made it clear they would stand firm for their chief and friend, no matter the strange circumstance. It warmed Idrys and Emyr's hearts.

"It's her!" A new voice said, and an old bald man crept to the edge of the circle of people. Madoc Moel pointed an accusing hand at Áine. "That Fey bitch. It's a trick somehow, I told them before that she's up to no good and now she's cast some terrible fairy spell."

"Hush you, Madoc Moel." Hafwyn appeared, her eyes ablaze with joy and relief. Eirian followed behind her with a very confused look on her face as she stared between the twins.

"Mother," Idrys said softly and smiled.

"Idrys. Áine." Hafwyn smiled back and then raised her voice. "Hear me, people of Llynwg and people of Rhufon. We will have no more secrets now, no more lies. They were necessary once for peace, but now I think the truth is needed."

"But that Fey bitch, look! She's covered in blood. It's a curse I tell you, turning that dog into a likeness of the chief. I saw it myself with my own damn eyes." Madoc charged forward, waving his arms.

"Judging by her scars, I'd say there's a fair chance that blood is hers," Eirian said as she stepped forward to lay a hand on Emyr's arm. "Please." Her eyes fixed on Emyr's face and a flush crept up her neck. "Let us go within and sort this out. I think you all have a very interesting story for us, do you not?"

Emyr nodded and bit his lip. He looked to Áine who shrugged.

"All right, everyone, into the hall." Emyr said and turned, pushing down the emotion clogging his throat. He was chief here and his people were worried. He could find the words to talk to his brother and Áine afterward.

The people parted for the three as they walked together into the hall. Caron, having gotten over her initial shock, had taken the initiative to grab a tunic from the chief's room for Idrys and he smiled at her warily when she handed it to him and murmured his thanks.

Áine tugged at her ragged dress as she sat awkwardly on a bench near the great hearth. Idrys, having hastily covered his naked body with a tunic, sat next to her, taking one of her hands in his. Emyr seated himself on the other side of Idrys, leaning slightly against his brother.

They waited, sharing glances between them, as the people slowly filed into the hall and settled on every available seat, some, like Urien and Llew, standing or leaning against the walls. After some long moments it was quiet and every eye in the hall was turned toward the twins and the strange woman who had appeared in their midst.

"Ten years ago," Emyr began "My twin brother and I went hunting alone in the forests. There was a rockfall, that much is true, but neither of us died in it. We were mostly uninjured but lost our gear. Not wishing to go home empty-handed, when we spied a lovely white deer the next morning, we gave chase."

"I gave chase, Emyr had little choice." Idrys cut in. He ducked his head for a moment and took a deep breath. "The deer led us to the glen of a Fair

One, a Lady. There we fell under her spell and were trapped. After a few days, or so it seemed to us, we escaped, but she hunted us down and commanded one of us to stay with her. Commanded that I stay. I refused, as did Emyr. For our apparent insult, the Lady cursed us. By day I would be a hound, by night Emyr would have that fate. We returned home and let it be known that I had died rather than risk ill will by having it known the Brychan's heirs were cursed."

When Idrys's voice turned guttural with emotion, Emyr took up the thread.

"Over three years ago, we met a wisewoman injured in a flood, Áine here. With her knowledge and wisdom she managed to figure out the curse, and today returned and somehow broke it. I think from here the story is hers to tell." Emyr turned and looked at her. Every other set of eyes followed his and Áine flushed.

She swallowed, then nodded. "There is not much to tell. I was gifted with a dream, as wisewomen sometimes are, and traveled to see the Lady who had cursed the twins." She hesitated and a shadow grew in her eyes. "After…" She took a deep breath. "After some time I convinced her to give me the means to break the curse. The Fair Folk ever love their sport, and so to make the task more difficult, she cursed me that I should appear in the guise of a mute crone and not change back until both my loves had recognized me. The curse had to be broken at sunset on the longest day of the year, today. And so we come to where we are."

Idrys looked at Áine and squeezed her hand. *She's leaving a great deal out, isn't she? But then again, so are Emyr and I. It seems some secrets are not for sharing, not here at least.*

Hafwyn stood and raised her arms to quiet the wave of questions and comments that started to build as it became clear the story was finished. "And so the terrible shadow over us is lifted. If our actions here cannot be understood, at least accept that the curse is gone, thanks to the strength and bravery of the wisewoman, Áine." She smiled at Áine. "She has performed a remarkable gift of healing here this eve."

"Mother," Idrys said and he rose. "The curse is not lifted, not wholly."

"What? What do you mean?" Hafwyn said.

"Idrys?" Emyr looked up at his brother. "But you stand before us, both of us men."

"The necklace did not fall over my head; in my desperation, thinking it might miss me entirely, I bit it, breaking the band and it dissolved away. I fear that, come sunrise, I will be Cy again." He hung his head.

"Idrys, quit that now." Áine rose and threaded her arm through his. "It was my poor throw that missed you both, my terrible timing that put me back here years later. If any blame is to fall, let me take it. You have borne enough burdens for your lifetime."

"Curse broken or half-broken, what does all this matter?" Gwideon stood and slammed a fist onto one of the tables, making the congealing dishes of food jump. "Which of these men is then Chief here? We have a contract. what means all this for that? There are lies within lies told here; how can I abide?"

"Emyr is Chief," Hafwyn said and Idrys echoed her.

Emyr looked between them and then nodded. "Aye, I am chief. Though only by daylight for the last ten years, Idrys ruling as myself when it was dark and I was a hound. As for the contract, I understand if you wish to withdraw it. There are things here that you were unaware of and though it pains me, I recognize the damage this might do for our relationship with you and Rhufon."

"Spoken just like a just and worthy chief." Eirian's clear voice rang through the hall and she made her way around the crowd to stand before Emyr. "But what of the man? I think perhaps we should talk in private."

"Eirian, this is none of yours," her father started to say but Eirian cut him off with an uncharacteristically sharp gesture.

"It is all of mine, father. The lawgiver has observed the contract of marriage and trade between our cantrefi. Until it is otherwise decided, that contract has been bound and witnessed. Thus, I am no longer your subject, but belong now to my husband. And this matter is a family one, I believe. It should be discussed and decided among his family." She looked pointedly at Emyr and added, "I am his wife unless and until he decides to set me aside."

"Use my chambers," Hafwyn said and motioned toward the private areas off the great hall.

Apparently shocked into silence by his daughter's firm and considered remarks, Gwideon made no more sound of protest as the little group left the hall. Behind them Llew took up a set of pipes and started a merry tune, trying to lighten the mood as the crowd broke into smaller groups and a hum of discussion swirled through the hall.

Áine and Idrys seated themselves by the hearth, while Emyr and Eirian took the narrow bed. Hafwyn settled in her sewing chair. The room was silent for a long moment as each gathered thoughts and searched for the perfect words to dispel the tension around them.

Eirian took the moment to study her husband's twin. She realized that he had been the man she'd known in the evenings, the man who'd played half-hearted games of Tallfwrd with her some nights.

Looking at him in contrast to Emyr, she wondered that she'd ever thought them the same person. Idrys had thin lines of care and worry worn into his face, and skin paler than his brother from his lack of exposure to sunlight. There was also a deep grief in his eyes, though it was lighter now as he looked upon the strangely scarred woman with the short, blood-red hair. The woman her new husband clearly loved.

"Eirian," Emyr said finally, "I understand if you wish to be set aside and freed to make a less complicated match." His warm brown eyes watched her with concern and his face showed his conflicted heart.

"Do you wish to stay married to me?" she asked baldly.

"I made a contract," he said. He turned to Áine and pain tightened his features. "I also broke faith. Áine told me she would return, but I gave up in my heart too soon."

"No, Emyr, please." Áine shook her head. "It hurts that you have married another, but years have passed. You are the chief here; you had to do what is best for your people." Her stomach clenched, hating her for being reasonable.

Áine wanted to rage, to demand that he set Eirian aside at once. If she'd been the same girl who'd arrived in the midst of grief and loss, the same girl who'd ridden her first horse with Emyr's smiles encouraging her along, she might have demanded such. But Áine was not the same; guilt and secrets pulled at her heart and she understood far better now the workings of the world. Emyr was chief, and Áine no longer had even the status of a wisewoman to offer him.

"I agree with Áine," Hafwyn said slowly "The reasons for your marriage to Eirian still stand, regardless of these events."

"And I agree with both," Eirian stated clearly. "You and I have forged a contract through our marriage that will benefit both our peoples. Not even knowing that I married a man cursed will put aside that truth."

"And what of you, Idrys? You are very quiet." Emyr looked at his brother, torn between duty and his heart and hoping that his twin would find a way to forge the two back together.

"Whatever you decide, Emyr, it is your decision and I will support it. As for me, I stay with Áine if she'll have me. Hound or man, I shall never let her from my sight again." He wrapped an arm around her shoulders and pressed his nose into her soft red hair.

Emyr rose and paced the small chamber. The others watched him, each with their own heart and want for his decision, each wise enough to stay silent and let him make his own choices. Finally he went to Áine and his brother and knelt before them, digging into his belt pouch.

He produced the little pearls of Áine's tears. "These are yours, Áine. I have held them too long with too little faith attached. And though I hold you in my heart and am more grateful to you than I will ever find the words to tell, I think I must stand by my word and the contract witnessed and given this day. But you and my brother will have a home here, no matter the curse that remains or the feelings of small-minded men like Madoc Moel." Emyr gripped Áine's hand in one of his own and then took his brother's in the other, reveling in the simple fact that he could touch his brother, look him in the eye, and know that Idrys would be able to respond in kind.

His joyous recollections of their boyhood teasing and friendship faded as Eirian rose and spoke.

"No," she said. Her words chilled Emyr and he turned, releasing the hands of the two people closest to his heart in all the world.

"No? You do not wish to keep the contract?" Emyr stared at her, confused and wondering how he'd mistaken her clear words from only a moment before.

"No, they may not stay. I will heed the contract as I said before. I think it best for our people. I know that it is painful for you, and for Hafwyn as a mother, but Idrys is cursed and he cannot remain. And Áine, well, she may not be one of the Fair Folk, but she has a strange look and strange history. She, too, will cause much trouble by her presence." She raised a hand to stall Emyr's angry protest. "Please, Emyr, think about this. It is one thing to have a tale of curses and adventure in your family's past, but quite another to live with a magical reminder of it each and every day. While those here might grow accustomed, what about the wintering folk? Or visitors from other cantrefi? Is not half the purpose of this marriage to bring fresh trade to both our peoples? If this shadow lives with us, each dawn reminding us of how it happened not long ago at all, how can we expect to have fair treatment?"

Áine's heart punched her chest as she stood and stared at the woman Emyr had wed. Eirian was lovely and by her words she was also intelligent and strong. Idrys rose beside Áine and looked down at her with a slight nod. Áine took a deep breath.

"Emyr," she said, touching his shoulder. He was tense and shaking with unspoken emotions. "She is right. At dawn each day, Idrys will shift. Between my strange heritage and his living proof that the Other is among us, it will be too much for many folk. If you are to prosper, we must hide ourselves away."

"Where will you go? How will you live?" Emyr turned to her, his eyes full of loss and fear.

"I do not know," Idrys said, "But I will go with Áine. She lived her whole life on the road; we can do so again. With me by her side to protect her and hunt for her, she will never want or suffer." He said this half to his twin, half to the woman clutching his hand.

Áine remembered Blodeuedd's words to her on the road and smiled at the memory of the warmth and lush bounty of the Ilswyn.

"We need not live on the road," she said. "I made a friend while I was away, and she has offered to share her valley with me. There we will be hidden and safe, but it is only a long day's journey to find if you ever have need of us."

"So it is decided then." Emyr raised his eyes toward the ceiling and blinked back tears. "On the very day I gain my brother, I am to lose him again."

"Emyr, my heart." Hafwyn threw her arms around him and Idrys followed.

"Be easy my twin, I think your wife is not so cruel that she will not allow us to meet in the wood on occasion. We will share many evenings together, more than we've had until now, I think." Idrys gripped Emyr in a hard embrace.

"I am not so cruel," Eirian murmured. She took a step back and looked at Áine, her body language stiff and uncertain.

"I will not meet with them," Áine said to Eirian, reading the fear and question in the younger woman's eyes.

"What is this? Why not?" Emyr looked between the women.

"I need to know that you are true, Emyr. You loved her first and deeply." Eirian looked down at her hands and twisted them in her embroidered skirts.

"Indeed," Áine said with a bitter smile as she touched her scarred face. "It would hardly be kind to put such temptation as I in your path, Emyr. Idrys will bring me news of you, and I will be content."

"And I will try to be content as well." Emyr sighed. "But you do not leave tonight. This night I will have to talk with my brother. The opinions of others will be damned."

"It will be so," Eirian said and she turned toward the door. "Please, catch up with one another. I will go speak to the assembled and calm my father. He will see reason and it will be settled. Gwideon ap Rhys will care to have it said he does not honor contracts witness and bound by a lawgiver."

The feast finished far more subdued than it had begun, and Áine, Idrys, and Emyr were conspicuously absent from much of it. The hour grew late and finally Emyr took his bride to his chamber. Hafwyn gave her own bed over to Áine and Idrys, staying instead with Melita, as all the guest spaces were filled with visitors for the wedding.

Áine and Idrys slept in each other's arms, too exhausted to do or say more. Idrys woke in the predawn as his blood tingled, a familiar harbinger of the change. Áine sighed and shifted next to him on the narrow bed. Her green eyes opened and she smiled up at him.

"I can feel the change coming." Idrys pulled away from her and sat up.

"I am here for you, Idrys, in whatever form you take. I care not." She sat up with him and pulled him into her arms.

"What is it that haunts your eyes, Áine? What gave you those scars?" he whispered into her soft, milk-pale skin.

"I will tell you. But not today. Come with me to the Ilswyn and I will find a way to share the tale with you, I promise. It is not a good one, but I think perhaps you might best of all understand what it is I have done." Her voice caught on the last part and he felt her shiver.

"Áine, my love, my heart," Idrys said and he pulled slightly away to stare into her shadowed eyes. He recognized the tension in her face, her body. She burned with guilt and longing. "Aye, Áine, I do indeed understand, best of all."

Epilogue

Emyr rose from the same restless dream he'd had for the last twelve years and, carefully removing Eirian's soft arm from his chest, slipped from the bed. The fire was banked low and he shivered in the winter air. He pulled on a thick woolen tunic and turned to look at his sleeping wife and children. They were a perfect picture of domestic contentment in the wan light of the little oil lamp that burned on the windowsill.

The two youngest twins slept on the other side of Eirian, curled under the thick covers in such a way that only their dark curls showed. His wife opened her eyes as he started to turn away again.

"Going to see Idrys again, are you?" she whispered.

He hadn't even known that was what he'd risen to do until she said it, but her words struck him and he knew their truth. He nodded.

"I will return in a day or two," he said quietly.

"No," Eirian said, "this time, I think you will not return."

In his dream, there was always a white owl waiting on a strange forest path marked with iridescent lights. Warmth waited at the end of that path, his dreaming self knew, warmth and completeness of a sort he never felt here in his home.

"I always return." Emyr crossed his arms.

"Follow your heart, Emyr. I cannot keep you longer, I know this now. Your heart left me twelve years ago. Find it again and be whole." Her voice and eyes brimmed with sorrow.

"Our children? I cannot leave," he said, feeling the old rift within of duty and desire.

"You have given Llynwg three strong sons as heirs and a beautiful daughter. You mother and I will see to them, as will Urien and Llew and Caron. They will not want, and when he reaches sixteen, Brychan ap Emyr will rule as you did when you reached his age. They will be strong; they will do well enough without you. I will be well enough without you."

"Eirian, I have loved you. You are bright and beautiful and full of too much wisdom. You break my heart with this wish. I cannot stay, nor can I go. I am lost."

"Hush, my husband. You are lost because your heart was broken years ago. Go to it; find your twin and your lost love. Be whole, go with my blessing. I have kept you as long as I could, but I understand now and I will fight this battle no more. This is a war I lost the day we wed and the curse was broken."

He knelt at the side of the bed and kissed her gently, murmuring to tell his mother and children where he'd gone and that he loved them deeply. Then, with only a few backward glances, he swiftly dressed and left the chamber.

In the hall he paused, wondering if this is how Áine had felt all those years ago, creeping away in the dead of night with nothing but hope and a dream. He looked around at the dim, familiar room and sighed. His sweet wife was right, as she'd often been. This place had ceased to feel like home as soon as his brother left, and the only times he'd felt even close to belonging anywhere had been on the lone hunting trips spent with Idrys by his side.

Movement by the banked fire startled him. Hafwyn rose and walked toward her son, her face shadowed and sad in the darkness.

"Good-bye, my son," she said, her voice breaking on the final word.

"Mother," Emyr said. He shivered as she touched his arm and then pulled her into a tight embrace. "I, I cannot stay. And I do not see how I can go."

"You have lived split apart long enough. Find your joy where you may, Emyr. There have been too many years of longing and sorrow here. Go toward your heart."

His throat burned with a strange mix of grief and happiness as something inside came loose at her soft words.

"I love you, mother. I will give your love to Idrys." He paused and pulled away from her, looking down on her white-haired head. "Take," his voice caught. "Take care of them for me. I don't know that the little ones will understand."

"Go, go before the chance passes." Hafwyn looked up at him. Then, slowly, she turned away.

Emyr took his cloak from its peg by the door and slipped out of the hall, heading into the wintery night, heading toward his heart.

He went to the woods, reaching them as dawn broke across the moor, and was unsurprised when a white owl alighted on a branch before him. The branch lit up with soft white light and slowly more trees ahead glowed as well, illuminating a clear path through the woods just as they had in his dream. Emyr nodded to the owl and walked into the woods, no longer looking back.

He walked through the day, following the white bird as the sun rose and the soft light on the path faded away. As darkness fell again the glimmering path returned, guiding him on his journey. He paused only once, stopping at a stream to drink before crossing it. Emyr's hands and face were chapped with cold and he pulled his cloak tight around his body as his boots soaked through slowly from the snow.

Finally, as if he passed across an invisible threshold, the snowy landscape gave way to a lush valley. The air warmed noticeably and beneath his feet the crunchy, dry snow was replaced with thick grass and tiny blue flowers. The stars shone bright above and he had no trouble picking his way down toward a lovely stone cottage nestled among apple trees that were in bloom and fruit all at once.

The owl disappeared and his glowing trail ended at the thick oak door of the large cottage. Emyr took a deep breath and knocked, looking about himself in wonder at this odd place. After a moment, the door opened and a young girl with soft brown hair peered out at him. Her leaf-green eyes went wide and she opened her mouth, but no words came.

"I greet you," Emyr said, realizing that this must be one of Áine and Idrys's four daughters. Though he knew their names, he was unsure which stood before him.

"I greet you, but you cannot be my father?" she said and turned to look within the cottage with a comically confused expression.

"I am not he," Emyr said, controlling his own grin. "But I seek him."

As if in answer to this, he heard Idrys's voice within. "Braith, who is at the door?"

Braith stepped back, clearly unable to tell who he might be, and allowed Emyr to step within.

Idrys sat on the edge of a large stone hearth, carving tools in his hands. At a table to one side sat Áine and two smaller girls with dark curling hair, gathered around a beautifully carved tallfwrd board. Next to the hearth was a girl who matched Braith's looks exactly, except for a single blood-red curl tucked behind one ear. She was slowly feeding wool into a drop spindle from the pile in her lap but stopped to stare at Emyr.

For a moment, no one spoke. The three adults stared at each other, frozen with emotion too deep to voice. Then Idrys and Áine rose almost as one, moving around their children to throw their arms around Emyr and each other.

Áine pressed her cheek into his chest and wept, her strong arms clinging to him. Idrys, who had aged somewhat more gracefully than Emyr, as Emyr observed in that moment, leaned his dark head in close to his twin's.

"Welcome home, brother," he whispered, "welcome home."

The end

Also by Annie Bellet:

The Gryphonpike Chronicles:

Witch Hunt

Twice Drowned Dragon

A Stone's Throw

Dead of Knight

The Barrows (Omnibus Vol. 1)

Chwedl Duology:

A Heart in Sun and Shadow

The Raven King

Pyrrh Considerable Crimes Division Series:

Avarice

Wrath

Hunger

Envy

Lust

Inertia

Vainglory

Short Story Collections:

The Spacer's Blade and Other Stories

River Daughter and Other Stories

Deep Black Beyond

Till Human Voices Wake Us

Dusk and Shiver

About the Author:

Annie Bellet lives and writes in the Pacific NW. She has a degree in Medieval Studies and her stories have appeared over two dozen magazines, anthologies, and collections. She is currently working on a new urban fantasy series. Follow her on her blog at "A Little Imagination" (http://overactive.wordpress.com/).

If you want to be notified when Annie Bellet's next novel or collection is released, please sign up for the mailing list by going to: http://tinyurl.com/anniebellet. Your email address will never be shared and you can unsubscribe at any time.

CPSIA information can be obtained at www.ICGtesting.com
Printed in the USA
LVOW10s1547021014

406990LV00009B/1357/P